HECTOR'S REVENGE

To Rick

Best wishes

from

John

John Pendleton

To Wendy, Colin and Trudi

Chapter one – Hopes and rebuffs

"She's no better than she ought to be," whispered an elderly woman to her husband as they watched the grieving widow walking by behind the coffin.

The husband nodded.

The willowy widow was clad in black from head to toe with a stylish picture hat and veil. She walked alone with a dignified and measured gait, followed at a respectful distance by a long train of relatives and friends.

Leading the procession from the ancient village church to the waiting grave was the Vicar of Marshyard, a portly, bearded figure with a pronounced limp. Progress was slow and, on a sunny, mild and windless late autumn day, with birds singing in the tall trees surrounding the churchyard, time almost seemed to stand still.

A soberly dressed middle-aged man in the middle of the line of mourners was slyly glancing around him as he trod the gravel path. A few yards behind was a group of three smartly dressed women, one about his own age, the other two in their twenties. He caught the eye of the older woman and she smiled and quietly mouthed the word "Hector".

"Hello," he replied in a similarly hushed and appropriate manner. He returned her smile, gave a wave and then continued along the route to the graveside.

****

Hector Ratcliffe was born on April 3rd, 1950, the only son of Charles and Margaret Ratcliffe, at the popular

English east coast holiday resort of Sanderholme.

Margaret was the eldest of two daughters of a farming family called the Ashburns.

Sanderholme had been a busy tourist destination since the railway came to the town in the 1870s. Hundreds of thousands of people, mainly from the East Midlands and Yorkshire, came on day trips. As time went on, many hotels and guest houses sprang up with people staying for their annual holidays of a week or even a fortnight.

Then, in the 1920s and 1930s, arose a significant new phenomenon – holiday caravan sites. Eventually there were scores of them. And the people who most benefited from this new trend in tourism were local farmers. Caravans became a much more lucrative crop than wheat or potatoes, and cattle and beach donkeys were moved out to graze on pastures further inland.

The Ashburns were one of the families who cashed in on this novel way of making money, developing a large caravan site on their land at the edge of the town. On the death of their parents, Margaret and her younger sister, Christine, took over the running of the site.

Margaret had married Charles, a tall and startlingly handsome young man whom she met while studying for a business degree at university. He was academically gifted, gaining a master's degree in the Classics. He qualified as a teacher and for many years taught Latin at Sanderholme Grammar School. Then he took early retirement and fulfilled a lifelong dream of owning a bookshop. This gave him a small income and the time and opportunity to further his Classical studies.

Margaret was a devoted wife and a caring mother to Hector and a thoroughly decent person, never flustered and always thinking of others before herself. She was a rock, both for her family and the family business, less glamorous, quieter and more stable than her formidable, likeable but eccentric sister.

Hector's father was his hero, a gentle, calm and interesting man, who always had the time to spare for his son. He played games with him, took him fishing and swimming and instilled in him a sense of curiosity about the world around him.

Hector was a shy child, thin and of moderate height. From an early age, spurred on by his father, he became an avid reader, lapping up everything from the Beano and the Dandy to "difficult" books on philosophy and art history. But, again influenced by Charles, his great passion was for Greek mythology and Roman literature. He loved to read about gods and goddesses and their interactions with human heroes and heroines. By the age of seven he had read Homer's "The Iliad" and "The Odyssey" and by eight he was engrossed in Virgil's "The Aeneid".

"The Iliad" was by far his favourite book. He reread it time and time again throughout his childhood and in later life, marvelling at the majesty of the poetry and the vividly drawn characters. On his first reading he had questioned his father as to why he had been called Hector – the name of a Trojan prince – instead of Achilles, the Greek warrior who vanquishes Hector in battle and kills him.

Charles explained to him that, despite his sticky end,

Hector was the real hero of "The Iliad". He was noble, a good husband and loving father – a courageous yet human hero who did not like war and was respected by his army for his mature judgement.

Achilles, on the other hand, was proud, petulant, cruel and sulky. He sadistically mistreated Hector's body, dragging it through the dust behind his chariot for 12 days in front of the Trojan's wife and children.

Our Hector understood this and was pleased to have been named after the better man. Even as a seven-year-old he determined, despite his unpromising physique, that he would try to live up to his name.

He was especially enrapt in the myths of the Greek deities, who seemed so much more alive and exciting than the Christian God and his meek and mild son, whom he found quite annoyingly insipid by comparison.

Take Zeus. Now there was a bold fellow. He might have had an ethereal fluid, ichor, running through his veins but he behaved just like a red-blooded male of the human species. He would stop at nothing in his conquest of the opposite sex – turning himself into a swan to seduce Leda, or, even more amazingly, a shower of gold to overcome Danae.

Even as a young child Hector was well aware that the classical myths were no more plausible than the fairy tales he had been told since he was a toddler. But when he listened to the news on the radio, and later on television, and looked at the world around him, he was impressed that the Greeks and Romans had an understanding of the imperfectability of both men and gods.

Despite all its nonsensical stories, mythology did at least recognise that gods, who, for example, allowed and actively participated in wars, inflicted cruel punishments on human beings and seduced luckless virgins by disgraceful subterfuges, were as morally imperfect as the people they had created.

Hector contrasted this with the Christian God, worshipped for being both good and omnipotent, and yet allowing all kinds of depredations and suffering to assault mankind. As a mere seven-year-old he had yet to be presented with the arguments about free will.

One of Hector's best friends at primary school was the son of a Methodist lay preacher. He talked to his father about Hector's preoccupations with mythology and was quickly told: "That boy will come to nothing if he believes that kind of ridiculous rubbish."

At the Sunday service the preacher related the story of the loaves and fishes.

Looking at the illustrations in his mythology books, often of gods and goddesses in various states of undress, Hector had experienced strange stirrings in the loins. He really didn't know what was going on and, this being the 1950s, he dared not ask anyone either.

By the time he was 11, the same excitements arose when Barbara Plumhills, the most well-developed girl in his class at Sanderholme Grammar School, started to show some of his friends her black bra, and enticingly, something of what was inside it.

As time went on, several other girls in the class started to emulate Barbara by displaying pieces of their underwear to the boys.

The sort of help from female classmates described above, and some useful dirty jokes told by more knowing boys in the class, provided Hector with the lion's share of his sex education. This was supplemented by school biology lessons about reproduction, which started with the dull asexual habits of the amoeba and never progressed further than the rather more racy behaviour of the rabbit.

Outside of school, time playing out in the town's streets was an almost daily occurrence. Hector and his school friends would play football in the road with jumpers laid down as "goalposts". Quirkily, a form of French cricket was another favourite game. It was ideal for playing on the road as there was no need for wickets to be pitched.

These games went on for hours at a time, often with a changing cast of players, as some participants were called in by their parents at teatime, to be replaced by others who had already had theirs.

The age groups were mixed, with players ranging from four or five-year-olds to those soon to be school leavers. Girls frequently joined in with the boys' games or sometimes watched admiringly from the pavement, often with their minds on other things than the older boys' footballing or French cricketing prowess.

There were few interruptions to these sports. A motor car might hold up proceedings every half hour or so. And there was the odd moan from a neighbour fed up with youngsters going into his garden to receive stray balls.

Another occupational hazard was Mossy, a big English sheepdog who lived along the same street as Hector's best friend, Matthew Copson. The dog had a very long coat, which meant when he lay down, he took up the whole width of the pavement. Although he probably went through his whole life without actually biting anyone, he would growl fiercely at any child who got too close to him. And, although his hair completely covered his eyes and he invariably appeared to be snoozing, uncannily he always noticed if someone was trying to pass by him. As a result children gave him as wide a berth as possible.

Despite these minor drawbacks, the street games were much enjoyed in an atmosphere of fun and good companionship.

For a short period these Lincolnshire lads and lasses were able to have a taste of the Latin flair of Italian football. One house along the road where Matthew lived was rented for a season by a local holiday centre for some young Italian men working there. Local parents were a little apprehensive at first, not being quite used to washing being hung out to dry from bedroom windows or the singing of operatic arias at all times of the day and night. But the friendly nature of the men and their kindness to the local children soon made them popular additions to the community.

Italians were not the only "foreigners" to take up residence in Matthew's street. A number of American air force personnel, stationed at a nearby air base, lived there for several years with their families in the 1950s. They brought with them such exotic things as refrigerators, home-made ice lollies and pumpkins. Their children, with such alien names as Clay and Butch, were warmly welcomed to join in the street games.

The biggest playground, though, was the beach, with its flat areas for ball games and its thickets adjoining the sandhills, which were perfect for playing hide and seek, cowboys and Indians, Robin Hood against the Sheriff of Nottingham, and the OAS versus the Muslims, a niche game which arose from the Algerian crisis happening around that time.

By the time Hector was 13 he began to have a series of crushes on girls in the Grammar School. But because of his shyness he could never pluck up the courage to ask any of them for a date, let alone suggest a kiss.

Then, when he reached the age of 15, Penelope Douglas became the focus of his attention. She was the cleverest girl in the class and the most beautiful. Slim and graceful, she had the best figure in the school, in a discreet kind of way. She had a lovely pale complexion, rich dark brown hair, doleful brown eyes and a queenly bearing. She was an English rose by looks, deportment and manners. To add to her alluring charms she had a smile which could light up the gloomiest castle dungeon.

Penelope's older sister, Susan, had also made a big impact on the school. She was just as bright and beautiful as her sister and had been head girl before leaving two years earlier. She won a place at Oxford University and gained a languages degree there. But during the summer holidays prior to starting her course she had surprised everyone, and appalled some, by revealing she was pregnant, consequently giving birth to a daughter at the end of the first term.

Although acutely embarrassed and very angry with

her, Susan's parents stepped up to the plate and provided financial help with childcare. There had inevitably been tremendous gossip and speculation among their daughter's friends as to the identity of the father. But this was never disclosed.

Boys loved her sister Penelope, although girls sarcastically dubbed her "Lady Penelope", referencing the aristocratic puppet in the Thunderbirds television series popular on British television at that time.

Penelope was always friendly to Hector, and he was quick to notice this. Up until now his feelings for girls had been largely confined to, shall we say, his nether regions. Now feelings of a different sort overtook him.

To begin with he would experience an excitement, a heightening of his spirits, every time Penelope stepped into a room. This was followed by an uncontrollable desire to see her as much and as often as possible.

Not content with ogling her in the classroom and on the school field at break time, he purposefully joined several of the school societies which Penelope already belonged to – the Film Club, the Debating Society, the Bridge Club.

As the weeks went by this fairly normal schoolboy crush was overtaken by much more traumatic feelings. He experienced a distressing physical reaction every time she appeared, a lump in his throat which made him fear he might vomit all over her – or "chunder" as was the schoolboy parlance gleaned from Private Eye magazine. He sweated profusely and almost felt he was going to faint.

The next stage was that he felt sick even in

anticipation that he might see Penelope. His distress was so obvious that he sometimes actually swerved to avoid her in case she saw the pitiful state he was in.

This latter symptom of his "illness" was something of a mystery to Hector – and a cause for concern.

He even consulted the Home Doctor book (every sensible family had one at that time) and convinced himself he was suffering from consumption. He was an avid reader of the works of the Romantic poets, famously susceptible to that fatal condition, so that may have helped convince him of that diagnosis.

It eventually dawned on Hector (he was not too bright in some respects!) that the malady afflicting him was Love of Penelope Douglas. Lovesickness.

Sigmund Freud once posed the question: *"Isn't what we mean by 'falling in love' a kind of sickness and craziness, an illusion, a blindness to what the loved person is really like."*

Later, Frank Tallis, a researcher on lovesickness, identified a list of common symptoms, including mania, depression, hopelessness, helplessness, nausea, tearfulness, insomnia, lack of concentration and loss of appetite. Hector was suffering from all of these.

He was feeling so ill, so thoroughly miserable, that he knew he must do something about it.

Reading one of his books on ancient magic, he came across a piece about a traditional method of attracting a loved-one. This involved placing seven red beans on the road along which the loved-one travelled and then collecting them up again after she had passed. This having been successfully achieved, the young lady would be incapable of resisting her admirer at the next meeting.

Hector decided it was worth a go.

Although he was a romantic, he did have a prosaic, practical side to his nature. There were no red beans to be had in the Ratcliffe household. His paternal grandmother, Nellie, who had passed on a few years before this, often used to have red beans in the pantry, but these were a vegetable seemingly unknown to Hector's mother, Margaret.

Hector didn't feel confident enough about the efficacy of the magic spell to actually go out and buy some red beans. He therefore made do with some baked beans out of a Heinz tin. They might not be red, but orange was the next best thing.

He dutifully placed the beans at the side of the main road where Penelope's school bus travelled. Then after the bus had passed he collected them up again.

The experiment, sad to relate, had no tangible results.

In his desperate search for some sort of reassurance, Hector would pick up a handful of playing cards and lay them one at a time on his bedspread, chanting "she loves me, she loves me not" until the last card he laid provided him with the answer. If he failed to get the right response the first time, he would do "best of three", "best of seven", "best of nine" to give himself more chance of success. Little was gained by this experiment either.

Six months passed and still nothing had been achieved.

****

Hector's recent sad demeanour was a source of concern to two people in particular, his mother and his Aunt Christine.

Christine raised the subject with Margaret at coffee time at the caravan site office.

"What's the matter with Hector these days? He looks really down in the mouth."

Margaret replied: "I'm not sure. Although… no, I'd better not."

"Come on. You know you can tell me anything, sis."

"Well, I was hoovering round Hector's bedroom the other day and I came across a love letter. Really full on. Quite desperate. It almost had *me* in tears. He obviously hadn't sent it – at least not yet."

"Who was it addressed to?"

"Penelope Douglas."

"Oh, my God. That needs nipping in the bud," said Christine. "That's not going to go anywhere, is it? I know what to do…"

****

Instinctively Hector knew that Penelope was "too good for him". She was the brightest and best looking girl at Sanderholme Grammar School and was well aware of this but too much of a lady to ever let on that she knew. Hector, on the other hand, was undistinguished, both as a student and in his personal appearance. Physically he had filled out a little. He was pale and had some teenage acne but was proud of his fine, brown shoulder-length hair.

Hector was intelligent but, at this particular stage of his life, lazy. Both he and Penelope were in the "A" stream at school; Penelope was top of the class, but he was near the bottom. He had become neglectful of his studies in most subjects and had lately immersed himself in his beloved Romantic poetry.

He still followed his father in being passionate about Greek and Roman mythology and sometimes took this to extremes. For instance, he shocked his religious instruction teacher by openly mocking Christianity and strongly reasserting his preference for the pantheon of Greek gods. Some classmates mocked him for this eccentricity, while others had a sneaking regard for his bold individuality.

He kept on good terms with Penelope, who found him pleasant and interesting, if not at all on her wavelength. He confided his love for her to a couple of his best friends, but the fact that he had written "I Love Penelope" in black ink on the flap of his satchel, embellished with a heart with an arrow struck through it, rather gave the game away. Penelope knew that Hector loved her and Hector knew that she knew, but nevertheless they were able to converse freely without ever mentioning the thorny subject.

One day in the classroom Hector overheard two girl classmates discussing Penelope in a disparaging way.

"Have you heard the latest about Lady Penelope?" asked a plain, freckly girl.

"No, what is it?" asked her plain, plump friend.

"She told Sylvia that she fancies Stuart Broadlake."

"Huh, you must be joking. She wouldn't stand a chance with him."

"No, not with her old-fashioned clothes and fuddy-duddy attitudes. He likes girls with a bit more oomph than her."

"Who does she think she is – Little Goody Two-Shoes?"

"She's like something out of Jane Austen. Stuart fancies himself as a blond Beatle! I can't see him going for her."

"No, more Penny Plain than Penny Lane", she giggled.

"Ooh, I like it. Our new nickname for her."

Hector was angry. How could they talk in such a manner about an angel? They were so ignorant they didn't even know that The Beatles' Penny Lane was about a road, not a girl!

But even more annoyingly, how could she possibly fancy Stuart Broadlake?

Stuart, the school's head boy, was a hunk of a young man, tall and muscular with an impressive mane of golden blond hair to which he had recently added a Beatle fringe à la John Lennon.

The much-loved eldest child of a family with a long military tradition, he was bright and very athletic, shining in the school's football and cricket teams and an impressive middle distance runner.

He was most schoolgirls' dream. But he was also arrogant and moody, too sure of his own good looks, sporting prowess and intelligence. Usually he was amiable enough, but he had a frightening temper when things didn't go his way. Woe betide any teammate who failed to perform on the sports field, as Hector himself had experienced on a number of occasions. Once Broadlake had even smacked him hard on the head after he muffed a goal scoring chance. It was a shock and humiliation which Hector never forgave or forgot.

However, even worse in Hector's eyes, Stuart was known to treat girlfriends badly, sometimes leaving them in floods of tears through his selfish behaviour.

Hector's nickname for him was Achilles, but he kept this as a secret from all but his best friends, who shared his contempt for Stuart.

For just a flicker of a moment Penelope went down ever so slightly in Hector's estimation. He had just bought prog rock group Cream's new "Disraeli Gears" album. The lyrics of the song "Swlabr" bemoaned *"the rainbow has a beard"* and *"the picture has a mustache"* (sic). He felt for an instant that Penelope was similarly imperfect in fancying Stuart Broadlake. He was quick, though, to dismiss this ridiculous thought.

On those occasions when he did manage to put Penelope to the back of his mind, Hector found life in the sixth form at Sanderholme Grammar School interesting, stimulating and often fun. It was a school at the top of its game.

His favourite subject was English and he had an inspiring teacher, Mr Plunkett, who broadened and deepened his interest and knowledge in its literature.

Hector had been obsessed with the Romantics for some time but now his horizons stretched to the Augustans, such as Pope and Swift and the great Dr Samuel Johnson, through to modern writers such as William Golding, Iris Murdoch, Joseph Conrad and T. S. Eliot. He also gained an insight into the genius of Shakespeare.

Hector particularly enjoyed the theatre trips which Mr Plunkett organised, including some memorable visits to Stratford-upon-Avon. The teacher was a bon viveur and introduced his students to the pleasures of fine dining and a glass of wine. He organised boat rides down the river and impromptu games of mixed football and cricket.

The highlights of these trips were their visits to the Shakespeare Memorial Theatre. For many of the young people, the plays they saw there awakened their imaginations and inspired future creativity. However, a number of the students found that the wine they drank at pre-theatre dinners at their hotel had consequences for their theatre experiences. Some unexpectedly found themselves canoodling in the stalls with school friends of the opposite sex they hardly knew. For Hector, though, the problem was keeping awake after imbibing, even through performances starring some of the greatest Shakespearean actors of the period, such as David Warner, Ian Holm or Diana Rigg.

He never did find out whether "Hamlet" had a happy ending!

During one of these trips Hector spent a good deal of time with Humphrey Gibb, who was to become a lifelong friend and confidant.

Humphrey was a new boy at the school, having joined it in the last term of the fifth year. He came from an upper middle class background and had been at Eton when his father, John, a merchant banker, made some unwise investments and fell into financial difficulties. The result was that the family moved out of their Hampshire manor house to live with John's parents in Sanderholme. There was no money for school fees and so Humphrey transferred from Eton to the Grammar School.

Humphrey was a good-looking fair-haired boy, slim and of above medium height. He was a snappy dresser, wont to wearing tweeds out of school hours in contrast to the blue denims favoured by his new schoolmates. He quickly persuaded the games teachers to introduce rugby to the curriculum.

Some classmates were suspicious of the new arrival but when he introduced them to the pleasures of his own secret wine cellar, he quickly won them over.

His lasting claim to fame in the history of Sanderholme Grammar School, though, was the introduction of the fart machine.

This ingenious device involved a rectangle of wood with a piece of elastic stretched between two eye hooks. A metal washer was placed in the middle of the elastic which was then twisted round tightly. The whole gadget was strategically placed underneath a pupil's bottom as he or she (usually he, as boys of that age are genetically more likely to be immature) was seated behind a desk during a class. The pupil waited until the teacher turned towards the blackboard and then slowly rose up. This released the elastic and the washer would knock against the wood, causing a sound identical to that of a fart. The teacher would invariably turn round but would be too embarrassed to say anything. Result: general laughter throughout the class.

Humphrey's version of the fart machine, devised at his prep school some years previously, was so successful that other pupils at the grammar school soon devised and produced their own versions. The machines got bigger and bigger so that the later designs could be anything up to two feet long with huge washers. These produced mega-loud farts.

One brave soul even took one of these gigantic machines into morning assembly, which was led by the school's fearsome headmaster, Mr Grout. It produced a huge sound during a hushed part of the proceedings between the bible reading and the singing of the school hymn. The perpetrator was caught by one of the prefects and ended up being given three strokes of the cane by the incandescent headmaster.

That was the end of the fart machine experiments. But it left Humphrey Gibb as a hero of his schoolmates. Previous prejudices were forgotten and he became one of the most popular boys in his year group.

One abiding memory Hector had was of an end of term school play, produced by Mr Plunkett. The lead parts in Shakespeare's "Romeo and Juliet" were performed by none other than Humphrey and Penelope. Humphrey, as might be expected, gave a bravura performance as Romeo, while Penelope was a controlled, demure and delectable Juliet.

The scenes where Romeo got to kiss his lover were a source of some envy on Hector's part.

His other bosom buddy, whom he had known since he was a toddler, was Matthew Copson, overtly a regular sort of a chap, even-tempered and loyal, a Boy Scout and chorister at the town's parish church. He had, though, a cynical streak which sometimes put him at odds with

Hector's romantic leanings.

Superficially the three lads, Hector, Humphrey and Matthew, had little in common, except a shared interest in music. They all enjoyed prog rock, classical music and jazz. Despite their different characters and appearances the three became close friends.

These friendships helped Hector to preserve his sanity despite his overarching lovesickness.

He was, though, stricken with grief when Penelope had several dates with another boy in the class, an ungainly oaf called Thomas Strawson, who had nothing to recommend him except rich parents.

Penelope hailed from a respectable farming family in the small market town of Hayfleet, about six miles from Sanderholme. She was doted on by her parents, who were not "pushy" people but at the same time were ambitious for both of their beautiful, talented daughters. Their father, Richard, was the scion of a long-established dynasty of Hayfleet farmers, churchgoing and a pillar of a number of community organisations. Their mother, Pamela, was a leading light in the Hayfleet Parish Church, the Mothers' Union and the local Women's Institute.

Hector's rival, Thomas Strawson, lived on a neighbouring 3000-acre arable farm, his parents being considerable landowners in the area. The Strawsons were well known in the community too but were a different kettle of fish from the Douglases. They spoke with broad Lincolnshire accents and had acquired none of the refinements which wealth could have brought them. The father was a rough-speaking, badly dressed man and the mother dowdy and old-fashioned in her appearance with a downtrodden air.

Thomas was intelligent but lacking in charm. He was a dull dog and inclined to be ill-mannered.

Penelope's parents had rather reluctantly allowed her to go on dates with Thomas, but everyone knew that this would be a passing phase and that basically he was not her "sort".

Although the sight of Penelope and Thomas together revolted Hector, even at this tender age he was perspicacious enough to realise that this was a liaison which would not last long.

However, it did last for another year and Hector began to panic. They were all now in their final year at school, doing their A levels.

Penelope, who had followed in her sister's footsteps as head girl, was certain to take up a place at university in the autumn. Hector, on the other hand, had decided to go straight into the family business. This was a cause of some disappointment to his father, who had long entertained the hope and expectation that his son would follow in his footsteps and take a Classics degree. His mother and Aunt Christine, on the other hand, were keen that the caravan site should stay in the family and helped to steer Hector in that direction.

Because of the very different path that Penelope would be following, the chances were that she would be lost to him for ever.

Then came his opportunity to strike. He heard from a friend that Penelope and Thomas were no longer "seeing each other". Theirs had been merely a convenient friendship, involving trips to the cinema and a few school dances. There had been very little meeting of minds and nothing remotely approaching a romance.

Still shy, but now steely in his determination, Hector decided to act. He would ask Penelope for a date.

In those days taking a girl to "the pictures" was the most common form of dating. Parents also thought it reasonably safe, although some may have been shocked by what took place on the back row.

A film showing at Sanderholme's Regal Cinema that week appeared to be a suitable choice for a first date. "To Sir, with Love", starring Sidney Poitier and the film debut of the pop singer Lulu, was unlikely to be a controversial choice either for Penelope or her parents.

Hector failed to find a suitable opportunity to approach Penelope at school, as there was always someone else within earshot. So he decided on a phone call. He waited until there was no one in the office at the caravan site and made his move.

Penelope's mother answered the call, politely but frostily, and handed the phone over to her daughter.

"Hello, Penelope. It's Hector here."

"Hello, Hector."

"I'm going to the pictures tomorrow night to see 'To Sir, with Love' and I wondered if you would like to come with me."

"Oh, thank you very much. I would like to come but I'm very busy at the moment revising for the exams. I don't think I'll be able to make it. Thank you for asking though, old bean."

"Oh, okay," said Hector. "I hope you didn't mind me asking you."

"No. Thanks very much."

"I'll see you at school then."

"Yes, see you at school."

 "Bye for now."

"Bye."

That was it then. Penelope had been her usual polite and friendly self. But there was nothing in her tone of voice, or in anything she had said, that gave him any hope. He slumped down on to the office desk – and shed a tear.

Back at school the next day everything was as normal. When Penelope entered the classroom she smiled gently at Hector but no words were exchanged. At break-time they chatted in their usual friendly way, but no mention was made of the phone call. It was obvious to Hector that there was to be no follow-up. He was simply out of his league.

At the end of the school year Penelope took up her place at York University, studying law. Hector was trained up by his mother in caravan site management. Thomas Strawson went on to agricultural college.

****

At this period of his life Hector was very much given to introspection and self-analysis. His experience with Penelope, he had decided, amounted to a pathetic lovesickness.

His love for her had been hopeless yet unconditional. He recalled a passage he had read in Dickens' "Great Expectations" about Pip's love for Estella:

"The unqualified truth is, that when I loved Estella with the love of a man, I loved her simply because I found her irresistible. Once for all; I knew to my sorrow, often and often, if not always, that I loved her against reason, against promise, against peace, against hope, against happiness, against all discouragement that could be. Once for all; I love her none the less because I knew it, and it had no more influence in restraining me, than if I had devoutly believed her to be human perfection."

Dickens had articulated exactly how Hector felt about Penelope. He knew that if, at any time during the rest of his life, she showed any faintest flicker of interest in him he would be overcome with joy. The sickness would return.

Freud had been "spot on" in describing falling in love as craziness, Hector concluded. His crushes on other girls in his earliest years at Grammar School had brought him no satisfaction at all and his love for Penelope, beautiful and honest though it undoubtedly was, had brought him misery, despair and a feeling of worthlessness.

One night as he lay awake in bed he asked himself if, at the age of 18, it would be better for him to give up on women altogether. After a few seconds' thought he rejected that notion.

He had reluctantly begun to accept that to continue his pursuit of Penelope would be futile. He also realised that other women would come along whom he would, in his choice of term, "fancy". He found many girls sexually attractive but had thought of Penelope in a completely different way. He believed that his love for her went to the very depths of his soul.

To try to understand his emotions he looked to the ancient Greeks, always a source of inspiration to him, and remembered that they had identified a number of different types of love. He discovered that in their concept of "eros" there appeared to be no differentiation between romantic and sexual love. This was not what Hector had expected, or hoped, to find. Rationally, he had always thought of his love for Penelope to be pure and innocent. He reverenced the perfection of her face and her body but had never consciously wished to defile this beauty with impure desires.

Now he started to question his motives. He would have given everything for a single kiss from Penelope's sweet lips. But if he had achieved that, would he have been satisfied? For the time being, at least, he kidded himself that he would.

However, he resolved that he would never put himself through the same pain for any other woman. His idea of romantic love was reserved for Penelope alone and if it were to be unrequited, then so be it.

Penelope aside, from now on his goal would be the other component of "eros" - the sexual part. Love of the body.

****

Since the age of 11 Penelope had been aware that she was different from the other girls in the school year group. Even at that age she was pretty, graceful and soft-spoken; by comparison the others were plain and awkward, although she would never have dreamt of using that description of them. She enjoyed herself as much as anyone but was never silly. She was mature beyond her years but never sought to belittle anyone who was not as grown up.

These qualities went unappreciated by most of the girls in school. To them "Lady Penelope" was snooty, conservative in her dress and attitudes to the point of dowdiness, and aloof and smug, despite her best efforts to be friendly.

The fact that she was attractive to the boys further alienated her from her female peers. And her comfortable and respectable background provoked further jealousies from the more mean-spirited among them.

All this did not trouble Penelope. She had a couple of loyal and understanding girl friends, both daughters of the farming community, and a devoted following of admirers who were boys.

She was a hard-working student who spent much of her free time revising for exams. She was determined to get to a good university, gain a top degree and then go into law. Encouraged by her sensible parents, she also found some opportunities for socialising and taking part in the life of the community.

She had been a Brownie and Girl Guide and then later secretary of the local Young Farmers' Club. One year she was crowned as their Dairy Queen – much to the disgust of her female critics at school.

Unsurprisingly, she was often asked out on dates by boys from school and from among the Young Farmers. She occasionally agreed, going to the pictures or to a local dance, but this was to be polite. She had no intention of "getting involved" and being distracted from her school work.

Then one day, at a Young Farmers' event, Thomas Strawson had asked if she would go swimming with him and a group of friends at the Sanderholme outdoor pool. After giving the matter some thought, Penelope agreed. In doing so she was being at best pragmatic, at worst cynical. She was not in the least attracted to this unprepossessing "farmer's boy", whom she found lacking in charm or poise, but who was nonetheless not especially objectionable either.

The Douglases and the Strawsons, although poles apart culturally, were both influential in the farming fraternity and so there was little in the friendship for her parents to object to, confident, as they were, that this could never be a long-lasting relationship. The main benefit from Penelope's angle was that it would help her to keep at bay other more persistent, unsuitable or importunate suitors. She would be able to "drop" Thomas politely when the time was right.

Thomas had been egged on by school friends and to some extent by his own parents to ask Penelope for a date. He had no illusions that she was to become "the love of his life".

It has to be noted that Hector was never counted by Penelope among those admirers to be kept at bay. She liked him because he was gentle and polite towards her. On the day she was told that he had her name etched on his satchel she at first blushed but then quietly dismissed the news with a smile. After all, she was used to such worship.

Then came the day when Hector asked her to go to the cinema. Penelope was surprised that he had plucked up the courage to telephone her, and just a little flattered. The general opinion of the girls at school was that Hector was rather an insignificant individual, bookish, a little dishevelled and quite shy. Penelope shared some of those opinions but was perceptive enough to recognise two things – that he was truly and madly in love with her, and that he had a quality which she prized: that, like her much-loved father, he was a gentleman.

She had been surprised that her mother, Pamela, had reacted quite badly to Hector's telephone call.

"He's not really our type of person," she had said.

Penelope quizzed her a little about this opinion but didn't get a satisfactory answer. She had never for a moment thought that her mother might be a snob, but her attitude towards Hector might have suggested that she was.

Pamela just brushed off her questions with: "I don't know, dear. He just doesn't seem your type somehow."

Her evasiveness annoyed Penelope and she even considered ringing Hector back and telling him she had changed her mind. Instinctively, though, she knew that if she agreed to go on a date with him he might never leave her alone. And that was definitely not on her life's agenda.

Chapter two – Playing with fire

Hector was standing next to the jukebox in the local disco, one of several bars in the Stag's Head, a typical Victorian town centre commercial hotel.

During his two years in the school sixth form, the psychedelic lighting effects had sometimes provided an exciting accompaniment to the rushing through of homework in a dark corner of the bar. Algebraic formulae and Latin declensions were washed down with a pint of best bitter shandy.

The walls of the disco were adorned by a jungle scene, with African warriors, lions, tigers, monkeys, elephants and crocodiles in vivid colours. Part of the wallpaper, which formed the underbelly of a huge lion, had been peeled off, and some juvenile graffiti artist had replaced it with a gigantic penis larger than the remainder of the animal's body.

The room was dark with the windows blacked out. But when the DJ started up the music the dance floor was illuminated by strobe lighting. This made for an exciting atmosphere but was also a source of embarrassment for young dancers who suffered from dandruff as this sparkled on their shoulders like a mini galaxy of stars.

It was in this disco that Hector and some of his school friends chose to celebrate the end of their A level exams.

On a summer Saturday night, the dance floor was a seething mass of hot and sweaty gyrating bodies. There was a good smattering of young males. As was the vogue in the late '60s, some were almost indistinguishable from the girls due to their Cavalier flowing locks. Hector's were not exactly flowing, but at least shoulder length.

The majority of the dancers comprised girls in the 14 to 20 age group. Many were in the bar illegally, but no one cared.

They were in various forms of '60s-style undress. Some had short mini-skirts barely covering their bottoms. They sometimes provided a quick flash of red or black knickers when the dancing got energetic. Some wore 'point-em-out' dark coloured bras, which, under the psychedelic lights, showed up clearly beneath thin white tee shirts or unbuttoned white blouses. Others wore hot pants, so short and tight that little bulges of buttocks protruded from them.

Hector and his friends loved it! They had devised an amusing little game to keep them occupied when, as usual, their novice attempts at seduction had proved unsuccessful.

The disco was often so crowded that physical contact with other drinkers and dancers was unavoidable. The aim of the lads' game was to score points according to which part of a girl's anatomy they could come into bodily contact with. For instance, brushing up against a girl's leg would score one point.   Bottoms were two points. Tits were three. If the tits belonged to Big Linda five points were chalked up. A kiss from a girl scored ten.

The lads never knew whether the girls had a similar game, although it seems unlikely.

On this particular Saturday night, though, two new pieces of female "talent" appeared on the dance floor. Hector and his sidekicks – with eyes like lasers for "totty" – were quick to home in on them.

One of the girls, a brunette, was in her late teens. She was wearing a relatively modest short skirt and quite unrevealing top. A nice girl, but a plain Jane.

But her companion, who looked older than most of the other females in the room, was a very different kettle of fish and took centre stage on the dance floor.

She was a tall, slim, pale-faced blonde, a couple of inches taller than her friend. Her face had perfect bone structure and an engaging pout and her hair was sleek, thick and almost waist-long. She was wearing a white blouse raised and knotted in a bow at the front so that a tantalising area of flat stomach was exposed. The blouse was unbuttoned as far as reasonable modesty would allow but she was wearing no bra and her nipples stood out, neat and firm. She had tight fitting denim jeans and her figure looked magnificent as she whirled energetically to the frenetic disco beats.

Hector's friend Matthew nudged him and commented: "Wow. She looks like Brigitte Bardot!"

Hector nodded in agreement, captivated by this vision of sublime womanhood.

After half an hour or so, Matthew, who was more confident than Hector, turned to his friend and said: "Let's have a dance with those two, shall we?"

Hector, still a shy soul at that time of his life, was reticent. Left to his own devices, it has to be said, he would probably have stood there all night, not daring to take to the dance floor.

But a few pints of bitter shandy had enabled him to shed enough of his inhibitions to acquiesce to Matthew's wishes.

"Yes, okay then," he said. "But only if I can dance with the blonde."

Matthew, a kindly soul who had his friend's best interests at heart, agreed and beckoned Hector on to the floor.

Matthew strode up to the younger woman and started to dance with her. Dancing with someone in those days largely comprised flailing one's arms about to the music somewhere vaguely in the direction of the partner.

Hector sidled towards the blonde. He was preparing to do the gentlemanly thing and ask: "Would you like a dance?" But he was spared that embarrassment when she happily waved him towards her. This type of welcoming gesture was something Hector had rarely experienced in his short life and it filled him with happiness and confidence.

He was proud as a peacock to be dancing with this blonde-haired beauty. His moves became as wild and uninhibited as hers.

On most occasions in the past when Hector had asked a girl to dance, his partner would end the experience after a couple of three-minute records. The blonde, though, was content to dance continuously for about three-quarters of an hour. The occasional warm flashing smile would reassure her partner that she was pleased to have his company.

She would sometimes beckon Hector towards her so they could hold hands and dance close together. Then she would fling him away to pursue more exuberant moves at arms'-length.

Eventually Matthew and his brunette partner approached Hector and his blonde and said: "We're going to have a drink now. Are you coming?"

Hector looked towards his companion in a questioning way and she replied: "Yes. I could do with a drink."

"I'll get them in," said Matthew. "What would you two ladies like?"

"We'll both have Bacardi and Coke with ice," said the blonde.

"I'll have the same," said Hector, in the belief that this would appear more sophisticated than asking for another shandy.

"All right. I'll get them. Let's have a seat down there," said Matthew, pointing to a vacant table at the relatively quiet end of the bar.

The four chatted together contentedly for a few minutes before Matthew said: "What are your names?"

"I'm Tricia and this is my sister, Hannah," said the blonde, "And you are?"

"Matthew."

"I'm Hector."

When the two boys eventually revealed that – at least for the next two weeks – they were still at school, they were pleasantly surprised that this did not appear to faze the women.

Tricia was much the more talkative of the two, oozing a self-confidence born both of an awareness of her attractiveness and her greater age and worldliness.

She said they both lived at Sheepsville, a small marsh village seven miles from Sanderholme.

Matthew knew the place quite well as he had aunts and uncles living there.

"Whereabouts in Sheepsville?" he asked.

"Oh, Rose Cottage, near the church," replied Tricia.

When it got to 9.30pm Tricia announced that they were planning to go on to the Buckthorn Arms, a rather upmarket pub at the quieter end of town which attracted some of the wealthier young people of the area.

"Oh, that's a pity," said Hector with a hangdog expression.

"Why don't you come with us?" asked Tricia.

"How are you getting down there?" asked Matthew.

"We can go in my car," said Tricia.

"Are you sure?" said Hector.

"Of course."

"If you can stand her driving," laughed Hannah.

"Cheeky!" said Tricia. "Come on then. Drink up. Let's go."

Parked along the nearby main road was her car, a new silver Ford Capri. Hector was mightily impressed. It seemed he was going up in the world.

After a decidedly hairy journey in a car driven at breakneck speed through town they arrived at their destination.

It was a quiet night at the Buckthorn Arms and, after buying drinks, our quartet settled for a game of darts. It was fun! Tricia was effervescent, Hannah calm and friendly, Matthew his usual amiable self. And Hector? He was shyly pleasant but starting to scheme. Eros was raising his head. He had never met anyone like Tricia before, overtly highly sexual but in an entirely natural, unthreatening way. Hector was determined not to fall in love with her. But, oh, how he wanted her!

Closing time came and it was time to say goodbye. There was no cause for Tricia to offer the lads a lift home as they both lived nearby. There were pecks on cheeks all round and everyone agreed it had been a good night.

"See you around," said Tricia.

This was said in such a tone of voice that Hector felt it was genuine – not just a brush-off.

As he and Matthew walked home they discussed the evening's events.

"I liked them," said Hector. "Especially Tricia. She's hot – and good fun too."

"Yeah," said Matthew. "You're not wrong. Great figure. Her sister was nice too, in a homely sort of way."

"Do you think we should try to see them again?" asked Hector.

"Yeah, why not?" said Matthew.

"Would you be happy to go with Hannah, if I had a crack at Tricia?" asked Hector.

"Yeah, don't see why not. Except…." Matthew paused, searching for the right words.

"Except you would rather have Tricia?" asked Hector.

"No, I'm realistic," said Matthew. "But do you think you might be playing out of your league with Tricia?"

"I'm sure you're right. I would probably make a complete idiot of myself. But, nothing ventured, nothing gained, eh?"

Matthew laughed.

"I suppose so. But it's a big leap from having no

girlfriend at all to someone as gorgeous – and most likely as experienced – as Tricia. But, as you say, nothing ventured, nothing gained. We do have a problem, though. How do we contact them?"

Hector frowned.

"Ah, that is a problem. All we know is that they live at Sheepsville."

"Rose Cottage, near the church," added Matthew.

"You're a genius!" said Hector. "I'll borrow my dad's car and we'll have a ride out there. On Sunday, maybe?"

"Suits me," replied Matthew. "If we find the cottage we could just knock on the door and see what happens."

"Okay."

****

The following Sunday afternoon the pair set off in Hector's dad's Vauxhall Victor, following the A road which led from Sanderholme to Sheepsville. The village, which in centuries past had boasted of being a market town, straddles the main road between Sanderholme and its rival resort of Sandytoft.

The High Street mainly comprises old terraced houses and cottages. The frontages of several of these have incongruously large front windows, suggesting that they had once been shops at a time when the village was of greater commercial importance.

The only significant building along this road is the impressive parish church, built in local limestone and greenstone, and with a large tower dating from the 12th century.

Hector parked the car at the front of the church and

the two lads got out to start their search for Rose Cottage. They walked up and down the High Street two or three times but couldn't find a property displaying that name. Nor could they see any silver Ford Capris in the neighbourhood.

"Perhaps it hasn't got a house sign with the name on it. Maybe it just has a number," suggested Hector.

"Let's knock on a door and ask someone if they know where it is," said Matthew.

They chose a cottage on the opposite side of the road to the church and rang the doorbell. A cheery middle-aged woman greeted them. When they asked her if she knew of a Rose Cottage she replied that she had never heard of such a place, adding: "But you've asked the right person. I'm the village postmistress."

"Oh, right," said Hector. "In that case you might know who we're looking for – two young sisters, called Tricia and Hannah. Tricia, the older one, drives a silver Ford Capri – quite a noticeable car."

"No," said the postmistress. "I don't know of anyone like that in the village."

Hector looked crestfallen. He thanked the woman and the pair slouched back to the car.

"We've been duped," said Matthew.

"You're sure they definitely said they lived at Sheepsville?" said Hector, who was very much put out by this setback.

"Yep, quite sure. And you thought so too, didn't you?"

"Yeah, 'fraid so."

As they drove home they had to admit they were beaten. Even if by chance they met the two young women again it would make no difference. They had clearly lied about where they lived in order to prevent any further contact.

Hector was less sanguine about the situation than Matthew. He was much more intense than his sensible, and more cynical, friend. And anyway Matthew didn't have "the hots" for Hannah in the same way that Hector did for Tricia.

Two weeks later when the two lads ventured once more into the Stag's Head disco Hector got chatting to a young "man about town" called Desmond whose parents owned a caravan site next to Hector's family's.

It so happened that Desmond had been in the disco the fortnight before and had seen Hector dancing with Tricia.

"You were dancing with Tricia Stanmore last time I saw you," he said.

"You know her?"

"Yes, most people know Tricia. I think quite a few have *known* her too," joked Desmond.

"Oh really," said Hector. "Is she a bit of a goer, then?"

"I think you could say that. She likes a good time. Did you get anywhere with her?"

"No, we got on all right, though. I'd like to see her again. Do you know where she lives?"

"Oh, yes. At Havenside. Bank Farm."

As Desmond said this a pretty young woman grabbed him by the arm and led him away.

Desmond turned around to Hector and said: "Sorry, I've been told we've got to go."

Hector would have liked to have asked him more

about Tricia and her sister. But at least now he had an address.

He turned to Matthew and said: "Did you hear all that?"

"Yeah, but it doesn't get us anywhere does it? They told us a false address because they obviously wanted to get rid of us."

"Suppose so," said Hector, dejectedly.

That should have been the end of the matter, but the powers of Eros drove Hector on. He was determined not to be beaten. That night in bed he weighed up the pros and cons.

Matthew was no longer interested in pursuing what he now believed was a fool's errand. With his friend at his side Hector had been quite willing to knock on any door at Sheepsville to achieve his goal. Now, though, he would have to go-it-alone.

Havenside was a tiny hamlet at the side of the arrow-straight Marsh Eau river, about three miles from Sanderholme. Bank Farm would be very easy to find – probably the only sizeable property in the hamlet. Hector was too shy to turn up on the doorstep on his own and ask for Tricia. The name Stanmore might well be in the telephone directory, but he feared he might become tongue-tied on the phone and ruin his chances.

There was only one thing for it - a letter...

Dear Tricia, You may remember me. My friend Matthew and I recently spent a very pleasant evening with you and your sister Hannah at the Stag's Head disco and then the Buckthorn Arms. We enjoyed the evening so much that we wondered if we might possibly meet up again at some time in the near future.

If you are interested in doing that, then perhaps you might drop me a line or give me a ring suggesting a time and place for a meeting. We are available most evenings.

My address is Marshview Caravan Park, Marsh Lane, Sanderholme, and my telephone number is Sanderholme 2235.

I look forward very much to hearing from you,

Kind regards,

Hector Ratcliffe xx

Hector's heart was pounding as he slipped the letter into the nearest post box. He was then impatient for a reply. In fact he thought of little else during the next few days. But no reply came.

Two weeks went by and Hector and Matthew were sitting in a local coffee bar called "Becky's", the name of the owner. This was where the local youth gathered to chat and play the jukebox.

A group of four girls was sitting at a nearby table and Hector became aware that they were looking furtively in his direction. He heard one of them say: "That lad over there wrote a letter to my sister – and she's married."

Hector observed the speaker closely. She was not Hannah and, as a redhead, bore no obvious resemblance to either Hannah or Tricia. He strained his ears in case she said anything else about him, but she apparently became aware that he was listening and lowered her voice to a whisper.

Matthew had heard her remark too.

"What was that all about?" he asked.

Hector had not told Matthew about the letter, being sure that his sensible friend would try to talk him out of sending it. Now he had to confess.

"I sent a letter to Tricia, asking if she and Hannah would like to meet up with us again."

"And she's married!" said Matthew. "I think you'd better keep your head down, mate."

"I think you're right," said Hector, smiling nervously.

Over the next few days Hector made some tentative enquiries among school friends who came from the adjacent farming area to find out what information he could about Tricia, and particularly about her husband. He wasn't especially frightened of any repercussions there might be from his letter, but curious to know "how the land lay".

He gradually began to build up some sort of picture of the inhabitants of Bank Farm. The farmer, and Tricia's husband, was Derek Stanmore. He was older than his wife by ten years, his first marriage with another local girl having ended acrimoniously, with accusations from her of cruelty and unfaithfulness.

Derek was a well-known local figure, a Round Tabler, keen golfer and member of the Drainage Board. He had lots of friends and associates to whom he was loyal and supportive. But he was also known to be a rather grumpy individual, liable to get himself into feuds with neighbouring landowners over farm boundaries and such like.

Tricia, for obvious reasons, was very popular in Round Table circles. At their mixed functions she was always the first on the dance floor, and often the last off it. She was noted for rarely wearing a bra and for the shortness of her dresses.

There were rumours that she also enjoyed nights out with female friends when she would take off her wedding ring. Hector could testify to that rumour being correct. No one could name any specific man she had had an affair with, but everyone asserted that she must have had numerous trysts.

There was one particular rumour which several people mentioned. There were Round Table parties where people would throw their car keys into a ring on the floor and then pair off with whichever member of the opposite sex picked them up. It was said that Tricia was a regular participant in this game. On one occasion this had led to a punch-up between her husband and a prominent local GP.

****

The day after Hector overheard the conversation in the coffee bar he was wandering down Sanderholme's main street, on the lookout for eligible girls, when he received a tap on the shoulder. He looked round to see the girl from the coffee bar who had said she was Tricia's sister.

"Do you mind if I have a word with you?" she asked.

"That's okay," said Hector.

"I'm Tricia Stanmore's sister."

Hector interrupted: "I know actually. I overheard you say so at 'Becky's' yesterday."

"Did you know that she's married?" she asked, in an

accusing tone.

"I must admit I overheard you saying that at 'Becky's'. I didn't know before that, though. I thought she and her sister were both single."

"Well, she is married. I'm her sister. I'm not married."

"Does she have more than one sister?"

"No, just me."

"When me and my friend Matthew met her at the Stag's Head she said she was with her sister, Hannah."

"Hannah's just a friend of ours. She's not our sister. But anyway this isn't why I stopped you. I wanted to warn you. Tricia's husband has found your letter and he's on the warpath. He says he is going to shoot you!"

"Literally?"

"Literally. He's got such a temper, he could do it."

"Phew. Has he told you that?"

"No, but he's told Tricia."

"Has Tricia explained that I didn't know she was married?"

"No, she wouldn't, would she? She'd be frightened of what Derek might do to her."

"What has she told him, then?"

"That you're just a schoolboy, who for some reason has a crush on her."

"Could you tell her husband that I didn't know?"

"I'm keeping out of it. The atmosphere's pretty tense in that house at the moment. I just thought I should warn you off. If you see Derek coming just go the other way – quick."

"Oh, God. I seem to have dropped myself in it, don't I? If your sister and her friend had told us the truth to start with, we would have steered clear of them."

"I don't know what went on between you all. I just don't want anyone to get hurt. That's all."

After saying that, the girl walked quickly away.

Hector called after her: "Thanks."

****

Now that school holiday time had arrived, Sanderholme was buzzing with holidaymakers. The beaches, amusement arcades, pubs and clubs were teeming with people and the hotels, B&Bs and caravan sites were full.

Most of Hector's Grammar School peers were preparing to leave the area to go to university or teacher training college. Some thought that he was the taking the easy way out by choosing to go straight into the family caravan site business. However, in his own way he was ambitious, the plan being that he would learn the business on the job with the ultimate aim of taking full charge of an expanding site. His mother and Aunt Christine would remain in supporting roles, mainly working in reception.

The day after his conversation with Tricia's sister, Hector busied himself delivering Calor Gas to various caravans before returning to reception which was being manned by his aunt.

As soon as he entered he saw that Aunt Christine was in an agitated state.

"Hector," she said. "There's been a very angry man in here looking for you. You haven't seen him have you?"

"No," said Hector. "What did he want?"

"He wouldn't say. He just demanded to know where you were. He was very rude."

"Did he say who he was?"

"No, I asked him but he wouldn't say. I could see he was looking for trouble, though. So I told him I didn't know where you were and that you might have gone off site for something."

"Did he give any clue what it was about?" asked Hector.

"No, I asked him that as well, but he just stormed off and said he would be back."

"What did he look like?"

"A biggish man with a good mop of black hair. About fortyish I would guess. I think he went off in a Range Rover or something like that."

"Oh, thanks," said Hector.

"Have you any idea who he could have been?" asked Christine. "He did seem very aggressive."

"Not a clue," replied Hector.

But Hector was lying. He was a gentle soul who usually went about his daily life without attracting any hostility, so he immediately concluded that the visitor must have been Tricia's husband. The Range Rover, a favourite vehicle for farmers, only served to confirm this. Not normally a fearful type of person, Hector began to get a little worried.

"I don't like the sound of him," said Hector. "Just warn me if you see him coming again, will you, Aunty?"

"Yes, of course," said Christine, looking bemused.

That night as his mother drove home with Hector to the family's four-bedroomed detached home at the smarter end of Sanderholme she noticed he was quiet and withdrawn.

"Everything all right with you?" said his mum. "You're a bit quiet. Are you worried about that man who came to the office?"

"Oh, no. I don't know what that's all about. No, everything's fine," he reassured her.

In fact he was deep in thought. He was worried that Derek Stanmore had him in his sights and he feared for the consequences. He appeared to have two options, to sit back and wait for his punishment, or to be proactive. He decided on the second course.

He was keen to avoid a man-to-man confrontation with Derek, either physically or verbally. As he saw the trouble had been caused by a letter, written as the result of a misunderstanding, he decided that the best way of putting things right would be through another letter explaining the situation. But if he posted it, would it get to Bank Farm before Derek got to him? He had heard of letters taking two days to reach some of the remotest hamlets in the area.

He would have to take a risk. He would write the letter and deliver it straightaway to the farm himself. The risk was that he might meet Derek as he approached the letterbox. If so, he would hand him the missive and offer his profuse apologies, grovelling as much as necessary. He reckoned that at least the fact that he was meeting the problem head-on might help to pacify the husband.

As soon as he got home he started to write:

Dear Mr Stanmore, I am writing to you to express my

45

sincere apologies for a misunderstanding that appears to have arisen. As I believe you may be aware, I recently wrote to your wife suggesting that she and her sister might meet myself and a friend. This was written on the understanding that I believed your wife to be a single lady. I give you my word that I would never have contacted your wife had I realised her marital situation. I would also like to stress that absolutely no blame attaches to her for this unfortunate misunderstanding on my part, Yours sincerely, Hector Ratcliffe.

Brief and to the point, thought Hector. He knew he was being unduly gallant regarding Tricia, as she had brought this problem upon them by being dishonest. She had given no indication that she was married and had provided a false address. And she had invented a sister she didn't have! He had also heard the story that she was in the habit of taking off her wedding ring when she went out on the town. He realised he was letting her off lightly in his letter to Derek, but he was so susceptible to her gorgeous looks and enticing personality that he might have forgiven her anything.

That evening Hector borrowed his father's car and set off for Bank Farm, armed with the letter. His journey took him along a main road and then on to a narrow lane which followed the route of the Marsh Eau river on its journey to the sea. The river itself was obscured from the lane by a high grass bank. On the other side of the road was a large flat wheat field which stretched as far as the eye could see.

It was a lonely road on this sunny and warm summer's

evening, the only company being a handful of seagulls wheeling away on the wind and a tiny field mouse which scurried across the road to avoid the car.

Eventually Hector could see in front of him a substantial and quite secluded farmhouse set amongst trees, with a range of farm buildings surrounding a large crew yard at the rear of the house. There was a tall red brick wall with a double gate leading to a gravel drive which went past the front door. At the side of the gate were two high brick pillars topped by a pair of fierce and weather-beaten stone lions.

The gates were open and Hector could have driven through them but he didn't wish to be so presumptuous as to do that. The thought also struck him that he needed to make the quickest possible getaway. The lane went to a dead end some 200 yards past the farmhouse. So that he could make a fast exit after delivering his letter, he sought to turn the car around and point it in the direction of the main road. The lane was too narrow for a three point turn so he edged forward past the farmhouse looking for a convenient opening. He spotted a field gate with a short muddy track leading to it. He turned the car there and then drove back to the farmhouse, parking in front of the double gates.

To his alarm as he got out of the car, a Range Rover appeared and pulled up in front of him.

A burly man, carrying a shotgun, got out and asked him: "Can I help you?"

This is the usual way that Lincolnshire farmers address people when they find them on or near their land. "Can I help you?" is not a polite enquiry from a fellow human being wishing to assist someone who may be lost or need some other kind of assistance. It is a euphemism for "What the hell are you doing on my land? Are you a thief or one of those damned ramblers who thinks they can just go anywhere they like, even though they can't afford to buy any land themselves?" Hector knew that. He had used the same sort of phraseology himself when he had seen strangers walking on the public right of way which crossed the caravan site.

"I was just delivering a letter to Bank Farm," said Hector timidly.

"All right. I live there. I can take it. What's it about?"

"It's for Mr Derek Stanmore," said Hector, now shaking slightly.

"That's me. What's it about?"

Derek's tone had softened when he asked this question a second time. He was satisfied Hector was not a thief and he had no wish to frighten him.

"There's been a misunderstanding and I wanted to clear it up."

"Misunderstanding? Let me have a look."

Derek tore open the envelope and read the letter.

"It's you, is it? I've been looking for you," said Derek.

"Is this true?"

"Yes, it's all true. I'm so sorry."

"I've calmed down a bit now," said Derek.

Pointing to his gun, he added: "I was all for giving you a bit of this earlier. Next time I think you ought to ask a woman if she's married before you ask her out. I'll let you off this time. But don't let it happen again, lad."

"I won't. Thanks."

"Right. Off you go, then."

"Bye," said Hector, shamefaced.

A sense of utter relief overcame him as he drove home. Eros was not for him, he decided.

****

Derek Stanmore was happy that his honour had been satisfied. A potential rival had grovelled in front of him. Hector had been the main target of his anger but in his heart he knew that the real culprit had been his wife.

In truth, he was far more captivated, and captured, by Tricia, than Hector could ever have been. He instinctively knew that she was unfaithful to him but never felt able to tackle her head-on about it. If he ever tentatively broached the subject she would sidestep the conversation by, quite literally, seducing him. A strong man in most situations, he was too weak to resist.

When he had had his pleasure, though, the nags and doubts returned. As time went on he changed from being the proverbial "hail fellow well met" to being suspicious, sour and melancholy.

Derek was ten years older than his wife. He first met her in the Buckthorn Arms when she was a tipsy teenager on the lookout for some casual sex. Their relationship was consummated in the passenger seat of his E-type Jaguar within a few minutes of their meeting.

Tricia came from a working class background, being brought up on a Sanderholme council estate. Her father was a landworker and her mother a cleaner at the local hospital. But her stunning good looks had already made her a favourite among the area's sports car owning rich set.

Four previous generations of Derek's family had farmed the same land at Havenside. His parents had died within a year of each other, leaving him, their only child, to live alone at Bank Farm and to run the business with the help of a foreman. He had a substantial inheritance which gave him the opportunity to be a socialite, at least in the relatively closed community of the Lincolnshire "county set". He liked fast cars, skiing holidays in Switzerland and expensive clothes.

From its very beginning his relationship with Tricia had its ups and downs. To Derek's friends it appeared that she used him when it suited her, enjoying being seen emerging from his expensive car on their nights out, but often neglecting him to engage with someone she found younger and more attractive.

In fact Derek was using her as much as she was him. He loved to be seen with this sparkling, seductive creature on his arm. And he was blissfully unaware of the sniggering going on behind his back, particularly by those who knew of her "availability" to a number of his so-called friends.

When, three years after they first met, Derek and Tricia announced their engagement those of their acquaintance treated the news with a mixture of incredulity and barely hidden mirth.

Derek was wealthy, with a strong physique and by no means bad looking but had a reputation for being something of a dullard.

"He will never tame her," was the general opinion.

However, the couple did get married and, despite Derek's constant jealousy when Tricia showed interest in other men, the relationship had already lasted far longer than most people had forecast. This was largely because Tricia got her own way most of the time.

For instance, it was a great disappointment to Derek that she had shown no interest in having children. She was a good-time girl and children would just have been in the way.

When they first got together, Derek, who fancied himself as something of a playboy, was of the same mind. However, as time went on he felt a void in his life which only an expansion of their family would have filled. This had been just another of the many fault lines in their marriage.

When Tricia had picked up Hector's letter from the doormat and read it she simply smiled to herself that she had made another easy conquest and gave it little more thought. Absentmindedly she popped it into a kitchen drawer with the intention of adding it to her secret stash of love letters later.

Unfortunately for her, Derek had rifled through the kitchen drawer looking for a torch battery and come across the letter. In a rage after reading the contents, he stormed into their bedroom where Tricia was sitting in front of her dressing table putting on her makeup ready for a night out.

He roughly grabbed her by the shoulder and yelled into her ear: "I found this. Who's bloody Hector Ratcliffe?"

"I don't know any Hector Ratcliffe," she replied,

angrily pulling his arm away.

"Don't bloody lie to me," shouted Derek. "There's a letter here from Hector Ratcliffe asking you out on a date."

"Let me have that," she said, snatching the letter from his hand.

She read it and said, gently : "Don't worry about this. I think he's just some spotty Grammar School kid I ran into at the Stag's Head. He's obviously got a crush on me. But I haven't given him any encouragement. He's just a daft young lad."

"I don't bloody believe you," snapped Derek. "I know what you're like when you've had a few drinks down you. It's anybody with trousers for you, isn't it?"

Tricia replied calmly: "No, it's not. Yes, I might have had a few drinks but I didn't give him any encouragement. He's just a kid. I was having a dance and he came on to the dance floor and started dancing with me. I didn't ask him to."

"But you know his name."

"He told me his name. I didn't ask him to do that either. Nothing happened – nothing at all. He just had a dance with me and got some silly ideas. That's all. Now come here."

She pulled her husband towards her, kissed him on the cheek and fondled his bottom.

"You know you're the only one I love. Shall I show you?"

Her hand slid up his tee shirt and she gently stroked his back. The couple embraced and, a few moments later, they were on the bed, vigorously making love.

Tricia had used this tactic many times before to divert her jealous husband's anger. And it had worked again. As always, he told her he forgave her.

The couple enjoyed a night out together with friends at a nearby country pub and restaurant, both drinking heavily and then stumbling into bed together at midnight.

The next morning, though, Derek's anger about the letter came flooding back. His ire was now directed towards Hector.

He rose early to do some work in the fields, returning to the farmhouse two hours later to have breakfast with Tricia.

"I'm going to find this bloody Hector Ratcliffe," he declared as he attacked his fried eggs and bacon.

"Don't be silly," said Tricia. "He's only a silly young boy with a crush. He's no threat to us."

"He's got some damn nerve asking my wife out. He's going to pay for this."

"Please drop it, love."

"We'll see," replied Derek.

Tricia gave him a hopeful smile.

Derek gobbled up the remainder of his breakfast, got up from the table and violently slammed the kitchen door as he left the house to return to his work.

Over the next few days the feelings of resentment built up inside him resulting in a number of further heated exchanges between him and Tricia. Even her most seductive charms were now insufficient to win him over.

"I'm going to shoot that young bastard," he eventually

threatened.

Tricia screamed at him not to be so stupid.

"You're mad. Absolutely bonkers. You could find yourself in prison for life over a silly little schoolboy. Nothing came of it. Nothing would ever come of it. Please, please, calm down."

But Derek would have none of it. His wife's flirtations had sent him to the end of his tether and he needed to take out his anger on someone. That someone could not be Tricia herself, because he was still madly in love with her. So it had to be Hector.

This time the door which led from the kitchen to the rest of the house was slammed, almost falling from its hinges, as he ignored his wife's pleadings. Derek went upstairs to the locked spare bedroom where his gun cabinet was located. He took out a shotgun, loaded it with cartridges which he kept in a nearby chest of drawers and went downstairs again. He left the house through the front door, avoiding Tricia, and then drove off in his Range Rover.

Derek was still ablaze with anger as he approached the Marshview Caravan Site on his quest to find Hector. But he still possessed just enough rationality to have decided during his journey that he would only threaten the young man with the shotgun, not fire it at him. He realised that even then he would be risking a considerable prison sentence. It was his nuclear option to try once and for all to control his wife's excesses.

When he went to reception and discovered that Hector was off the site he was inwardly relieved that he had been denied the opportunity of going through with his foolish mission. He also decided to tell Tricia where he had been in the hope of scaring her into improving her behaviour.

So by the time he met Hector in the process of delivering his second letter his red mist had subsided and he was able to forgive the young man. After all, he knew what Tricia could be like and the effect she could have on any red-blooded fellow.

Chapter three – Moving on

When Hector reached home following his confrontation with Derek he pondered on the lessons to be learnt from his unfortunate experience with Tricia.

He realised he had been incredibly naïve. He should have given up on her as soon as it became clear that she had lied about her address. He had been extremely foolish in writing a letter to someone in such unpromising circumstances.

He had tried the romantic side of erotic love with Penelope with no success at all. He had been hoping for the physical variety with Tricia but that had been an utter disaster.

But, at the tender age of 18, would Hector give up altogether with women? Of course he wouldn't. To help him decide what to do next he once again consulted the Greeks – and once again those wise old people appeared to have an answer – *ludus*.

Ludus has been described as a playful, child-like, flirtatious and teasing kind of love, perfect for people who just want to have fun together.

He determined to return to the Stag's Head and wait patiently for a suitable "playful" encounter. Not one to let the grass grow under his feet, the very next night after his Bank Farm visit, he walked round to see his friend Matthew, who lived with his parents and two sisters in one of Sanderholme's many leafy grid-patterned roads.

He told his confidant about what had happened regarding Tricia.

Matthew, a lanky lad with a shock of ginger hair, combined an unerring self-confidence with a strong measure of common sense, a thoroughgoing decency and a strong streak of cynicism. He was not one to mince his words and was scathing about what Hector had done.

"You're a complete idiot. Why did you write to that woman after she lied to us? Couldn't you see she was just a lying cock teaser?"

"I know. I know. But she was so gorgeous."

"Yeah, she was gorgeous. But she was dangerous. You should have realised that, you twat."

"I know. I've learnt my lesson. But you've got to get back in the saddle, haven't you? Do you fancy going to the Stag's Head, to see what's about?"

"There's no hope for you, is there? Yeah. Let's go to the Stag's then."

It was mid-week in summer and the disco, which at weekends was heaving with sweaty bodies and teeming with what lads in those non-PC days described as "crumpet", was just about half full. It was how Hector liked it. You could see the wood for the trees.

The two lads bought their Newcastle Brown ales and took up their position at the side of the dance floor. They stood there for an hour enjoying the view of the girl dancers in their miniskirts, tight-fitting hot pants and crop tops.

Then Matthew felt a tap on his shoulder. Standing behind him was a pretty, 5ft 2in brunette, with a lovely trim figure and a broad cheeky smile.

"Hi Matt," she said, putting her arm around his waist, "will you buy me a drink?"

"Sorry, Bernice. I'm skint," said Matt, who was doing a poorly paid pot washing job at a local café while deciding on his first career move.

"Who's your friend?" she asked.

"This is Hector."

"Pleased to meet you, Hector," said Bernice. "You couldn't buy me a drink, could you?"

"Yes, I'll buy you one. What would you like?"

"Could I have a snowball, please?"

"Yes, of course you could."

"Thanks," said Bernice, kissing him on the cheek.

A snowball, the cocktail made from Advocaat and lemonade, was an expensive drink in the '60s. Hector had enough left of his weekly wage from the caravan site to just about be able to afford one.

Bernice thanked him for the drink, kissed him on the cheek again and went over to the far side of the dance floor to rejoin some female friends.

Matthew smirked at Hector, who well understood the meaning of his expression. It said: "You've just been taken for a mug, mate."

Some minutes later Bernice joined three other girls for a dance to the Rolling Stones' "Satisfaction". Her cheerful demeanour gave her an air of boundless vivacity and she looked so enticing in her pretty flowery mini dress.

Hector decided it was time to take the plunge and ask her for a dance. The music was so loud that speaking was well-nigh impossible. So he caught Bernice's eye and merely mouthed the words: "Like a dance?"

She nodded her agreement.

Hector did his signature "Moves Like Jagger" routine, which caused Bernice much amusement. She joined in with gusto, smiling, laughing and giggling the whole time. As the music changed from track to track the couple carried on dancing.

This filled Hector with hope. His usual experience had been that after one three-minute record had finished, the girl he was dancing with thanked him, picked up her handbag from the dance floor and scurried off to reunite with her friends. This time the lively dancing went on and on until the DJ signalled the approaching pub closing time by slowing down the tempo of the music.

Hector knew this was crunch time. Would Bernice allow him to get close to her to have a smooch? To his delight, she beckoned him towards her and he felt the warmth of her body as she joined her hands around his back. He returned the compliment and their dance soon became a warm embrace.

He felt a gentle bite on his neck as Bernice hung her head across his shoulder. Bliss! He put his hands on her shoulders, leant forward and kissed her on the lips. She responded with enthusiasm and playful tongues were soon brought into use.

When they eventually left the dance floor they looked around for Matthew, but he had gone.

"I think Matt got fed up," she said. "We've been dancing for ages."

"I really enjoyed it," said Hector.

"So did I," said Bernice, still smiling. "I'd better be going now. I've got a bus to catch."

"Can I walk you to the bus stop?" asked Hector,

growing in confidence.

"Yes."

The couple left the disco hand in hand and walked across the road to a covered bus stand.

"Where do you live?" Hector enquired.

"At Sheepsville," she said.

A faint nanosecond of déjà vu entered Hector's head as she voiced this reply. For that was where Tricia had said she lived when she lied to him about her address. But this was of no consequence.

"Do you live in Sanderholme?" asked Bernice.

"Yes."

"Are you still at school?"

"No, I went to the Grammar School, but I've just left. I'm working now."

"Oh, so you're a gooseberry!" she laughed.

Grammar School pupils were known as gooseberries because of the colour of their school uniforms.

"Yes. Are you still at school?"

"Yep, the secondary modern."

"So you're a plum-bum then?"

Again a reference to the colour of uniform.

"Yes, I guess I am," she giggled.

"How old are you?"

"Sixteen. How old are you?"

"Eighteen."

"Quite old then."

"Yes, positively ancient. We've had a good night, though, haven't we?" said Hector.

"Yes."

"Can we meet up again?"

"Yes, we could."

"Do you have a phone number?"

"Yes."

Bernice scrambled in her handbag and came up with a pen and a scrap of paper, on which she scribbled her number.

"Look, my bus is coming. Give me a kiss."

She gave him a deep, sweet kiss on the lips. It was a best kiss Hector had ever had in his life.

****

As Hector lay in bed thinking about the night's occurrences he was in a quandary. He had set out to find a playful *ludus* girlfriend to have some fun with. And yet already he could feel the first stirrings of a romantic attachment. He thought Bernice was a delightful girl. He had been a little put off by her cheekily asking Matthew and himself to buy her a drink, but that first impression had soon passed as he became captivated by her infectious smile, easygoing charm and elfin features.

He knew only too well that he could be very weak-willed when it came to the opposite sex, but told himself he was determined not to fall in love again so soon after his disappointments over Penelope.

He eventually decided he would phone Bernice and ask for a date but at the same time "screw his courage to the sticking place" and ward off any arrows that Cupid might let fly in his direction. He would only look for a good time – a bit of harmless fun.

The next evening he did phone Bernice. His normal instincts would have been to ask her on a formal date, perhaps a trip to the pictures or a meal at the one and only Chinese restaurant in Sanderholme. This time, though, he would act casual and just ask her if she would be going to the Stag's Head disco any time soon and, if so, could they meet up there?

Luckily, Bernice answered the phone herself. She instantly acknowledged Hector and seemed pleased to talk to him.

She rattled away, telling him all about what she had done that day, how her sister had annoyed her in a petty squabble over some missing makeup and how her mother had, even more annoyingly, taken her sister's side in the argument. It was all said in a cheerful, gossipy kind of way, with no real malice.

Hector, however, was not one to linger on the phone. He wished to get straight to the point: when could they meet at the disco?

It was now Thursday and she said she would be at the Stag's Head at around 8pm on the Saturday. She would look out for him.

"You can buy me another drink!" she joked.

"And we'll have another dance?" Hector replied.

"It's a date!" she declared.

"See you then."

"See you."

Hector had a wide satisfied grin as he put down the phone.

At home early that Saturday evening he had a bath, cut his fingernails and toenails, washed and blow-dried his shoulder-length hair, shaved and sprayed himself liberally with cheap aftershave. He put on his best flowery shirt, a favourite gold-coloured medallion and a freshly ironed pair of blue jeans.

He left his house feeling proud as a peacock and soon entered the busy disco. At first he found the comfort blanket of a group of his friends, including Matthew, who were, as per usual, standing sipping their beers and gawping at the girls on the dance floor.

Hector's eyes moved laser-like around the room in the hope of catching sight of Bernice. She didn't disappoint, coming over to him within a couple of minutes of his arrival.

She looked as alluring and cheeky as on their first meeting, introducing one of her own friends, Sally, and suggesting that Hector would like to buy them both drinks. He was only too willing to oblige.

Sally was a sultry, almost morose looking brunette with a flawless dark skin and gipsy origins. She had a slow, placid smile, in sharp contrast to her chirpy companion. Beneath that exterior, though, was a wry, almost dark, sense of humour.

When Hector returned from the bar, he was pleased to see that Bernice had already acquainted Sally with Matthew and they were making pleasant conversation. Hector felt this gave him the perfect opportunity to give his undivided attention to his new conquest.

The night went swimmingly even though most of it was a duplicate copy of the couple's first encounter. The main difference was the addition to the mix of Sally, who got on really well with Matthew and disappeared with him half way through the night. Matthew gave a knowing wink to Hector as they left arm in arm and subsequently

Hector was told that they had enjoyed a passionate time on the sandhills.

For Hector and Bernice, the night ended as before, with a delicious kiss at the bus stop and a promise that they would meet again the following Saturday.

For the time being this new experience suited Hector very well. It became a regular Saturday night event for a couple of months. Hector sometimes found himself getting frustrated, and a little jealous, when Bernice would occasionally leave him standing or sitting alone while she chatted and danced with her girl friends, and occasionally with other men. But generally he accepted that this was part and parcel of her outgoing friendly nature, which he otherwise greatly admired.

He had gone out searching for ludus – and that was exactly what he was getting. What was there not to like?

Matthew, meanwhile, was getting very attached to Sally, and she to him. Their personalities seemed to be perfectly matched. They were constantly canoodling in a darkened corner of the disco and spent a good deal of time together on weekdays as well as on Saturdays.

Sometimes Hector envied his friend for the deeper relationship he appeared to be experiencing. He kept telling himself that this was exactly the kind of thing he was trying to avoid. He had wished for a no strings attached, fun relationship and Bernice was supplying just that. And yet he had enough self-knowledge to realise that he was deceiving himself. He wanted more.

Three months after he first met Bernice, one particular event was to bring this yearning to the fore.

She was sitting on Hector's knee and chatting away

about some trivial happening in her life when she was approached by Terry, one of the local "greasers".

One side of the Stag's Head disco was populated by the motor cycling fraternity. The opposite side was dominated by scooterists. For this was the era of mods and rockers. In the disco, the two rival groups just about tolerated each other for most of the year. But woe betide any "newcomer" from either group who mistakenly sat down at the wrong side of the room. Usually they were just given a warning and told to move on. If they didn't take that hint, they might be picked up by their arms and legs by several of the opposing gang and "escorted" to the pavement outside.

At bank holiday times, matters could take a more serious turn. The opposing groups, bolstered by hundreds of extra recruits from among the "day trippers" from the Midlands and North, would congregate outside sea front pubs and there were often clashes, including fights between individuals and running battles between groups. These confrontations had to be broken up by a reinforced police presence in an attempt to protect the "family" image of this seaside holiday resort.

The Stag's Head was well away from the sea front but its disco still provided a magnet for both mods and rockers, or greasers as they were referred to locally. At bank holidays, one group felt it should have exclusive use of the pub. When mods were in the majority, they held sway and ejected greasers brave enough to venture inside, and vice versa. Tables and chairs were often thrown around and some beer glasses and heads got broken.

For the rest of the year "neutrals" such as Hector and Matthew were in the majority in the disco and left alone by the mods and rockers.

Terry was one of the leaders of the rockers, well respected for his immaculately turned out 500cc BSA Goldstar bike, his top of the range leathers, his craggy features and his spectacularly long black hair. He had an arrogant swagger but compensated for this with an open and friendly face. The girls adored him.

It was apparent that he was well known to Bernice and when he came over to talk to her, she drooled over him in a quite blatant way. She also showed an interest in his motorbike, which he was only too keen to boast about.

"I've got it outside," he said. "Won't you come for a spin on it?"

"Wow. Yes please," said an excited Bernice.

He immediately led her away. She didn't say a word to Hector or even give him a glance as she left the room.

Hector waited anxiously for her return until pub closing time. She didn't come back.

He was a forgiving person with a generally optimistic nature, but he sensed that this could signal the end of his relationship with Bernice.

In fact the following Saturday they did meet again at the Stag's Head and they danced the night away as usual. Bernice had said not a word about Terry, although Hector had been expecting something in the way of an apology.

He had begun to realise that the superficial attraction of *ludus* was never going to be enough for him. He needed a girl who would give him some commitment. It was time to move on to another Greek love category.

****

Agape has been described as love of the soul, selfless, unconditional love – the love for humanity, "the compassionate love that makes us sympathise with, help and connect to people we don't know".

This appealed to the better side of Hector's nature, for, beneath his laddish desire for sex for its own sake, he had a serious and compassionate outlook on life.

It was by a total coincidence that the next girl who came into his life appeared to complement perfectly this side of his personality.

After a few months of dalliance with Bernice it had become obvious to Hector that there was there no real love between them. They liked each other and he still fancied her. But she had shown clear signs that she was not looking for a physical relationship with him. When his hand occasionally strayed on to her leg it was quickly removed and a playful but at the same time meaningful slap was delivered.

They never rowed. They just gradually drifted apart, until one night in the disco Bernice introduced him to a 17-year-old mod called Martin, whom she announced as her boyfriend. Hector felt a little downtrodden and a tad jealous but shook Martin's hand and accepted the situation with good grace.

Bernice kissed him on the cheek and took Martin on to the dance floor.

****

Humphrey Gibb, who was studying English Literature at Cambridge University, was home for the Easter vacation and so this gave him the opportunity to meet up for a drink with his best school pals, Hector Ratcliffe and Matthew Copson.

Like Hector, Matthew had shunned the chance to go to university and instead was pursuing a long-held ambition to be a journalist by taking a job as a trainee reporter on the Sanderholme Times.

The quiet snug at the Stag's Head was the ideal venue for the three friends to get together for a chat and a few pints.

Having just ended his relationship with Bernice, Hector was in a subdued mood at the start of the evening, becoming more talkative as the drink cheered him up. Humphrey was as effusive and upbeat as always and Matthew dry and cynical as was his wont.

Humphrey had enjoyed his first year at university enormously. He had signed up for the rugby club, the rowing club and the Light Entertainment Society and had been invited to lots of parties.

After regaling his pals with amusing stories of his experiences, he expressed an interest in Matthew's job on the newspaper.

"Does it get boring being a cub reporter on the local rag? Or do you get to meet some quirky people?"

"Plenty of quirky people, that's for sure," said Matthew, bristling somewhat from being described as a cub reporter.

He said he had been put in charge of chasing up the army of village news correspondents, an admirable bunch of worthies who were often leaders in their communities, getting themselves involved in many of the organisations which breathe life into villages – the Women's Institute, the parish council, the local churches and schools. Except for one or two exceptional individuals who managed to turn their role into a cottage industry, and who could make a reasonable sum from their twopence a line recompense, most of the correspondents worked purely for the love of their communities.

Having an eye for the bizarre, Matthew had a few anecdotes to share with his friends.

There had been a murder in one village, something which happened less than once in a lifetime in a quiet part of Lincolnshire. Matthew had been told by his editor to find out a few personal details about the victim. He naturally contacted Mrs Phelps, the village correspondent, for some help, but was met with the firm response: "No, I'm afraid I can't help you, duck. It doesn't do to go spreading news about in villages."

This response from *the village news correspondent* had left him completely nonplussed.

Most village correspondents put in a monthly linage claim to the paper but the editor had noticed that one of them, Mrs Milburn, was in the habit of sending in an annual claim for only one line, at twopence a line! This line had merely stated the amount raised in the village by the annual Royal British Legion Poppy Appeal.

However, this particular year no claim had been sent in at all and no information had been forthcoming about the Poppy Appeal. Matthew was put on the case. He rang the correspondent's home telephone number and got to speak to Mrs Milburn's husband, an elderly farmer. Mr Milburn sincerely apologised for his wife's lack of diligence that year, explaining that she had been ill in November. He promised she would provide her normal good service the following year.

Matthew had questioned whether anything happened in the village other than the Poppy Appeal, but Mr Milburn assured him that was the only event of any significance.

Matthew reported back to his editor, who reacted with a resigned shrug of the shoulders. However, there was a sequel. A few weeks later Mr Milburn phoned Matthew to inform him that, with great regret, his wife would have to retire as village correspondent, as the stress of the job had been getting too much for her.

Matthew asked the husband to pass on to his wife the newspaper's thanks for her sterling service over many years and then set about finding a successor.

A Mrs Adams was duly appointed, and having received useful training from her predecessor, come November, duly provided the one and only line about the Poppy Appeal. She then sent in her letter of resignation, having found the role to be too onerous.

"I see you are living life in the fast lane, mate," quipped Humphrey. "Tell me, is there anything more exciting in your job?"

When Matthew revealed that he especially enjoyed covering the proceedings of the local magistrates' court, Humphrey could hardly contain his mirth.

"Steady on, old boy, you will give yourself a heart

attack with all these thrills you are getting," he declared.

"No, seriously," said Matthew. "Sitting in court is just like watching a drama unfold. All human life is there to observe. Life in the raw. With your love of theatre, you would appreciate it, Humphrey. You really ought to come and sit in on a session. It's all done in public, you know. Two old ladies come to watch every week. They sit there doing their knitting while the magistrates are out making their decisions."

"Sounds like something from the French Revolution," chipped in Hector. "The women who sat knitting as the guillotine did its work."

"I suppose so," said Matthew. "But, believe me, it can be better than a night with the Sanderholme Players.

"I met an interesting chap at court the other day," he continued. "He was there to give evidence against a tramp who had set fire to a pile of rubbish and nearly burnt down the block of flats the bloke lived in.

"Anyway, this witness was a really dapper middle-aged chap, wearing a smart dark suit and looking every inch like one of the solicitors.

"While the magistrates were out he came over to me and introduced himself as Cecil Roberts. He showed a lot of interest in my work and then revealed that he worked in the newspaper industry himself, for the Nottingham Post. He spoke with some authority and seeming experience about newspapers and I imagined that he must have some important managerial job with The Post.

"The next day I was walking down the High Street and heard the loud cry 'Nottnam Post, Nottnam Post, read all about it, Nottnam Post'. I looked over to the newspaper seller standing at the side of the pavement outside Lloyds Bank and immediately recognised the little man I now knew to be Cecil Roberts. So he did, indeed, work for the Nottingham Post. He didn't have his best suit on this time but he was still well dressed for a newspaper street seller, with a respectable sports jacket, shirt and tie and carefully creased grey trousers.

"He said 'hello' very politely, had a long conversation with me and asked me my name.

"Anyway, a couple of days later he came into the reporters' room at our office, full of smiles, and announced he was engaged to be married to his landlady, a woman called Pat. We all shook his hand and wished him all the best.

"We were quite surprised about his news as several of us know of Pat. She's the landlady of a well-known house of multiple occupation in Newton Mews. She's a good-hearted woman, quite attractive in a busty sort of way and a lot younger than Cecil. After he'd gone, all of us agreed that he was a little eccentric but a very nice man in a funny kind of way.

"Then, a few days afterwards, he came in again. This time he was in an agitated state. He said Pat was having second thoughts about getting married to him, even though she had accepted his engagement ring. He asked us if he could sue her for breach of promise.

"We tried to persuade him that that wasn't a very good idea, so he came up with another one. He suggested that if we put something in the paper to announce their forthcoming wedding that would put pressure on her to go ahead with it.

"We told him that we would all get the sack if we did such a thing, but he was adamant about it. When we refused again, we saw a different side to his character. He became loud and just a little threatening and then came up with his ultimate weapon: 'If you don't put something in the paper then I will report you to The News of The World!' Then he stormed out of the office in a huff.

"Fortunately, he didn't carry out his dire threat and turned up at our office a couple of weeks later."

Matthew described what happened:

The efficient receptionist went scurrying into the reporters' room asking for help with a customer whom, she said, had either bamboozled her, or himself.

Matthew followed her into reception and was confronted by Cecil Roberts, who was back to his friendly, smiling self.

"Hello, Matthew," he said. "Can you help me? Your staff in this office don't seem to understand what I want."

"I'll certainly try to help," said Matthew. "What's the problem?"

"Well since I last saw you the wedding's off. I have fallen out with Pat, my landlady. She doesn't want to marry me. I don't know why. I think she's got somebody else.

"I think she wants me to move out of my flat. So I'm looking for somewhere else. In your paper I found this…"

Cecil pushed in front of Matthew a dog-eared cutting from the Sanderholme Times classified advertising section.

"Accommodation wanted: One bedroomed flat, Sanderholme. References provided. Box No. 20."

Cecil continued: "I thought if this person wanted a flat we could do a swap. I could have their flat and they could have mine."

Matthew grinned as he tried to fathom out Cecil's logic and eventually replied: "But we don't know if this person has a flat they could swap for yours."

"We could ask them, couldn't we?" asked Cecil.

"Well, no. That isn't the way it's done, I'm afraid. Have you looked in the Accommodation to Rent section?"

Cecil was becoming confused and a little annoyed.

"No, I thought we could ask this person if they wanted to swap."

"No, sorry," said Matthew. "I'll tell you what. Give me your address and if we come across any flats to let I'll try to let you know about them."

"It's Flat B, 21 Newton Mews. Come and have a cup of tea with me."

"Thanks. I might do that," said Matthew.

Cecil turned on his heels and left, leaving Matthew and the reception staff to share some laughter at his expense.

"He sounds like a wonderful character," said Humphrey.

"I like him," said Matthew. "But I haven't finished yet.

"A few weeks later Cecil came into the reporters' room again, this time in exuberant mood and greeting us with wreaths of smiles."

Matthew recalled this new encounter:

"I've got some good news for you," said Cecil. "I'm

getting married."

"That's great," said Matthew. "So Pat changed her mind, did she?"

"No, not Pat. She's a horrible woman. Another bloke's moved in with her. She'll regret it. I think he's one of those paedophiles. I'm getting married to Anne. We get on really well. She's a lot older than me and she's not very good looking. But she has said she will marry me."

"That's great news," said Matthew.

The two young female reporters in the office offered their congratulations too.

"I would like you to be my best man," Cecil said to Matthew. "And you two ladies could be the bridesmaids."

The three reporters were stuck for words. They didn't exactly relish the prospect of being the main attendants for this very eccentric individual whom they hardly knew. At the same time they felt curiously proud to have been asked and had no wish to be rude to their simple new acquaintance. The two young women giggled in a girlish way.

Matthew asked: "When and where is the wedding, Cecil?"

"At the register office next Wednesday morning at 10 o'clock."

"Ah," said Matthew, sensing the chance of a get-out. "Wednesday is a working day, so it's unlikely we would be able to get time off work to come along."

Cecil was not so easily fobbed off.

"I could speak to your boss and tell him he has got to let you have time off," he insisted.

"No, no. It's okay," said Matthew. "We'll speak to the editor and see what *she* says. Give us a couple of days and then come back in and we'll give you an answer. But tell me, don't you or your wife-to-be have any friends who you could ask to be your best man and bridesmaids?"

"No, she hasn't got any friends. And I don't believe in having friends. All friends are interested in is having sex with you or stealing your money. I want you three to come. Your editor could come as well if she likes. We'll be having a little reception at the Starship Café afterwards. There won't be any drink. I don't believe in drink. It gets you into trouble."

"Okay, we'll see what we can do," said Matthew.

Matthew told Humphrey and Hector that this latest meeting had been two days previously and Cecil had not reappeared at the office since. He said the two female reporters were resolute that they were not going to be bridesmaids. He, on the other hand, had decided that if it came to the crunch he would agree to be the best man. He had tentatively raised the idea with the editor, who had found the whole scenario highly amusing and had agreed to give Matthew time off to do his duty. She had even agreed to send the newspaper's photographer to take a photo of the happy couple for the newspaper. Matthew was just hoping that Cecil would have a change of mind and drop the whole idea.

Humphrey and Hector were becoming intrigued by these tales of Cecil Roberts. They insisted that Matthew must do the right thing and be best man.

"All right then," he said. "If necessary I'll do the

bloody thing. On one condition – that you two come with me."

"Us?" said Hector. "We've never even met the man. We can't just gatecrash his wedding."

"I'm sure he would love you to come along," said Matthew. "I don't mind asking him. I think you chaps should come and give me some moral support – and support Cecil."

"I'm game if you are," said Humphrey to Hector. "It should be a laugh."

"Oh, go on then," said Hector. "But you will ask him first if it's all right, won't you, Matthew?"

"Yeah, I'll ask him. I know he'll agree."

****

The day of Cecil Roberts' register office marriage arrived. The venue was a grim pre-war building along a main road in Sanderholme, its austere furnishings and plain décor giving it more of the atmosphere of a courtroom than a setting for a celebration.

Cecil looked smart in his best suit, sporting a new, sharp, short back and sides haircut. He looked proud and very happy, an expansive smile never leaving his face during the whole proceedings.

His wife-to-be was a diminutive figure, much older looking than him, her grey hair having been specially, and very tightly, permed for the occasion. She looked deathly pale, shy and almost apologetic for being there, clutching a small bouquet of white lilies and looking ill at ease in an A-line dress which looked two sizes too big for her. Her demeanour spoke of poverty and ill health.

Standing behind the couple as the matronly and severe looking registrar put them through the ceremony were Matthew, best man and keeper of the wedding ring, and Hector, both wearing conventional smart suits, and also Humphrey, resplendent in a purple suit, bright yellow shirt and broad matching tie.

Making up the party was none other than Pat, Cecil's erstwhile fiancée, who had agreed to act as one of the two witnesses. In spite of hard words having been exchanged between Cecil and herself, they were now on better terms and it was a matter of some relief to Pat that she was now merely a witness rather than the blushing bride.

And bringing up the rear was the towering, glowering figure of the Sanderholme Times' staff photographer, who looked as if he would rather be anywhere else.

Cecil spoke his vows in a loud assertive voice while Anne whispered hers in a mouse-like squeak. Then a few photographs were taken outside the office by the impatient photographer, who said he had to be away quickly for another assignment, but who clearly felt that this event was totally unworthy of the professional expertise of a fully paid-up member of the National Union of Journalists.

Then it was all across the road to the Starship Café for cups of tea, salmon and cucumber sandwiches and a small wedding cake specially baked and iced by the proprietor.

Cecil thanked everyone for coming and vigorously shook hands with them, while Anne stood at his side, smiling meekly and weakly. All agreed the event had been a great success.

Chapter four - Metamorphosis

Two weeks after his final parting from Bernice, Hector was visiting the local library to pursue his interest in Greek mythology when he found himself standing next to a tall, svelte girl, who was searching the religion section for books on the occult. She had long black hair tied in pigtails and was wearing a purple bandana, a multi-coloured tie dye shirt, a long flowery skirt and leather sandals.

When she caught Hector's eye she smiled and said: "It's Hector Ratcliffe, isn't it?"

"Yes, replied," Hector, looking at her closely.

"It's Phoebe, isn't it? Sorry, I didn't recognise you."

Phoebe laughed.

"I'm not surprised. The last time you saw me I was probably in school uniform."

"I think you're probably right."

Hector had known Phoebe Barrington a little from the Grammar School, where she was in the year below him.

They had both been members of the school Debating Society and he recalled that she had proposed a motion that "This House believes that marriage is an outdated institution".

He remembered being quite surprised that she had favoured this motion, as she came from a strong Christian household. With her serious spectacles and school prize for RE he had thought of her as something of a swot and a goody-goody.

Now her appearance had undergone a metamorphosis and she had become much more worthy of close attention.

"What are you doing now?" she asked.

"Oh, I'm just helping the family to manage our caravan site. Nothing very exciting, I'm afraid. And you?"

"I'm still at school, doing A levels. I'm hoping to go to university. But I want to do a gap year first doing Voluntary Service Overseas."

"Oh, good for you. Where do you fancy going?"

"Africa. There's a crying need for help there. Starvation, disease."

"Yeah, I admire you. When you will be going?"

"Hopefully in September. I'm intending to have a great summer first. I'm going to the Isle of Wight Festival in August. Should be fab."

"You'll have a great time, I'm sure."

"Yes, groovy music, drugs, all that shit. What more could you want?" she laughed.

Hector was a little shocked by her mention of drugs. This was not the Phoebe he knew from school, at least not the girl he imagined he knew.

Although curious as to whether she actually took drugs herself, he felt too embarrassed to quiz her about that. So he asked her about music instead.

"What sort of music are you into?"

"I'm into flower power music – Californian stuff – but I dig progressive music too – The Doors, Love, that sort of thing."

"Yeah, I like them too," said Hector. "I'm very much into progressive music – Cream, The Nice, they're a couple of bands I like."

"Oh, yes. That's cool too."

"I've just bought a couple of new albums, one by Pink Floyd and one by Jethro Tull."

"Oh, yes. I've heard of both of them," said Phoebe. "I've not heard any of their albums, though."

"I could lend you them, if you like."

"That would be good, thanks."

"If you could tell me your address I could pop them round to you."

"Sure, give me a second and I'll write it down for you."

She opened her multi-coloured shoulder bag, took out a pen and piece of paper, wrote down her address and passed it to Hector.

"The Old Hall, 23 Toft Drive."

Hector was impressed. The Old Hall! Toft Drive – the poshest road in Sanderholme. He remembered now that Phoebe's father, George Barrington, was a well-known local solicitor.

"Oh, fine. I'll pop round."

"We could listen to the albums together, if you like," said Phoebe.

"I'd like that very much," said Hector, instantly warming to the idea. "Would you be at home tomorrow night?"

"Yes, come round any time after six o'clock."

"Seven, then?"

"Seven. I'll look forward to it."

****

Hector was excited by the prospect of visiting Phoebe, but at the same time strangely nervous.

He had seen hippies but never really met one before.

He liked their looks, their flowers and their music, but their mantras of peace and love had never interested him and their use of LSD and marijuana slightly frightened him. Despite his kooky enthusiasm for Greek mythology, he was, in essence, a respectable, rather conformist English trainee caravan site manager. The "new" Phoebe he had just been introduced to seemed to be a free spirit, possibly a little dangerous.

However, her address certainly had an appeal. Hector was not a materialist but, although he would never openly admit it, he was not entirely hostile to a little social climbing. An Old Hall, a solicitor's daughter – those things certainly gave Phoebe a certain cachet.

Toft Drive was quite a short distance from Hector's home so he walked there, albums under his arms. He passed some of the most desirable residences in the town, a mixture of large houses with balconies and long sweeping, manicured front lawns, interspersed with the odd space-eating bungalow.

As he approached number 23 he immediately recognised the house as being the most impressive along the whole road. Leading to it was a long drive bordered by an avenue of tall poplar trees. The view from the roadside afforded a glimpse of a magnificent three-storey, Tudor-style house. This sight alone gave Hector butterflies in the stomach.

As he reached the front door, with its enormous brass knocker, a golden retriever came bounding towards him, its welcoming tail swaying eagerly. It was followed by a smiling middle-aged man wearing dungarees and a white floppy sun hat. Hector took him to be the gardener.

The heavy front door was suddenly flung open and there stood Phoebe, wearing a short cheesecloth dress and looking even more attractive than she had in the library.

"Hi, Hector. Good to see you."

Pointing to the retriever, she said: "This is Henry. Oh, and this is Daddy."

Oops, not the gardener then, thought Hector.

Pleasantries having been exchanged, Phoebe led Hector upstairs to her bedroom. He was surprised to be admitted to her "inner sanctum" so readily and without any reticence on her part. Clearly this was a liberated household.

The room had red and black walls largely covered with posters. There were adverts for various pop and rock bands and their albums, psychedelic prints in kaleidoscope colours, a large CND sign, an Oxfam campaign poster and, inevitably, the famous representation of Che Guevara.

Hector noted that everything in the room was artfully designed to show that Phoebe was a free spirit, intolerant of conformity. Cynically, he deduced that she was the ultimate conformist who had fallen hook, line and sinker for the fashions of the prevailing counter-culture.

Hector was self-aware enough to realise that he was a conformist himself, albeit in a different kind of way. He had done nothing in his life so far to rebel against his parents' world view. He shared his father's academic inquisitiveness and esoteric interests while inheriting his mother's practical common sense. Simultaneously, he fitted in tolerably well with the majority of his peers. He was neither mod nor rocker, neither school swot nor useless idler. He was a middling sort of a chap on the outside but, inside, his head was a bubbling maelstrom of ideas and aspirations.

Accepting his own conformity, he found himself smiling inwardly at Phoebe's own version of it. But he did not think any less of her. She was interesting and very fanciable.

Underneath the bedroom window were two bean bags placed in front of a dressing table on which was placed Phoebe's stereo record player. They sat cross-legged on the bags and spent a couple of hours listening dreamily to their favourite music.

At the end of the session they went downstairs to the large kitchen/diner where Hector was introduced to Phoebe's mother, a slim and statuesque woman who looked like an older, understated version of her daughter. She offered Hector a coffee, which he was pleased to accept.

As Phoebe eventually showed him to the front door, he counted his first visit to her home as an unqualified success. As he stood on the doorstep he felt confident enough (and conformist enough!) to ask the inevitable question: "Can we meet up again?"

She took his hand and replied: "Yes, I'd really like that."

"I wondered if you'd like to go to the pictures. 'Rosemary's Baby' is on at The Gaumont."

"Oh, fab. I'd love to see that," said Phoebe.

"How about tomorrow night?"

"Yeah, I don't think I'm doing anything."

"It starts at seven o'clock. Shall I walk round for you at 6.30?" asked Hector.

"Yes, that would be great."

Hector had a spring in his step as he made his way home.

****

Phoebe was just as excited as Hector as she anticipated their date. It was the first proper date she had had.

Her bright, self-confident exterior belied a deep insecurity. On the surface she had everything going for her. She came from a stable family with two intelligent parents and two older brothers who had already left home for university. She had attended a local preparatory school before passing the 11-plus and winning a place at Sanderholme Grammar School.

However, most of her classmates came from state primary schools and none of her friends from the prep school accompanied her to her new school. She was about to experience some culture shocks which oppressed her.

The school PE mistress was her particular bête noire. A tall, red-faced "jolly hockey sticks" type of woman, she was a sadistic bully who would not have been out of place as a German concentration camp guard. On her second day at the school, Phoebe was introduced for the first time to the joys of the forward roll and pieces of gymnastic torture equipment, such as the vaulting horse, the box and the medicine ball. Her classmates, who were all well acquainted with these joyful aspects of school life, found it laughable that someone should be so pathetically ignorant.

Phoebe felt isolated and became shy and withdrawn, concentrating on her school work and making no friends. For the first three years at Grammar School she was relentlessly bullied. This gradually died down as the bullies became bored with her lack of response. She tried as well as she could to ignore her tormentors and eventually, as most of them became more mature, they began to have a grudging respect for her.

As she entered the fifth form, the metamorphosis occurred. Phoebe, who up to now had considered herself to be a plain, bespectacled beanpole, looked in the mirror one day and realised that what she had always considered to be her minus points had become definite plus points. Her legs were long and shapely, her shiny black hair, usually confined in a bun, cascaded to her waist when she let it down and she now had a woman's body. Her skin was smooth and her pleasant heart-shaped face had developed a striking bone structure.

When she wore a miniskirt she suddenly started to notice that boys were looking at her in a way they never had before. The butterfly had emerged from the chrysalis. This realisation of her physical attributes increased her sense of self-worth. She deliberately changed her image, wearing short skirts, going without a bra, and wearing trendy sunglasses whenever possible instead of her usual spectacles which looked as if they were specially designed for very serious study.

Her behaviour changed too. Instead of the reticent and subdued creature she had been, she now became louder, often shocking her schoolmates with bad language and her avant garde ideas on life. She was determined never to be bullied again.

Hector and Phoebe enjoyed their first date at the pictures. There was no canoodling on the back row but they were friendly and at ease in each other's company. On leaving the cinema they made for the Stag's Head disco where they both downed several pints of bitter and had a couple of dances.

Then Phoebe made a suggestion which took Hector by complete surprise.

"I said I'd meet some friends at the outdoor swimming pool for a midnight swim. Will you come along?"

Hector was hesitant.

"How will you get into the pool at this time of night?"

"We just climb over the wall. It's a bit of a stretch. But we can help each other."

"We won't get arrested, will we?"

"No, but even if we do, they won't send us to jail, will they?"

"No, I suppose not," said Hector, unconvinced. "What will we do for swimming costumes?"

Phoebe laughed.

"We won't need those, love. We'll be skinny dipping."

Hector began to feel excited, although Phoebe's forwardness so soon after they had met did rather astonish him.

"Ok, let's go for it," he said.

When they reached the entrance to the pool, which was next to Sanderholme's main beach, they were greeted by a group of eight other young people, five boys and three girls. Hector recognised several of the boys as lifeguards who worked at the pool during the summer. They were bronzed Adonis types, noted for being feckless and reckless and very attractive to the local females. The girls were equally athletic looking and tanned. Hector suddenly felt very "ordinary".

They helped each other to scale the six foot perimeter wall. They also smuggled in several crates of wine and beer and some plastic cups. As soon as they got poolside, out came the bottles and some spliffs. Hector poured himself a beer while Phoebe immediately lit up a joint, which Hector declined to share with her.

After 20 minutes or so one of the lifeguards shouted: "Come on – time for a swim." A cheer went up and all members of the group quickly stripped off. Phoebe was the first to get naked. Hector was the last and feeling acutely self-conscious as this was a totally new experience for him. He was not as lacking in confidence as he once had been but in this company he was a fish out of water, overawed by the sight of so much naked flesh, displayed with seemingly no inhibitions. The area around the pool was unlit but there was sufficient light from the nearby sea front illuminations for bodies to be clearly seen.

Phoebe plunged into the pool, closely followed by Hector. A number of the others quickly started to indulge in initially innocent horseplay. There was a lot of splashing and chasing. It was not long before this led on to some touching and groping and then some not so innocent coupling in darker areas of the pool.

Phoebe had been tormenting Hector by constantly splashing him. He took it all in good part and gave as good as he got. Then she grabbed him by the arms and pulled him towards her.

"Kiss me," she ordered.

Hector obeyed and kissed her passionately. His hand strayed to her right breast and she offered no resistance. She clutched his bottom and pulled him even closer. This watery encounter was to be the time when they both lost their virginity.

****

Phoebe, the speccy swot, had morphed into a Sixties wild child and she swept Hector off his feet. She was into everything that a good middle class girl shouldn't be – free love, soft drugs and hard drinks, dodgy music festivals and far left causes.

She wanted to change the world – free it from poverty, capitalism, orthodox religion and old-fashioned concepts of marriage and the family.

Hector, on the other hand, saw the world as a much more complex place. In his bedroom at night he would be transported into a different plane by the Romantic fancies of Keats, Shelley and Byron. In the cold light of day he was businesslike and practical as he toiled to make money for the family caravan site. He dreamt of a better planet where imagination was the force majeure; he lived in the world of ordinary men and women, whose idea of paradise was a week in a caravan by the seaside, with perhaps a beer and a game of bingo for themselves and buckets and spades for the kids.

That said, there was undoubtedly a chemistry between Hector and Phoebe. This was partly physical and, although it could never be said there was a meeting of minds between them, they found each other very interesting.

What remained of that summer was a rollercoaster ride for Hector as Phoebe led him astray in so many different directions. There were Bohemian parties, wild outdoor sex, and trips to music events which attracted poets and faux poets, abstract artists and piss artists, hobos, drug addicts and boy burglars. Typical sixties really.

To Phoebe, this was her idea of heaven on earth. For Hector, it was a bit of shallow fun with a woman he was beginning to fall in love with.

September arrived and with it the realisation that they could soon be parted, as Phoebe was due to start her Voluntary Service Overseas in Uganda in a couple of weeks' time.

Then came the bombshell.

One evening Hector rang the front door bell at Phoebe's home to be greeted by her mother. He sensed a froideur towards him as she invited him in.

"She's upstairs. You'd better go and see her," she said in a peremptory tone which he had not encountered before.

Hector went up to her bedroom and knocked on the door.

"Come in," she said.

"You, okay?" Hector asked.

"Why?" she replied, brusquely.

"Oh nothing. It's just that your mother seemed not quite herself."

"She's had a shock," said Phoebe.

"Oh?"

"I'm pregnant."

Hector was dumbstruck for a few seconds.

"Are you sure?"

"Quite sure. I've been to the doctor's and had a test."

"But we've been taking precautions."

"Except for that first night. At the swimming pool."

"Oh, Christ. No, sorry. I don't mean it like that. I mean, it's good news isn't it?"

"You ask my parents that."

"And you?"

"It's not something I wanted. But I suppose I'll get used to the idea. And you?"

"Yeah. Yeah. Why not? A baby. Why not? I think I'd like a baby."

"Good. What about *your* parents?" asked Phoebe.

"I can't think that they'll be over the moon. But yeah. I think they'll come round to it. Will yours?"

Phoebe hesitated: "Um, yes. I can usually talk them round. There's just a couple of things which I regret, though."

"What are those?"

"I won't be able to go to Uganda, or to university."

Hector gave a long sigh, signifying his empathy with her disappointment. But inwardly his spirits rose because he had dreaded the prospect of her going away.

"I understand. You were so looking forward to your gap year. Maybe it can be a postponement rather than a cancellation."

"Perhaps so," she replied, looking unconvinced.

She was sitting on the edge of her bed while he had remained standing near the door. He walked forward and sat next to her, putting his arm around her tightly and kissing her.

"We'll be all right. You see," he said.

"Yes," she said. "We'll be all right, babe."

She patted his leg.

****

And they were all right. Both sets of parents reacted in the way enlightened parents did in the latter part of the 20th century – accepted what had happened and looked forward to the birth of the child.

One aspect of the matter did cause some little controversy.

After initially being shocked, but then accepting the news with good grace, Hector's mother, Margaret, turned to her son one day, smiling broadly.

"I'd better go out and buy a hat!" she declared.

"A hat?" said Hector, fearing what was to come.

"For the wedding."

"Mum, there's something you ought to know," said Hector, with some trepidation. "Phoebe doesn't believe in marriage. She thinks it's just a piece of paper."

"I've only met Phoebe a couple of times. She seems a nice enough girl. But she's well – a bit way out, isn't she?"

Hector smiled: "Yes, she is a bit way out. But she's lovely. You'll like her when you get to know her better."

"What do her parents think about it – no marriage, I mean?"

"I don't think they're any happier about it than you are. But we'll be okay. We'll look after the baby."

"I'm sure you will, Hector. But children need stability and that's what marriage brings."

"She won't change her mind. I know that. Trust us. We'll be okay. The baby will be okay. We'll be good parents."

Margaret grimaced.

"Be it on your own head, then. It seems as though I will have no say in the matter."

For Hector that *was* the end of the matter. His parents had never been ones to dictate to him and they cleaved to their normal policy.

The baby duly arrived. A healthy boy called Troy. He was loved by Hector and Phoebe and doted on by both sets of grandparents.

The new family moved into a three-bedroomed house on the caravan site which had previously been rented by the site's handyman who had recently retired and moved away from the town.

****

Matthew Copson had his head down at his desk, hard at work writing up Saturday's football match between Sanderholme Rovers Reserves and Hayfleet Athletic, a 15-0 wipeout win for Sanderholme even though play had been temporarily suspended when a herd of cattle invaded the Hayfleet pitch.

There was a loud knock at the door and in strode Cecil

Roberts. This was the first time in the 12 months since the wedding that Cecil had been seen by the Times reporting staff. To begin with they had imagined him riding off into the sunset with his bride and living happily in marital bliss.

But then Matthew received an intriguing report from his own new wife. A few months previously he had married Bernice's friend Sally. Ever since they had first met in the Stag's Head disco Matthew and Sally had clicked. His sardonic sense of humour perfectly complemented her own dry, restrained sense of the ridiculous.

Sally worked in Sanderholme Library and she had told of a visit paid there by Cecil a few weeks earlier. He had approached the reception desk and said: "Can you help me? I'm looking for a book?"

"Oh, yes. What kind of book were you looking for?" asked Sally.

"A book about men and women."

"We have plenty of those," she said. "Were you thinking of a love story, perhaps?"

"No, not a love story," he replied loudly.

"Come with me and we'll see what we can find," she said.

Sally escorted him into the body of the library and suggested all sorts of possibilities in various categories, none of which satisfied Cecil.

Eventually, in exasperated tones he declared loudly: "Have you got a book on how to do it?"

Sally laughed and took him to the Science section where she found a couple of suitable books.

"Will these do the trick?" said Cecil as he presented his library card to borrow the books.

"I hope so," said Sally, smiling. "Best of luck!"

As he entered the reporters' room Cecil looked miserable.

"How's married life?" asked Matthew.

"Not very good," said Cecil. "The wife's not interested in sex. And she's always quite poorly. It's disappointing."

"Oh, dear. Sorry to hear that Cecil."

"Could you come and tell her what she needs to do?" asked Cecil. "You're a married man, aren't you?"

"Yeah, I am. But I don't think I could do that. It's too... well, it's too personal, isn't it?"

Matthew was finding it impossible to keep a straight face as he could hear the two young female reporters giggling in the background.

Cecil became aware of them and turned round quickly.

"Could you two girls come and see my wife and tell her what she should be doing?" he asked.

Both women declined as politely as they could and then left room hastily so that they could giggle more freely outside.

"I think you'll just have to be patient with her if she's not very well at the moment," said Matthew.

"Nobody seems to want to help me," said Cecil. "To be honest, I wish I'd never got married. I don't think it's for me."

"Perhaps you should get a book from the library," said Matthew archly.

"I've got two books and I gave them to her. But she

can't read."

"Could you read them to her?"

With that Cecil waved his band brusquely and dismissively and walked out of the room, brushing past the two female reporters who were still convulsed by laughter in the corridor.

This story, and other bizarre incidents involving Cecil which he had heard second hand, were related with some relish by Matthew the next time he met up with Hector and Humphrey. They had now established a routine of meeting up for a drink and catch-up at the Stag's Head snug each time Humphrey came back to Sanderholme.

At this latest meeting, when several pints had been consumed and the lads' spirits were running high, Humphrey declared: "I would like to propose that we inaugurate a club, with just two rules: 1 That we three promise to meet together at least once a year for the rest of our lives; 2 That we consume a number of beers on each occasion."

"I'm all for that," said Hector. "I'll second it."

Matthew looked sceptical.

"Are you sure we'll be able to keep that up for all of our lives?" he asked. "For instance, one of us might move to the other side of the world and that would make it impractical."

"Nonsense," said Humphrey. "That would be part of the fun of it. However far apart we are we would have to meet the challenge of turning up for the meetings – at least once a year. That shouldn't be impossible."

"What if one of us has a wife who doesn't approve of

such an extravagance?" said Matthew. "After all, if we had to travel to the other side of the world it could get very expensive."

"Rubbish man. We can do it. We can take it in turns to meet up at each other's locations."

Matthew looked unconvinced but decided to "go with the flow".

"Oh, go on, then. We'll give it a try. But I propose that we have an Annual General Meeting so that we can change the rules if they become awkward or obsolete for any reason, such as death or something more serious."

"All in favour then?" said Humphrey.

They clinked glasses to show their approval.

Matthew sniggered, sensing that even if they remembered what they had agreed in their current inebriated state, a rule change would probably come sooner or later.

"Are we going to have officers in our club?" asked Hector, warming to the whole concept.

"Why not?" said Humphrey.

"Then I propose you, Humphrey, as chairman," said Hector. "Will you second that, Matthew?"

"All right then," said Matthew with a world-weary shrug.

"Then I propose you as secretary, Hector," said Humphrey. "You could send out dates of meetings, agendas, minutes, if there are any – that sort of thing."

"Seconded," said Matthew, with an air of total indifference.

"Okay," said Hector. "Then I propose Matthew as treasurer. He can look after the kitty when we're getting rounds in etc."

"Seconded," said Humphrey.

"That's all sorted, then," said Matthew. "Let's get another round in."

"Hang on a minute," said Humphrey. "Every respectable club needs a president. I propose Cecil Roberts."

The other two friends chortled at this suggestion.

"I'll second that," said Hector.

"I only support it on one condition," said Matthew.

"What's that?" asked Hector.

"That we never invite the president to any meeting."

"Agreed," said the other two in unison.

"What should we call the club?" asked Hector.

"May I suggest The Cecil Roberts Appreciation Society?" said Humphrey.

"Absolutely agree," said Hector.

"You're both as mad as Hatters," said Matthew.

"I propose we are the Mad Hatters' Cecil Roberts Appreciation Society, Sanderholme Branch," said Hector.

"Why the branch bit?" asked Matthew. "There aren't any other members to put in any other branch, are there?"

"Ah, but if one of us moves say, to Adelaide, then we could set up an Adelaide branch."

"That's mad," said Matthew.

"Exactly," interrupted Humphrey. "We are Mad Hatters. I second the name Mad Hatters' Cecil Roberts Appreciation Society, Sanderholme Branch. All agreed?"

They clinked glasses again to show their approbation.

Matthew's eyes looked skywards as he did it.

"What about having an initiation ceremony for new members?" said Humphrey.

"What new members. I thought it was just the three of us?" asked Matthew.

"Ah, yes. But there is a girl who works in your newspaper office that I wouldn't mind initiating," replied Humphrey.

"Meeting closed!" shouted Hector.

****

They didn't have to wait a full year for their next get-together, which was held five months later.

After they had ordered their first pints, Humphrey called the meeting to order.

"First item on the agenda is 'Does anyone have any stories about our esteemed president, Mr Cecil Roberts?'" said Humphrey.

Matthew said he did – and they were not going to believe it.

He recounted that a few weeks after Cecil's previous visit to the newspaper office, he had made a further appearance there.

He had been straight to the point.

"Good afternoon. I want you to put an obituary in the paper. How much is it?"

"Oh," said a surprised Matthew. "There's no charge for obituary reports. It's news."

"I don't mind paying," said Cecil. "I'm not short of money."

He took a brightly coloured purse from his jacket pocket and flashed a ten pound note.

"Here."

"No, no," said Matthew. "We don't charge for obituary reports. Is it perhaps a death notice you want?"

"A report to say my wife has died."

"I'm so sorry to hear that," said Matthew. "When did that happen?"

"She isn't dead yet," replied Cecil. "But she will be in a week or two."

"Oh, dear," said Matthew. "What on earth's the matter with her?"

"Stomach pains."

"But how do you know she's going to die?"

"She's bound to. She's very ill."

"Has the doctor said so?"

"He said she's very ill."

"But actually going to die?"

"Yes. Can you take down the details for the report?"

"We don't usually write obituary reports for people who are not dead yet."

"Well, if you got it ready then you could put it in when she does die."

"Okay, then, let me take down some details. I really am sorry to hear this."

The almost hysterical female reporters had to leave the room again.

Matthew produced an obituary form from a desk drawer.

"Your wife's name is Mrs Anne Roberts, yes?"

"Yes"

"How old is she at the moment?"

"Sixty-five. She's a lot older than me. I think that's

been one of the problems. I should have married somebody younger."

"And her address?"

"The same as mine. She's my wife."

"Do you still live at Newton Mews?"

"No, I moved into the wife's flat – at Park Road."

"Do you know where Anne was born?"

"No."

"Has she lived in Sanderholme long?"

"I don't know."

"Was she retired?"

"She doesn't work."

"What did she use to do? What was her occupation?"

"I don't know if she ever worked. She's been ill a lot."

"Oh, okay. Did she belong to any local organisations or have any hobbies or particular interests?"

"No, she used to stay at home. She watches television – Coronation Street. She's very quiet.

"Okay. Any other things she liked doing earlier in her life?"

"She used to look after her father, but he died a long time ago."

"Was she ever married before?"

"No, at least she never told me she'd been married."

"Did she have any relatives?"

"Only me."

"Is there anything else we can say about her – anything that the readers of our newspaper would be interested to know about?"

"No, it's none of their business is it? Can you put something in about the funeral?"

"You won't know about that yet, will you – as she's not actually dead yet?"

"I've been to see the vicar. He said he will have the funeral at his church."

"So it will be at St Leonard's Church, will it?"

"The one on the roundabout."

"Yes, that's the one. And will it be cremation or burial?"

"Cremation."

"At Sanderholme Crematorium?"

"Yes, I haven't got a date yet. The vicar said he couldn't tell me a date yet."

"No, I don't suppose he could."

"Will the report go in this week's paper?"

"No," said Matthew. "We'll hold on to the details until your wife passes away. Then we'll put it in. Hopefully, she might still recover. I do hope so."

"She won't get better. Shall I come in again when she dies?"

"Yes, please do that. In the meantime if you can find out any more details about Anne that we could put in the report it will be really useful. We don't have many facts about her so far."

"She's very quiet," said Cecil. "I should have found someone with a bit more life in them. I will next time. She's called Brenda."

"You mean you've already found someone?"

"Yes, Brenda. She lives next door. I haven't asked her yet, but I'm sure she'll have me."

"I think it would be best to wait until something happens to Anne," suggested Matthew.

"Yes. But you will come to the wedding won't you? And bring your friends again?"

"We'll see," said Matthew.

For the young, inexperienced reporter this had been a surreal experience and on returning home that night he couldn't wait to tell Sally about it.

She listened patiently, but with mouth wide open as he told his bizarre tale.

Then she had a startling revelation of her own to add to the narrative.

"Cecil came into the library again a few weeks ago. He asked me if we had any books on poisons."

"Oh my god," said Matthew. "Are you thinking what I'm thinking?"

"His wife?"

"That's what I was thinking. But we mustn't jump to any conclusions. Cecil is a wildly eccentric bloke – a nutter I would call him – but he's basically good-natured and an innocent abroad so I can't imagine for a moment he would harm anyone."

"Yes, I'm sure it's just a coincidence," said Sally, laughing.

"Our Cecil's the gift that keeps on giving," said Matthew.

This latest twist in the Cecil Roberts' saga had Humphrey and Hector in stitches. But beneath the laughter both of them had an unspoken sliver of doubt. Could he be a murderer? On reflection they largely dismissed this thought from their heads.

"Let's drink to our honorary president," said Humphrey.

They clinked beer glasses as Humphrey shouted: "To Cecil, our president and hero!"

****

Only a few days after this meeting, Cecil was back at the Sanderholme Times office to announce the news that Anne had died and that the funeral had been arranged for the following week.

He said this meant the newspaper could go ahead and publish the obituary report. Matthew enquired if Cecil had managed to find out any more details about his wife's life, but apparently there was nothing else to tell.

Matthew suggested that all the information could be included in a paid-for death notice in the classified advertising section. Cecil asked how much that would cost but when given the answer insisted on the obituary report.

It was clear to Matthew that Cecil was short of money, so he agreed to produce a free report which would run to little more than two lines.

"What did Anne actually die of?" he finally asked.

"A heart attack," said Cecil. "That's what the doctor said."

He thanked Matthew for his help and gave him a warm handshake.

"You will come when I get married to Brenda, won't you? You and your two friends?"

"Let us know when it is, mate, and we'll do our best."

There was something about Cecil that Matthew just loved and admired – an uncanny mixture of innocent affability and searing directness. This was honesty such as he had never experienced before. He told everyone that Cecil was "at least two sandwiches short of a full picnic" and he was sure that was correct. But this strange man had a unique attitude to life which appealed to the reporter's own iconoclastic view of the world.

Still lurking at the back of Matthew's mind, though, was the notion that Cecil was so "off the wall" and tunnel-visioned that he might just consider taking direct action to rid himself of an unsatisfactory wife.

Too soon for comfort after Anne was laid to rest came Cecil's second wedding. He was again loyally supported by the total membership of the Mad Hatters' Cecil Roberts Appreciation Society, Sanderholme Branch, but this time there was no Pat to be one of the witnesses. She had protested strongly about what she considered to be the untimely haste of Cecil's marriage to Brenda, a woman she considered to be of low moral standards.

The honour of being a witness therefore fell this time to Maisie Waters, the senior waitress at the Starship Café, which was again to be the venue for the reception.

Cecil arrived looking as spruce as he had at his first wedding, in a three-piece suit topped off with a large red carnation buttonhole.

None of the four guests had set eyes on the bride before so they were full of anticipation as she arrived outside the register office on the groom's arm. There was no limousine or horse-drawn carriage: the couple had walked to the office from their flat about half a mile away.

Anne's arrival had been something of an anti-climax. She had cut a poor, pinched figure and looked at least 20 years older than Cecil. The groom was in his mid-forties so it was a contrast, and something of surprise, that Brenda appeared to be perhaps 15 years his junior. She was short with a voluptuous, some might say frumpy, figure accentuated by her low cut ball gown-type wedding dress.

As she stubbed out her cigarette on the pavement outside the entrance to the office it struck those seeing her for the first time that she looked to be in a bad mood, clearly not expecting this to be the happiest day of her life and certainly not a blushing bride.

"She looks a bit of a handful," Humphrey whispered to Hector.

During the ceremony, the contrast between Cecil and Brenda could not have been greater. He was grinning like the proverbial Cheshire Cat and speaking clearly with a warm authority, while she was sullen, unenthusiastic and spoke in a barely audible monotone.

At the reception, their moods stayed much the same. Cecil was the genial host, talking to everyone in a friendly manner and expressing his sincere gratitude for their support. Brenda acknowledged the guests in a cursory way and spent much of the occasion outside on the pavement, smoking.

"Can't see this marriage lasting very long," commented Matthew as the three friends left the café together.

****

A month or so after this prestigious event Matthew was walking towards his office when he encountered

Brenda walking in the opposite direction.

There was instant recognition between them and this time Brenda was clearly keen to talk.

"How are you?" asked Matthew.

"I've left him!" said Brenda. "He's a madman. I'm leaving town to get away from him."

"Oh, dear," said Matthew. "I'm sorry to hear that. I was hoping you'd be happy together."

"Bloody happy? He's just stupid. I wish I'd never set eyes on him. I'm out of it."

With that she flounced off. Matthew could only speculate what might have gone on between the couple behind closed doors. Doubts he always had about Cecil's true character and motives came flowing back. There was much to report to the next meeting of the Mad Hatters' Cecil Roberts Appreciation Society, Sanderholme Branch.

Chapter five – Making a better world?

Two years after Troy's arrival a second child was born to Hector and Phoebe. She was, at Phoebe's suggestion, named Janis, after Janis Joplin. With some reluctance from their mother, the children were given the surname Ratcliffe.

They experienced adventurous early lives, being transported to numerous music festivals throughout the world.

Phoebe also became heavily involved in the International Socialists and later the Socialist Workers Party. While not sharing her passions, Hector was content to stay at home and look after the children while she attended conferences, party meetings and demonstrations, usually in London. He respected her principles, her commitment and her altruism but at the same time allowed himself a wry inward smile that her activities were being subsidised by the capitalist venture of a caravan site on inherited land.

Later Phoebe joined the Greenham Common protests against American Cruise missiles being stationed at the RAF base, sometimes joining the Women's Peace Camp there for months at a time.

Outwardly, Hector continued to give her his loyal support, despite strong mutterings of discontent from his mother and other family members. His father kept his own counsel on the matter. He had become a slightly distant figure himself, not geographically, but far away in thoughts of his books and Classical studies.

Margaret was particularly concerned about the

distance opening up between her son and Phoebe and was not about to keep mum. Her observations to Hector, though, were muted and restrained. The Ratcliffes were in many respects a typically buttoned-up lower middle class English family, not given to noisy outbursts or overt feuding.

Despite Hector's defence of Phoebe to his mother, as he lay alone in bed at night he began to have his own doubts about the relationship with his partner. He loved her, was still captivated by her, and believed she still loved him and her children. But he sensed that her family was not her top priority in life. She was beginning to remind him of Mrs Jellyby in Charles Dickens' "Bleak House", the philanthropist more interested in her African missionary project than her needy children and neighbourhood.

It is a common trait in the world's do-gooders and idealists that they care more for humanity at large than for those closest to them.

Sometimes he would wake up in the early hours and find his thoughts wandering towards his old love Penelope. To his dismay, he had recently learnt from his friend Matthew that she had committed the cardinal sin of marrying none other than Achilles. Well, not Achilles actually, but, in Hector's view, the worst possible choice of husband, Stuart Broadlake. How could she? What could she possibly see in that unpleasant hulk?

Hector wondered whether he should have tried harder to woo her himself. And, if he had succeeded, what would his life be like now? Those were the thoughts that kept him awake at night, but in the light of day he dismissed such ideas as mere fantasies. He had developed a hard shell of common sense since those schooldays.

Each time Phoebe returned home after one of her sorties she was affectionate to Hector and the children, almost cloyingly so for a few days. Her husband could sense, though, that she was dissatisfied with home life, bored with the humdrum existence of an English seaside resort.

She made token efforts to engage with the local community, getting herself involved in the Parent Teachers Association when Troy moved to secondary school but became disillusioned when she failed to get other parents to support her petition calling for a ban on caning at the school.

Although still active in the Socialist Workers Party she decided to infiltrate the Sanderholme Labour Party, only to be expelled for her extreme views.

At this stage in their relationship Hector sensed that she was getting "itchy feet". He noticed that she was receiving brochures and other correspondence about humanitarian projects overseas. She spent hours poring over them.

One evening she curled up close to him on the sofa in their lounge, looked intently into his eyes, and declared: "I have something I need to discuss with you."

She revealed that she wished to take part in a year-long project for Oxfam, tackling extreme poverty in Zambia.

Hector was appalled.

"But what about the children? You can't just up and

leave them for a whole year."

"They are okay. They both enjoy their schools. They've got you and their grandparents. They will be fine, I'm sure. Let's face it, they have a comfortable life here, no worries about where the next meal comes from. No problems with having to drink and bathe in dirty water. These people who I'll be helping are in dire need. They don't have enough to eat. They're ravaged by disease. They need our help."

"We need you here," replied an angry Hector. "I've been very patient with you over the years, but this is a step too far. Would you have suggested doing this if we were married?"

"What's that got to do with it?"

"Being married might have given you a little bit more commitment."

"That's crap, Hector, and you know it. God, you can be so bloody bourgeois sometimes."

"At least I'm human."

"So, I'm not human. I care so much about humanity. I cry sometimes when I think of all the people out there suffering – not having enough to eat, riddled with disease. Can't you see that?"

"Sometimes the humane can suffocate the human," replied Hector, recalling a quote he had read somewhere.

"That's rubbish and you know it."

Hector got up from the sofa, clasping his hands to his head in a show of frustration. He went outside to get some fresh air and to think about what had happened.

He felt he was losing his partner and that his children

were losing their mother. She *was* Mrs Jellyby.

His was not an uncommon fate. Throughout the history of mankind there have been people who care more about humanity in general than human beings in particular.

A notable example of this was the famous Christian medical missionary Albert Schweitzer. He did magnificent work setting up and running a hospital in Gabon. However, this was at the expense of a normal married life with his wife, Helene. She supported him and tolerated his priorities even though she was struggling with depression. Eventually she was compelled to accept that she and Albert would never have a satisfactory marriage.

George Eliot showed she understood the downside of prioritising humanity in general when, in "Middlemarch", she has a journalist saying: *"We all know the wag's definition of a philanthropist – a man whose charity increases directly as a square of the distance."*

For centuries there has been a debate over whether people are right to prioritise their family over the world at large. How often have we heard the maxim "charity begins at home"? It is so often spoken in a tone which suggests that the speaker's charity ends at home too... or doesn't even start either at home or abroad.

The very notion of charity has been attacked from both from the Right and the Left. Some of the Right take the "survival of the fittest" standpoint, maintaining that charity merely discourages people from standing on their own feet. To some on the Left charity means those with wealth patronisingly doling out a little of it in order to assuage their guilt, while at the same time helping to preserve the status quo.

In "Aaron's Rod", D. H. Lawrence, who is sometimes claimed by both the Left and the Right and more often disowned by both, wrote: *"From the 'liberal' point of view charity is mainly a soothing of conscience and a means of maintaining an unjust state of affairs."*

Perhaps, as in most areas of life, the best course is to aim for reasonable balances: between dispensing charity and changing the economic structure of society; and between charity at home and charity abroad.

Balance was a foreigner to Phoebe's nature; her will prevailed and two months later she left for Zambia.

There was a tearful scene at the airport. Hector, Troy and Janis cried. Phoebe kissed them all and was gone.

Hector was left with a sinking feeling of finality, which he tried his hardest not to transmit to the children.

For the first three months after her departure Hector and Phoebe took it in turns to phone each other once a week. The children, in particular, waited for these calls with great anticipation. They told their mother about things they had been doing at school and their activities at the weekends with their father, grandparents and friends.

Phoebe would excitedly describe the work she was doing with clinics for the under-fives. Hector would feign interest and long for the end of the year.

But as that year rolled on Phoebe sometimes "forgot" her turn to phone. On the first few occasions that this happened Hector would contact her instead. He began, though, to sense that all they were doing was going through the motions. He felt a growing coolness and detachment on Phoebe's part.

Summer came round again and Hector and the children started ticking off the days to mummy's return on a calendar.

Then, one July evening, Phoebe made an unexpected phone call home.

"This is a nice surprise," said Hector.

"Hector, I have something to tell you, and I am so, so sorry."

Her husband was struck with foreboding.

"I'm not coming back in September. There is so much necessary work to do here and..."

She paused.

"And I've met someone."

"What do you mean?" asked Hector, fearing that he knew exactly what she meant.

"I've met a man here and we've – how can say it? We've become an item."

"An item!" shouted Hector. "You mean he's shagging you?"

Phoebe was nonplussed as she had never heard Hector use such a crude term before.

"Yes, we're shagging each other."

"You can't not come back," said Hector. "What about the kids? Surely you're not going to desert them."

"I thought they might come and live with me and my friend, Adam."

"Did you not think I might have something to say about that? Did you not consider that *they* might have an opinion on the matter?"

"I'm sorry Hector. I'm so sorry to put you in this position. I know you don't deserve it. But you see I truly believe I've found my vocation here – helping others – and that I've found a man who shares my passions."

"Who is this man?"

"Well, as I said, he's called Adam. He's my age and he's so very kind. He's an American. You would like him."

"I bet I bloody wouldn't," was Hector's snarled retort.

"I think the kids would like him anyway. He loves the children here and they adore him."

"Have you thought about how you would wreck our children's education if they went to live with you?"

"They'd catch up. Adam and I could teach them."

"We'll see about that," said Hector. And he slammed the phone down.

He paced up and down, then slumped down in a chair at the kitchen table and broke into tears. The world was suddenly a bad place to be.

It wasn't just that his partnership with Phoebe had ended and that he might even lose his children. When he first met Phoebe he was committed to his "Greek" definitions of love. At the early stages of their relationship "eros" was in the ascendancy, but as time went on and Phoebe became preoccupied with her charitable and political campaigning this had transformed, at least from his point of view, into *agape* – selfless love. It seemed that whatever Phoebe threw at him he would take with a resigned good humour. Now he thought he had been a fool and that his selflessness had been in vain.

On the evening when he heard Phoebe's news his

self-esteem took an enormous battering. But his immediate concern was how he would break the news to the children. He called them into the kitchen and explained everything to them.

Troy, now a handsome 14-year-old, and Janis, a pretty 12-year-old, were surprisingly stoical in their reactions. Unlike their father, they shed no tears. It was almost as if they expected this to happen one day.

Janis, the feistier of the two, was the first to express an opinion.

"There's no way I'm going to Africa. Mummy's an idiot."

Troy nodded and merely added: "I agree. I'm staying here."

Hector, not easily moved to emotion, found himself welling up again. He tried to hide this from the children by rushing over to them, pulling them towards him and hugging them tightly.

"I'll always love you and look after you. You know that, don't you?"

Troy and Janis simultaneously replied "yes", Janis adding bitterly: "Well mummy doesn't love us does she?"

Hector said nothing in response.

****

With some justice it can be claimed that the relationship between Hector and Phoebe could only have been a product of the Sixties.

This was the time when all traditional values were challenged, whether they concerned sex, drugs, music, personal appearance or the notion of deference. Every long-established institution came under fire, including the family, the Government, the church, the monarchy and the class structure.

Instead it was the era of "love and peace" and an anarchic worship of "free expression".

In many ways it was the best time ever to be young. It was certainly easier to have relationships with the opposite sex, the poet Philip Larkin suggesting, no doubt tongue in cheek, that *"sexual intercourse started in 1963"*. There was a high degree of personal freedom – except freedom from high rates of personal taxation – and was a time of relative affluence.

In Sanderholme, for example, many young people could seemingly afford to go out and have a good time on most nights of the week. The car park of the Buckthorn Arms was full of sports cars owned by young men in their late teens and early twenties.

But there were casualties too. Too many young girls were having abortions or unwanted pregnancies and too many young men and women were becoming addicted to drugs or alcohol. There were horrendous fatal accidents caused by young drink drivers and householders were suffering from burglaries committed by those believing that "property is theft".

The essential foundations of a stable and prosperous society were being mocked and undermined in the name of abstract and unachievable ideals of love and peace and the redistribution of wealth. Authority figures such as politicians, the police, the armed services, parents and teachers were constantly being ridiculed and attacked.

And in the vanguard of this movement was one of the institutions itself – the BBC, which was casting off its sound Reithian principles.

Hector and his close friends had never been taken in by the inanities and neophilia of the sixties. They had enjoyed the trappings of the time without falling for the hype. Phoebe, though, had taken it all very seriously and genuinely believed she was on a crusade to make the world a better place.

****

At what had now become the annual meeting of the Mad Hatters' Cecil Roberts Appreciation Society, Sanderholme Branch, there was a subdued atmosphere as Hector acquainted his two fellow members with the problems in his marriage.

Matthew and Humphrey were as supportive as ever, although both were having difficulties of their own. Matthew and Sally desperately wanted children but were having difficulty in conceiving. Humphrey's problems, as per usual, related to financial matters. On the rare occasions when he managed to put a little money aside he found himself having to bail out his father who lurched from one unsuccessful business venture to another and who was always in danger of losing the family home. Humphrey could offer relatively small sums to help him out but the result was that the son could never afford to live in the manner to which he would have liked to be accustomed.

On this occasion, though, Matthew and Humphrey largely put aside their own problems to empathise with

Hector's plight.

"I always thought your missus was a nutcase," commented Matthew bluntly. "You'd be best off without her."

Eventually the beer-fuelled conversation got around to association president Cecil Roberts. This was usually the occasion for a laugh at Cecil's latest exploits in his madcap and confused world. However, this time Matthew entered a deadly serious note.

He said he had been talking to the pastor in charge of the local Pentecostal Church, who had revealed that, since the swift break-up of his second marriage, Cecil had been heavily involved in the life of that church.

The pastor had gone on to reveal some startling facts about their president's life. After giving birth to Cecil out of wedlock his mother had been committed to a mental home. Her baby was taken from her and, having learning difficulties, was himself committed to a mental hospital miles away. Incredibly, Cecil had lived at the same institution in Nottinghamshire for 45 years before being considered fit for release into the community.

Hector and Humphrey were shocked to hear this and Humphrey questioned whether it was plausible that a woman would be sent to a mental hospital merely for being an unmarried mother.

Matthew said he had been similarly sceptical and this had led him to do some research. He had discovered that there were cases of unmarried mothers still living in mental asylums, having been incarcerated there for decades. Mental defect was believed by some to have led to immoral behaviour.

Among the most influential proponents of this view was a prominent child psychiatrist called John Bowlby who condemned the "neurotic character" of the "socially unacceptable" unmarried mother.

"Did they just send out Cecil into the community without any support?" asked Hector.

"It certainly seems like that," said Matthew. "A bit of a scandal really."

"It explains a lot," said Humphrey. "Poor old sod."

The pastor had told Matthew that Cecil was often depressed and short of money and what he craved more than anything was a job. For some minor discrepancy he had been sacked from his newspaper seller's role some time previously.

The three men sat silently, pondering what they had just heard. Each felt a little ashamed that they had treated this unfortunate man as a figure of fun, when all he had been doing, in his often cack-handed way, was to try to forge a reasonable life for himself – almost from scratch.

There are many Cecil Roberts in our society, aspiring to make a very modest but decent way in the world, while seemingly consigned to a demi-monde of poverty and often ill health. Although worthy enough in themselves, they are degraded by the surroundings in which they have to live, a world of drug addicts, petty criminals and appalling housing conditions. Some come to be regarded as little more than tramps.

Cecil, though, despite all his shortcomings, had shown an admirable resilience. Having been unsuccessful in affairs of the heart, he had gained consolation and self-respect in his new-found religion. Among the local Pentecostalists he had found acceptance, compassion and a set of respectable God-fearing standards to live by.

After their period of reflection, and a certain amount of unspoken self-loathing, our trio put their minds to whether they could help Cecil in any practical way.

"Can we do anything for the old boy?" asked Humphrey. "Could he sell newspapers for your paper, Matthew?"

Matthew, who was now the Sanderholme Times' chief reporter, replied: "We don't have newspaper sellers. That's more for the big daily and regional newspapers than for small weeklies like ours."

"I have a germ of an idea," said Hector. "We need someone at the caravan site to clean toilets, look after the laundry and do some refuse bin collections. The site handyman and I do those jobs between us at present, but we could do with some help. I'll talk to my mother and see what we can do."

"That's sounds ideal," said Matthew.

"I'll drink to that," said Humphrey, who always found a reason to drink to something. "That way we could keep an eye on him and make sure he was all right."

"Don't have him making the tea for you, though," said Matthew, winking at Hector, and making an arch allusion to the 'poisons' story.

Hector was true to his word and an extremely grateful Cecil took up his position at the caravan site the following week.

****

Phoebe accepted the children's decision not to join her in Africa and was to become an increasingly distant figure in their lives. At the outset, every couple of years she would make a brief trip to England to see them. She didn't believe in Christmas or Easter so they got no presents or cards. Sometimes she would remember their birthdays.

As the years of her absence turned into decades her visits became less frequent and eventually stopped altogether.

Her relationship with Adam had lasted for only one year and after that she had a string of partners before resigning herself to living alone and having occasional one night stands. She eventually died of malaria in Zambia at the age of 69. She had taken part in Oxfam projects in various African countries for 37 years and in 2002 had turned down the offer of an MBE for her charity work. The British Empire was an anathema to her and the monarchy an outdated abomination.

When Phoebe first left her family, Hector was aged 34. His physical appearance had changed somewhat over the years, the main difference being that he had no longer had shoulder-length hair. He now had a short back and sides haircut with a slight quiff at the front. In the couple of years before he left school he had put on a few pounds in weight. Phoebe had become a vegetarian and, although she could not persuade Hector to follow suit, they both ate quite healthily. As a result Hector lost some weight and now looked slim, with handsomely chiselled features like his father's.

There was every reason to believe that he would have

no great difficulty in finding a new partner.

However, in the months immediately after he became "single" again Hector went through a period of introspection. He rekindled his enthusiasm for Romantic poetry and in particular the nature poems of William Wordsworth.

Earlier he had found little in Wordsworth to attract him. He preferred the panache of the younger Romantics, such as Byron, Shelley and Keats. He found Wordsworth stuffy by comparison and at school had laughed at what he believed were the poet's unsuccessful efforts to reproduce in his verse *"the real language of men"*.

Now more mature and open-minded in his outlook, he decided to give the poet another chance. In his melancholy state following the loss of Phoebe one particular quote from the poet struck home and moved him deeply: "Nature never did betray, The heart that loved her."

He needed something in life that he could rely on. Women did not fit the bill at this particular juncture. All he read of Wordsworth led him to consider that Nature could become his consort.

After work in the summer evenings, he started to go on solitary "nature walks": long and varied meanders in parts of the marshy countryside surrounding Sanderholme which had never greatly interested him until now.

He listened to birdsong, took a book with him to help him to identify wildflowers, plants and trees, and combed the beaches for interesting seaweeds and marine life. Sometimes he would lie on his back and contemplate the formation of a passing skein of geese or the mesmerising murmurations of starlings, or just admire the varying shapes and hues of the clouds.

Inspired by his knowledge of Greek mythology and Romantic poetry, he often drifted into a strange state of reverie, imagining himself surrounded by nymphs and other spirits of nature: dryads in the trees, naiads in the water courses and a mighty River God who protected the Marsh Eau river.

One summer's evening after work, Hector decided to take a walk along the bank of the Marsh Eau, following its course between Havenside and the sea. It was the first time he had ventured in that direction since he had travelled with a feeling of foreboding to deliver his letter to Tricia Stanmore's husband Derek.

The air was cool and refreshing, the sky blue and cloudless – the perfect conditions for a brisk walk. The river was busy with jumping fish and dancing insects and a couple of fishermen friends, with bulging keep nets, were enjoying a smoke and a joke together as they waited patiently for their next bites. Hector nodded to them as he passed.

As he approached Bank Farm, he wondered if he might catch sight of Tricia. He was in two minds whether he wished to see her. A glimpse of her wonderful figure would certainly be welcome but he feared this might rekindle his earlier desires. One person he certainly did not wish to see was Derek, someone he had happily managed to avoid since their encounter some years earlier. As it happened he saw no one as he passed the farm.

A few yards further along, on a broader stretch of grass at the top of the bank, was a feature he was surprised to see – a green wooden shed with a door and two windows facing the river. As there was no one about he was curious enough to peer through one of the windows. Inside was a wooden table and two wooden chairs, a couch which looked as if it had been used as a bed, a chest of drawers, a cooker, an oil heater and a small television set. Various plates, cups and saucers were spread around the room and a number of empty beer bottles. Looking through the second window he could see there was another very small room, containing a chemi loo and a wash basin.

Clearly someone lived in the shed for at least some of the time. Hector was intrigued by what he had found, guessing perhaps it might be used by farmworkers or as a modest holiday retreat.

He continued his riverbank walk for a further half hour before turning round and starting the journey home. As he came near to the shed he noticed that the door was open and he could hear someone moving around inside. As he passed by, a stocky man wearing blue denim overalls emerged from the shed and stared in his direction.

"Hello," said Hector. "Nice evening, isn't it?"

The man nodded and said: "Aye."

Hector suddenly recognised the speaker as Derek Stanmore. He was fatter than he remembered him and his thick black hair looked dishevelled.

Hector was about to carry on walking but Stanmore

called after him.

"It's young Mr Ratcliffe isn't it?"

"Yes. Mr Stanmore?"

"That's right. You'll remember me."

"Yes, I do. Are you keeping well?"

"Keeping well, yes. What brings you round these parts?"

"I'm just having a walk."

"Funny place for a walk, I should think. There's not much to look at down here."

"Oh, I like the peace and quiet. I've always liked rivers. I used to come fishing along here with my dad," said Hector.

"Oh, aye. The fishing's not as good as it used to be, I'm told. Too many small fish about. We don't get the anglers down here like we used to, thank goodness. You're the first person I've seen along the riverbank for months."

"Oh, I saw a couple of fishermen tonight, just this side of the bridge."

"There's still one or two who fish near the bridge. But nobody seems to come down here. I have beast grazing along here sometimes. I think that puts people off."

"You don't mind me walking along here, do you?"

"It's a free country, mate. You still work at the caravan site?"

"Yeah."

"Are you still with George Barrington's daughter?"

"No, I'm afraid not. She went off to Africa and left me and the kids."

"Oh, I see. Women. They're all the same," said Derek.

"Well, I don't know about that. But I haven't had much luck with them yet."

"Tell me about it. How's the caravan business then?"

"It's going pretty well, thanks."

"My cousin's setting up a caravan site along the bank there," said Derek. "Don't know if he'll do any good."

"Oh, that's interesting. Whereabouts exactly?"

"Along the bank here at the old Havenside Farm. Round the corner – just the other side of the bridge."

"Who's your cousin?"

"Richard Douglas."

"Is that Richard Douglas the farmer from Hayfleet?"

"Yes, that's the one," replied Derek.

"I went to school with his daughter, Penelope."

"Oh, yes. She's a decent girl, Penelope. Very pretty too."

"Yes, she certainly is," said Hector, warming to the subject.

"Are you in contact with her at all?"

"I last saw her at Christmas when her dad had a bit of a Christmas do."

"How was she?"

"She seemed all right, "said Derek. "She's got two nice kids, two girls, and she's doing well as a solicitor down in Stratford-upon-Avon. Not so sure about her husband, though. That Stuart Broadlake."

"Oh, what's the matter with him?"

"Well, he's in the army, you know, a captain. And he's always serving abroad somewhere. I'm told he does a lot of chasing after women when he's away from home."

"Is that so? He must be mad with a lovely wife like

Penelope," said Hector.

"Aye, I've heard when he is at home he can be a bit of a bastard to her. Gets drunk and then gets aggressive with her and the kids."

"Really? He always could be moody when he was at school. She doesn't deserve that."

"No, you're right. I know her mother and father are not very happy about it. He didn't even join them at Christmas. Mind you, perhaps he wasn't invited."

"The man's a fool," said Hector, with growing indignation.

"Aye, marriage is a funny business. Take my wife. Ever since we got married she's had roving eyes for the fellas. And of course they've got roving eyes for her."

"Yeah."

"There was a time when I used to get really angry about it. As you know. For a few hours that day I probably would have shot you. But by the time I met you I'd calmed down a lot. After all, I knew that she would have led you on. That's what she's like. Anyway that's well in the past."

"Are things all right now between you and your wife?" asked Hector.

"No, she's got a young fella living at the house now. That's why I'm staying in this shed."

"You live here?"

"Yeah, I've been here for nearly a year now. It's good to get some peace and quiet."

"And she's living with a chap?"

"Yes, I've just given up. I should have shot him but I'm almost past caring. There've been so many different blokes over the years. She's an attractive woman, you see. It's as if she can't help herself and men are just drawn to her."

"It doesn't seem fair on you," said Hector. "Having to live here while they're in your farmhouse."

"It's not bloody fair. But what do I do? I still love her, you see. I shouldn't, but I do. She'll tire of this latest bloke before much longer and then I'll be back in the house. She'll come on to me all lovey-dovey and I won't be able to resist her. Again.

"Anyway, enough of my problems. Can I get you a beer?"

Hector accepted the offer. He wasn't especially keen to hear more of Derek's sob stories but he could see that the farmer was starting to become emotional and he felt it would be unfair to leave at that point. He was also pleased to have established contact with someone with a connection to Penelope, albeit not a close contact.

Derek went into the shed and brought out the two chairs and a small fold-up table. He produced two cans of beer and poured them into glasses.

"So, you were telling me you're no longer with George Barrington's daughter," said Derek.

"She upped and left me last autumn. She's living in Africa with another man she met out there."

"Oh, dear. You can't trust women. So you're on your own?"

"Yes, me and the two kids. She left them behind. But I was pleased about that. I couldn't bear the thought of losing them too."

"Quite right."

"What about you? Do you get a social life? I know you used to belong to the Round Table and the Golf Club."

"No, I don't have any connections like that anymore. I'm too old for Round Table now anyway. The people I used to think were my friends, weren't really friends at all. They'd either shagged my wife or they were in a queue to be the next to shag her. They were just laughing at me behind my back.

"No, I just work on the farm during the day and then come here at night, have a few beers and watch telly. Not much of a life, I suppose you're thinking. But at least it's peaceful. Suits me for now."

The two men spent the next hour sympathising with each other's plight and sharing a second beer. Then, with the light fading and a chilly wind starting to blow off the sea, Hector decided it was time for him to go.

"Thanks for the hospitality," he said.

"Next time you're fancying a walk, come and have another beer with me," said Derek.

Laughing, he added: "Chin up!"

"Chin up!" said Hector, waving goodbye.

As he walked back along the riverbank on the way back to his car, Hector had plenty to think about. It had been a strange evening. He had met up with the man who once wanted to shoot him, and although Derek was rather a sad, diminished character, he had rather liked him.

Then there was the news he had had about Penelope. He felt sad for her as it appeared she was trapped in an unpleasant marriage. But her plight did give him a fanciful notion that one day he could be the man to pick up the pieces. This idea was a pleasant daydream to indulge in as he wandered back along the riverbank but, as reality set in again and he got back into his car, he told himself not to be such a ridiculous fool.

Chapter six – A new friendship

As Hector was sitting in the caravan site office the next day he received a surprise visit from his good friend Humphrey.

Humphrey, looking even more flamboyant than usual, was wearing a Cambridge blue striped blazer, blue slacks and sandals, topped off by a straw boater. It was an incongruous style for an east coast caravan site, but pure Humphrey.

Still a bachelor, he had enjoyed a varied life since leaving Grammar School. He had gained a second class honours degree in English Literature at Cambridge University, worked on a building site in London, been a skiing instructor in Switzerland and a tour guide in South America. Now he was a partner in his father's new financial advice company, which was also based in Cambridge. As someone who had come close to bankruptcy numerous times himself, his father believed he was just the right man to warn others of the pitfalls.

Hector was pleased to see his friend, who could always be guaranteed to cheer him up.

After they had exchanged a few pleasantries, it became clear that Humphrey had a particular reason for visiting on that day.

"The thing is, old chap, I'm going out on the town with a couple of girls tonight and I wondered if you'd like to come along. Just a bit of fun, you know."

Hector wished to know more about the "girls".

"They're called Esme and Miriam. Mine's a doll. Absolutely wonderful. Not so sure about yours, though.

Has a figure like the back end of a bus and a face like a bulldog licking piss off a thistle."

Humphrey paused and Hector grimaced.

"No, I'm joking. They're both lovely girls. Great sports."

"Okay, then. Why not?" said Hector.

"Righto. I'll pick the ladies up and then call round and collect you from home at 7.30. We fancy going to that new wine bar down Lifeboat Street. That okay?"

"Sure, I've not been there yet. Should be good."

"We could have a spot to eat there, perhaps?" said Humphrey. "I could buy us a bottle of champers. Oh, and mine's Esme by the way. See you later."

Hector would have liked to know much more about the two girls but Humphrey had bounded out of the office before he had chance to ask.

The evening turned out to be a great success. The young women were bright, intelligent and good looking and the conversation and the wine flowed easily. Humphrey was on his best form, full of hilarious anecdotes and teasing sarcasm.

Esme was a stunning blonde with an hourglass figure while Miriam was a slim brunette with a face notable for its good bone structure.

Hector learnt that Esme was a legal executive at a Cambridge solicitor's firm, where Miriam was a trainee solicitor. They had met Humphrey at a party held by his father to launch his new business.

Both girls were voluble and bubbly, clearly out for the best possible night.

The foursome stayed in the restaurant until it closed

at midnight. But none of them wanted the fun to end there. It had already been decided that Humphrey would leave his Merc in the restaurant car park and would order a taxi to take everyone home.

Then he had a better idea. He went to his car and produced a bottle of champagne.

"We've got this to drink yet," he said. "Is there any chance we might go back to your place, Hector, and have a little drinkie?"

"Yes, of course," replied Hector. "The kids are at my mum and dad's. So I'm a free agent."

"You up for it, girls?" said Humphrey.

"Yay, let's go for it. The night's young," said Esme.

"Yep, I'm up for it," said Miriam.

When they arrived at Hector's house all four were already tipsy so the champagne went quickly to their heads. There was a good deal of kissing and cuddling and finally Humphrey retired to bed with Esme and Hector with Miriam.

The next morning Hector made breakfast for everyone. Esme and Humphrey, who had clearly known each other for some time, said they must go to Humphrey's grandmother's house that morning as they had arranged to take her to a hospital appointment. It was agreed that Miriam would join them later at the house for lunch.

Miriam had been quiet over breakfast and Hector sensed she was embarrassed about what had happened the night before.

"Are we all right – after last night?" Hector asked her after the others had gone.

She smiled ruefully: "Yes, I had a good time. But I must tell you that I don't normally behave like that. We all drank too much."

"Yes, you're right. If you think I took advantage, then I apologise. It's not my style either."

"No, you have nothing to blame yourself for. We both got carried away. I don't want to spoil things. I know you have had a bad time, with your partner leaving you. You deserve a break."

Hector had not mentioned anything to her about Phoebe.

"Did Humphrey tell you about all that?" he asked.

"Yes, he wanted you to have a good time. That's what last night was all about."

"Oh, I see."

"Your aunt had been in touch with him apparently."

"My aunt?"

"Apparently. She suggested that you needed cheering up with some female company."

"That's incredible. How interfering is she?" said Hector. "So you just felt sorry for me?"

"That's not why I did it with you. I liked you. I like you."

"I'm pleased about that. Because I like you."

He held her hand.

"I can't believe my aunt, though. I didn't know she had even spoken to Humphrey. I'm a big boy now. I can handle all kinds of setbacks and still not go mental."

"I'm sure you can," said Miriam.

Hector could sense that she was uncomfortable, probably suffering from pangs of guilt. He was feeling that way himself, although he couldn't quite explain why. He was an unmarried man of a similar age to Miriam's and did not have any particular personal or religious convictions to worry about. Nevertheless, inexplicably, he did feel guilty – dirty even.

"Are you in Sanderholme for long?" asked Hector.

"Just until tomorrow. Then we are all going back to Cambridge."

When Miriam told him that this was her first visit to Sanderholme, Hector offered to show her the sights and they spent the rest of the morning walking through the town, along the sea front and on to the beach. Then he accompanied her to Humphrey's grandmother's home, leaving her at the gate.

"Will I see you again?" asked Hector, more out of politeness than from any conviction that he wished to.

"I'm sure you will. I expect Humphrey and Esme will come over to see his grandmother again some time. Perhaps we could meet up then. We'll keep in touch through Humphrey, I'm certain."

Hector perceived that she was far from certain. They both knew that they liked each other but the drink-induced chemistry of the previous night seemingly could not be sustained in the cold light of day.

They never saw each other again.

****

Hector felt it was time he had a conversation with his Aunt Christine. He had felt mortified that she had taken upon herself the role of matchmaker.

That same afternoon they found themselves alone in

the caravan office. Reception was quiet and Christine was busying herself by doing The Times crossword. She had been "doing" the cryptic puzzle every day since she was a student on a management course at the London School of Economics. She had never completed it.

On her daily commute into the city she, along with many fellow travellers, would tackle the crossword each morning. Having filled in the few clues she could solve she would put any sort of gibberish in the remaining spaces. Then she would ostentatiously throw the paper on to one side and sit with a contented, smug smile on her face having "completed" the puzzle. Other passengers, mainly pin-striped city gents, still struggling with their Times crosswords, would look at her in amazement. This happened every day for months without anyone suspecting that she was not the genius she appeared to be!

Christine Ashburn was what is often described as "a one-off". She was always immaculately turned out, with expensive clothes and carefully applied, thick make-up, long, false eyelashes and long, false fingernails.

She had a strong interest, almost an obsession, in maintaining the status of the Ashburn family, her forebears having been a long line of landowners and gentlemen farmers.

Although inclined to be a snob and quite bossily loud she was also kind and approachable. The caravan site owners whom she dealt with, mostly working class people from the Midlands and the North, looked up to her in a deferential sort of way but also genuinely liked her and would sit with her for hours telling her their stories and sharing their troubles. It never occurred to them that she was also a voracious gossip, who could never keep a good tale to herself.

Christine, noted for voluptuous good looks as a young woman, had been engaged five times but never married. This may have been due to her proclivity to take up various religions, often with all-encompassing enthusiasm, only to ditch them and go on to some new faith.

Sometimes there was an overlap which raised a few eyebrows. She was a fanatical Scientologist at the same time as playing the organ at the Sanderholme Methodist Church. She dabbled in Paganism much to the alarm of parents whose children were being taught by her at an Anglican Sunday School. Currently she was a Zen Buddhist.

Another of her passions was am dram and she had taken many leading roles in Sanderholme Players' productions, starting as a teenager. Her latest role had been as Lady Bracknell in "The Importance of Being Earnest".

Christine's lack of success in the area of matrimony did not stop her fancying herself as an unpaid marriage counsellor for her friends and acquaintances.

Hector loved his aunt and knew that she invariably acted from the finest of motives, but he now felt he had to put his foot down over her interference in his own affairs.

"Aunt Christine, may I ask you a question?" he said.

"Of course, my dear," she replied.

"Is it right that you've been in touch with my friend

Humphrey Gibb?"

"Yes, I did speak to him a few weeks ago."

"I didn't know you knew Humphrey that well."

"I don't really. I did know you were a friend of his, though, and he played a few parts with the Sanderholme Players when he was still at school."

"So how did you know how to get in touch with him?"

"Through his grandmother, Gloria. She belongs to the bridge club. A charming lady. I've known her for years."

"Why did you contact Humphrey, Aunty?"

"You seem to have been at rather a loose end since Phoebe left you. I know you do everything for Troy and Janis, but you need to have a life yourself. Humphrey's grandmother told me that he knows lots of nice young women so I thought he might be able to introduce you to one or two."

"Did you? Well he did introduce me to one of them."

"I know."

"You know?"

"Humphrey's grandmother told me that you and Humphrey had a night out with a couple of girls last night."

"Did she?"

"Yes, she rang me this morning."

"Did she?"

"Yes, she was quite worried about Humphrey because he didn't go back to her house last night. She wondered if you might know where he was. But then she rang back later on to say that he and his girlfriend had returned home. She is so pleased that he seems to have a proper girlfriend this time.

"Really. I'm pleased that he hadn't got lost."

"Where had he been?"

"He stayed at my house."

"Did the two young ladies stay as well?"

"Yes."

"So you had an enjoyable evening then?"

"Very enjoyable, thank you."

"So the two girls enjoyed themselves too?"

"I believe so. Aunty, may I ask you something?"

"Of course, dear."

"Do you know how old I am?"

"Yes, dear. I believe you're 34."

"And how old do you think Humphrey is?"

"I don't know. I suppose he must be about the same age as you."

"Yes, he's 34."

"Why are you asking me about ages?"

"It's just that do you think that you, and Humphrey's grandmother, need to be worrying yourselves about 34-year-old men, one of whom has two teenaged children?"

"So I'm being told off then."

"Just a little."

"All right. I am censured and am contrite. But just tell me one thing."

"Yes?"

"Are you going to see Miriam again?"

"You're a terror. You even know her name. I don't know if I'll see her again. She's gone back to Cambridge now."

"I know. Humphrey's grandmother told me."

"She rang again?"

"Yes, a few minutes ago. She said Miriam was very quiet over lunch. I do hope you will see her again. I'm told she's a very nice girl."

"I suppose Humphrey's grandmother told you that as well."

"No, actually it was Miriam's mother. A very nice lady. She sounded quite Home Counties."

"Miriam's mother!" declared Hector, "You've spoken to Miriam's mother! When?"

"Last night, dear. I was curious to see what kind of young lady Humphrey had found for you. I am sorry if you think I was interfering."

"Interfering! It's absolutely incredible. Please would you not interfere again. I'm quite capable of running my own life."

"That's what your mother said."

"When did she say that?"

"This morning. She told me off as well."

"Good for her."

Hector was completely nonplussed. Outwardly he was angry with his aunt. But inwardly he was laughing at the sheer outrageousness of it all.

He turned to leave the office but before he did so he said to Christine: "Okay. I've had my little moan. You're incorrigible. But we'll say no more about it."

His aunt replied: "Thank you, dear. Least said soonest mended. I just hope you took precautions in bed, especially if you're not intending to see Miriam again."

Hector slammed the door.

Christine picked up her phone and dialled.

"Hello Gloria Gibb here," came the answer.

"Hello, Gloria. It's Christine here. I've got some things to tell you...."

＊＊＊＊

Hector had a lot to think about as he went about his work on the site that day. He contemplated why his date with Miriam had ended on such a non-committal note. She was a lovely lady and, although she had been cool towards him that morning, he was pretty sure that he could have dated her again if he had really wanted to.

Deep down, though, he knew exactly what the problem was. His meeting with Derek Stanmore had rekindled his interest in Penelope Douglas.

The prospects of his ever winning Penelope were much worse than they had been when they were at school together. The biggest obstacle was, of course, that she was married, and married to a bad-tempered he-man. There was a distance problem too, as she lived at Stratford-upon-Avon.

What had given him a tiny sliver of hope was that the marriage appeared to be an unhappy one and that Penelope's parents may have taken against Stuart Broadlake. His pragmatic, mature, sensible self knew that he was being pathetic trying to hang on to such a flimsy thread. His idealistic, romantic, childlike nature instructed him never to give up. And, for the time being at least, this side of his character was back in the ascendancy.

His only small point of contact was Derek and so he decided he needed to exploit that as much as he could. He began to have regular meetings with Stanmore who was always pleased to have his company.

One of these visits was paid on a cold, crisp Sunday afternoon in January. The Marsh Eau was frozen over and lifeless, with only a gaggling skein of Canada geese flying overhead to break the solitude and silence as Hector walked along the bank.

Outside Derek's shed were a dozen sheep eating swedes provided for them as a tasty winter supplement.

Hector knocked on the shed door and Derek was quick to open it.

"Come in, lad. It's cold outside this morning. I've got the oil heater on in here."

Hector removed a backpack and opened it to take out two beer cans.

"Here we are. Something to warm us up."

"I don't know that beer will do that. If it doesn't, I have some Scotch here that might," said Derek.

"I didn't know if you'd still be here in this cold weather. I thought you might have retreated into the house," said Hector.

"Nah, I'm still here. Lover boy's still in the house. This one seems to be sticking around. He must have something she likes."

"Oh dear, I'm sorry about that. You shouldn't have to live out here in the winter."

"I'm hardy. I'm a farmer. We're a tough breed, you know."

"You must be.

"I see the sheep are tucking in well."

"Aye, they like swedes. Gives them something to eat when the grass is frozen up."

"I didn't know you kept sheep. I thought you were just into arable and cattle."

"I bought these from Richard Douglas. He had them at the old farm near the bridge. But there's too many there for the grazing, so he sold a few to me."

"It brings back a strange childhood memory for me," said Hector. "I was about 12 or 13 and I came fishing on my own for the first time. I was fishing near the bridge. I got a bit stiff sitting on my basket so I stood up for a few minutes.

"In the distance I could just see the garden at the front of the farmhouse – the one you said Mr Douglas owns. In the garden there were a few sheep and an elderly man, who looked like a farmer. He had the usual flat cap on. A collie dog was running round him, barking. The man picked up what looked like a piece of wood and, to my horror, appeared to beat the dog repeatedly. The dog fell silent and I didn't see it get up from the ground. I was sure it had been killed.

"I can't be certain of what I saw, because, as I said, it was a fair distance away. But I have never forgotten that image of the man beating the dog. I have often thought about it over the years. I wondered if the dog might have gone rogue and worried sheep. Or whether it might be an old dog which had outlived its usefulness.

"I might have lived a sheltered life, but this was one of the worst things I've seen."

"I don't know anything about that," said Derek. "Old Mr Douglas used to live at the farm, Richard's father. He was a tough old boy – dead now, of course – but I don't think he would do anything like that. I may be wrong."

"I hope he didn't do it. I hope my eyes deceived me."

Hector paused to consider the story he had just told. Old Mr Douglas may have been a very hard man, he thought. The notion came into his head that Penelope's treatment of him when she had refused his invitation to go to the cinema had also been a little hard. Perhaps it was a family trait. Then he mentally kicked himself for his silliness. How could beating a dog to death reasonably be conflated with Penelope gently turning someone down for a date?

He continued: "Talking of the Douglas family, did you see anything of them over Christmas?"

"Yes, I did. I was invited to their usual Christmas party. Penelope was there with her two lasses, but no Stuart again. I asked her where he was and she said he was busy working – on manoeuvres or something like that. I got the feeling she didn't want to discuss him."

Hector had come to consider Derek as a friend – someone who would listen to him without being judgemental and whom he could trust. He was confident now that he could confide in him enough to reveal his feelings for Penelope.

"You know when I was at school I was madly in love with Penelope. It never went anywhere. She didn't really want to know. But I've never really stopped loving her. I know it's stupid."

"Aye, it is stupid, mate. I had an inkling that you had a special interest in her. You do mention her quite a lot. But who am I to call anyone stupid when it comes to loving women?" said Derek. "I'm the stupidest bloke in the world when it comes to that.

"Do you know that when I was in my early twenties I had a lovely wife, Deborah. She was pretty and faithful. A decent girl. Good farming stock. But when Tricia came along I couldn't resist. I should have stuck with Deborah."

Hector was reminded of Dostoyevsky's The Idiot, where Prince Lev Nikolayevich loves the femme fatale Natasya Filippovna when the more sensible option is clearly Aglaya Yepanchin.

By Derek's tone of voice Hector feared that his friend was going to become maudlin very soon.

"Let's change the subject," said Hector. "We're only going to make ourselves miserable."

"You're right, mate. Let's get another can open," said Derek.

****

Fast forward 15 years….

Hector is a fit 49-year-old and now managing director of the Marshview Caravan Site. Margaret, 71, and Christine, 67, are still in harness, running the reception and looking after the money. Hector's son, Troy, has joined the business too and is unmarried. His daughter, Janis, is a primary school teacher, married to a police officer and with three young children.

Hector loves his children and grandchildren dearly and they love him in return. He is truly experiencing another of the Greek love categories – *storge* – love of family.

Cecil Roberts, who had been a hardworking and popular employee at the site into his mid-seventies, has retired. He has always been loyal to Hector and his family and eternally grateful for the job he was given. His eccentricities, and occasional irascibility, give all who know him an endless supply of amusing stories, eagerly recounted to this day at meetings of his Appreciation Society.

Cecil still lives in a caravan on the site with a Staffordshire bull terrier, which Hector, ever ready with his Homeric references, has named Ajax.

In spite of Christine's best efforts Hector does not currently have a woman in his life. He has had a few dates with a selection of divorcees but none have developed into anything serious. This has mainly been due to his unwillingness to commit

He is playing his part in the community, being chairman of the Sanderholme and District Chamber of Commerce and also a director of the local Nature Conservation Trust.

However, despite a routine full of hard work and activity and a family he adores, there remains a gaping void in his life – Penelope.

Not a day passes without his thoughts returning to his unrequited love affair with his former schoolmate. He has absolutely no feelings of bitterness towards her, blaming his lack of progress in the relationship on his own shortcomings.

He always rates Penelope as being a human being far superior to himself. When he thinks of her during the waking hours his sense of failure causes him to flush with embarrassment. He is also angry with himself for having given up without more of an effort. One measly request for a date and one polite refusal on Penelope's part was the pathetic limit to his endeavours. Why hadn't he fought for her? How could he have allowed that preening prima donna Stuart Broadlake to get the better of him?

In bed at night, though, it is an entirely different story. Almost every night Penelope features in his dreams. And they are pleasant dreams which he tries desperately to hang on to when daytime arrives. In them, Penelope is invariably sweet to him, a calming, dignified presence, who, significantly, actually returns his love. When he wakes up he tries to go to sleep again as quickly as possible, hoping, against all experience, to carry on with the dream where he left off.

In the theatre of dreams Penelope is Queen.

These night-time fantasies provide Hector with a kind of comfort blanket, protecting him against the harsh fact that he may never see Penelope again, and that even if he does it will be to no avail. A number of the girls they knew at school have been married and divorced, some more than once. But Penelope is not like that. He knows that she was always dutiful and respectful in her outlook and just not the type to give up on a marriage.

Hector is without hope, but he can always dream...

****

His friend, Derek, is back living in the shed after being to and fro between there and the farmhouse several times over the years. Tricia's "toy boy" left ten years earlier but she has had several more affairs since then. Although she is currently living alone the relationship between her and her husband has reached an all-time low.

Hector has noticed, with increasing concern, that his friend is struggling both mentally and physically. He has become gradually more depressed, he is drinking to excess, bottles of whisky having taken the place of the odd can of beer, and he looks scruffy. He rarely shaves or has a haircut and so has hair growing in all sorts of inappropriate ways and places. He has also lost weight alarmingly.

When he paid his most recent visit Hector was greeted by a distressing sight. Derek was laid on his back asleep on the grass at the front of the shed. He was a grasping an empty whisky bottle and saliva had dribbled on to the front of his shirt.

Hector waited a while but Derek did not stir. He decided he ought to wake him as, in good conscience, he could not leave him in that state.

He gently shook the prone torso and eventually it was roused.

"What the bloody hell? Who's this?" Derek slurred, wiping spittle from his chin.

"It's me, Hector. Are you okay?"

"Aye, I'll live. Had a bit of a session and fell asleep."

Derek raised himself from the ground and shuffled over to the dining chair he had placed outside the front door. He flopped down onto it.

"Ah, that's better."

Hector looked at him quizzically.

"You're sure you're all right now?"

"Yes, I'm fine. Go inside, fetch your sen a chair and get a can of beer. There's plenty in the cupboard."

Another aspect of Derek's deterioration was that his

speech had become rougher and more countrified. It was if he had completely given up trying to be the man-about-town of his younger days and returned to his natural state.

"You really should be in the house. The nights will start drawing in soon and it will get cold. You ought to have a proper warm bed to sleep in this winter," said Hector.

"I can't stand the sight of that bitch now. We just row all the time. Well, mainly I row with her. She just laughs at me now. I can't do anything for her these days. She needs another toy boy to keep her satisfied but I can't stand being around when she has her 'friends' there. I just cut up rough and retreat back over here. You know how it is."

"I've got an idea by now," said Hector, patting his friend on the arm. "I just worry about you."

"Don't you worry about me. Anyway I still get my invite to the Douglas's at Christmas. She doesn't get invited.

"I had a surprise visitor yesterday, Susan Douglas's son, Timothy. He's a good lad. Very interested in farming. He's come to live with his grandad and grandma and he's going to run their farm for them. He's run a farm before, down south. I gave him a few tips. A good lad."

"I don't remember much about Susan. She was a few years above me at school," said Hector.

Derek replied: "She was a bonny girl when she was younger. A bit of a goer by all accounts. Then she fell for the baby. That was her first kid, Jodie; Timothy came later. When she had Jodie it was a bit of a scandal. No one ever knew who the father was."

"I expect someone knew," laughed Hector. "Susan at least."

"Aye, she must have known. But no one ever let on anyhow. Might have been one of the lads from school.

"She's not had an easy life apparently – two divorces. She's never had any more kids. Anyway, I think she's brought up Timothy well.

"I wish I had a lad like that. Tricia was never interested in having children. It would have cramped her style. I don't know what'll happen to this farm when I die. I'll leave the house to the bitch. I might leave the farm to that lad Timothy. I think he would look after it. I don't have close relatives, you see."

"Sounds like a plan," said Hector. "But you won't need to implement it for many years yet. If you look after yourself."

Derek didn't answer. He just stared into his beer.

****

A week goes by and Hector sets off again to see Derek. He is so worried about the farmer that he has decided to visit him more regularly.

It is a late October afternoon and there is a chill in the air as he reaches the bridge and steps over a stile to get to the grassy bankside path. Two fishermen are spinning for pike from the bank opposite and give him cheery waves.

"Any luck?" he asks.

"Not yet," they both reply.

He doubts if they will have any.

He reaches the shed and knocks on the door. There is no reply so he tries again, and then a third time. He shouts: "Derek, are you there?" Still no reply.

He tries the door handle and, finding the door unlocked, pushes it ajar and shouts out again.

"Are you there, Derek? It's me, Hector."

No response.

He opens the door a little wider and is confronted by a sight which will haunt him for the rest of his life.

Derek is lying front down on the floor. Where his head should be is just a grisly mash of blood. A shotgun lies at the side of the body. Hector struggles not to vomit.

He runs out of the shed across the lane, past the stone lions at the head of the drive and knocks furiously on the back door of the farmhouse.

Tricia comes to the door, her hair dishevelled and wearing just a white dressing gown. She looks as sexy as ever. She doesn't recognise Hector.

"Yes, love, can I help you?"

Hector is shaking from head to toe and she realises he is alarmed.

"It's Derek. I've just come from his shed. He's dead."

"Dead? Oh, my god. How?"

"I can't be sure but it looks as if he's shot himself."

"Are you sure he's dead?"

"Absolutely. Will you come with me and look?"

"Yes, come on."

As they run along the driveway he warns her: "You're going to be shocked, I'm afraid."

When they get into the shed she lets out a shriek.

"Oh, my god. My god," she cries and bursts into tears.

Hector puts his arm around her shoulder to comfort her.

"I never thought he'd do anything like this," Tricia says between her sobs.

"We must ring 999," says Hector.

"Of course, let's go back to the house," says Tricia, already running at speed.

Back in the farmhouse kitchen she asks Hector to make the phone call and he immediately does so.

Tricia is pacing up and down, tearing at her hair, wiping away tears with the sleeve of her dressing gown and obviously still in severe shock. Hector does the English thing and asks if he can make her a cup of tea.

"I'd rather have a brandy," she replies. "There's a bottle in the cupboard over there and a couple of glasses."

Hector pours her a brandy and she begins to recover a little composure. She stares at him with a wild, questioning look.

"Who are you?" she asks.

"Hector Ratcliffe. I do know you. We met some years ago – at the Stag's Head."

"Oh, yes. I think I remember you. What were you doing at Derek's shed?"

Hector senses that he is under suspicion.

"I went to see him. I regularly do. I was worried about him, to be honest. He hasn't been the same lately."

Tricia looks at him closely.

"Are you a friend of his, then?"

"Yes, we've been friends for years. Has he never mentioned it?"

"No, never."

Hector believes this lack of communication must be emblematic of their incredibly peculiar married relationship.

Tricia continues: "I didn't know he had any friends these days. He was so miserable."

Hector felt like saying "I wonder why?" but restrained himself as she was still fighting back tears and shaking.

She becomes totally silent, keeping her distance from him as she gulps at her brandy, coughing as she almost chokes herself. Hector understands that she fears she is in the presence of a murderer. The arrival of the police at the door comes as a great relief to them both.

****

Forensic evidence all pointed to the obvious conclusion that Derek committed suicide. Further investigation revealed that three days before his death he had visited his solicitor, Phoebe's father George Barrington, and made his will.

When the will was subsequently read at Mr Barrington's office those invited to be present were Tricia, Richard and Pamela Douglas, their grandson, Timothy Grenville, and, to his own great surprise, Hector.

As they sat in the waiting room before the reading Hector felt ill at ease – that he didn't belong there. The reception he received from three of the others in the room was icy. The only friendly approach came from Timothy who introduced himself and warmly shook Hector's hand. Hector immediately took to this affable and well-groomed man and began to understand why

Derek had been so impressed by him.

It was revealed that, as he had indicated, Derek had left the house and its contents to Tricia and the farm to Timothy. Richard and Pamela Douglas were to receive £10,000 each and Hector, described as "my best friend", £20,000. The residue of the estate was to go to Tricia.

At the end of the proceedings Tricia left the office without a word to anyone, the elder Douglases just nodded peremptorily to Hector, and Timothy shook hands with him again and said: "See you at the funeral."

Hector was left feeling dejected as he drove home. He reflected on his strange friendship with Derek, which was an unlikely phenomenon considering that this was the man who had once threatened to shoot him.

Derek was not a particularly nice man. He could be brusque, his conversation was mundane and he had a great facility for self-pity, exemplified by the manner of his death. For all this there was something genuine and loyal about him which had appealed to the down to earth side of Hector's character.

His death had affected Hector much more than he could have imagined it would. Every time he thought about it he had to fight back tears. In the privacy of his bedroom the tears were uncontrolled and copious. The manner of Derek's death and his discovery of it had been horrific and it was inevitable that those images would stay with him for ever.

But there was far more to it than that. He came to the surprise realisation that he had come to love Derek, like a brother. His mind went back to the Greeks. Once more they had a word for this type of love – *philia*. It has been described as the type of love shared by people of the same dispositions. The two men's characters had differed in many aspects but what they had in common was a preoccupation with a woman. Despite his harsh words about Tricia and his inability to live happily under the same roof, Derek still had a love for his wife bordering on the obsessive. Hector's inner life was dominated by his unrequited love for Penelope.

Hector believed that his brotherly love for Derek was reciprocated and that this had been demonstrated by the generous bequest in the will.

It was obvious that this show of affection for someone outside of the family had not gone down well with the Douglases. That would have accounted for the frosty reception they had given him at the will reading.

This added to the overwhelming sadness he was already feeling over Derek's death. The last thing he needed was any ill will towards him from Penelope's family.

R. I. P. Derek Stanmore – a martyr to unwise love and a victim of cruel Eros.

****

Over the next few days there was much to be discussed by Margaret and Aunt Christine. They knew everything about Hector's involvement with Derek's tragic death and he had told them about the will reading and his unexpected legacy. They had given him a great deal of sympathy for his ordeal but had seemed somewhat perturbed about the legacy and the connection with the Douglas family.

"What's to be done?" Christine asked Margaret when they were next alone together in the caravan site office.

"What do you mean 'what's to be done?'" Margaret replied. "I can't see that anything needs to be done, or should be done."

"Well, I don't know. He keeps getting himself involved with those Douglas people," said Christine.

"He's hardly getting involved, is he? He just happened to make a friend of a cousin of theirs. That'll probably be the end of it."

"Huh, I suppose you're right," said Christine, sounding unconvinced. "There'll be a funeral, of course. They'll all be there for that. I think Hector should stay away."

"You can't expect him to stay away. Mr Stanmore had obviously become a very good friend of his."

"I can't understand him getting involved with that awful man," said Christine. "He's been living like a tramp for years. And that wife of his. Just a trollop. What on earth was Hector thinking about?"

"Don't be too hard on him. He's had a difficult time of things, as you know."

"You're right, of course. None of this is his fault, poor lad."

****

As we recounted at the beginning of this story, Derek's funeral at St Michael's Parish Church, Marshyard, was a dignified and controlled affair. The grieving widow looked stylish in her black outfit and her veil was sufficient to hide any tears – or lack of them.

Hector, well turned out in his best black suit, found his

stomach churning, just as it had at school, when he saw Penelope Douglas in the line of mourners. He was determined to stay cool, but at the same time show his delight at meeting her again after a space of more than 30 years.

After the interment, the funeral party made its way to the wake at a small village pub. Hector lost no time in reintroducing himself to his old school friend.

Penelope had removed her hat, revealing that her pageboy styled hair was still dark brown and glossy. Her face was as beautiful and flawless as ever.

She was standing at the side of the lounge bar talking to her two daughters when Hector plucked up the courage to walk over. He had decided to approach in a subdued manner as befitted the sad occasion.

"Hello, Penelope," he said, gently shaking her hand. "It's very nice to see you. A pity that it's on such a sad occasion."

Penelope smiled: "Hello, Hector. It's been a long time. You're looking well."

"Thanks. You hardly look any different."

"A few grey hairs, I'm afraid," she replied.

"I can't see any," he bantered.

"Can I introduce my daughters, Sarah and Jane?"

The daughters were just as pleasing to the eye as their mother, and a few inches taller.

When the introductions had been made Hector and Penelope went on to reminisce about schooldays and what had happened to various people.

"What's happened to Matthew Copson?" she asked.

"He went into journalism and he's editor of the

Sanderholme Times now," replied Hector. "He's married with one son and still lives in town."

"And what about Humphrey Gibb? He was a lovely character."

"Humphrey is fine. The same old Humphrey, just as flamboyant as ever. He lives in Cambridge and works for his father in his financial advice company. He married his long-time partner Esme and has two children."

"How's Stuart?" he asked.

"Oh, he's fine, thank you. He's retired from the army now. He's set up his own little firm, advising on events security. It takes him all over the place."

"Couldn't make it today?"

"No, he was too busy to come."

Hector got the impression that Penelope wished to change the subject.

"I heard that you married Phoebe Barrington."

"We never married, but she is the mother of my children. We were together for 13 years but then she left me years ago. She's doing charity work in Africa."

"What children do you have?"

"A boy and a girl, Troy and Janis, both grown up. They carried on living with me after Phoebe left and they still live locally. Troy is my right hand man at the caravan site and Janis is a teacher and is married with three kids."

"Oh, I'm sorry it didn't work out with Phoebe. She seemed a nice girl at school."

"Yes, but you wouldn't believe how she changed. She was more interested in saving the planet than in raising a family."

"That's a shame for you. Still, at least you've had the

children."

"Yes, they were good kids. They're the constants in my life — uncomplaining and totally loyal. They were a pleasure to bring up and they're really fulfilled adults."

"That's good to hear. My daughters are great too," she said sotto voce, making sure that they were out of earshot.

"I envy you living at Stratford-upon-Avon," said Hector. "I loved those theatre trips we used to have there."

"Yes, they were great fun," said Penelope. "It is a lovely place to live — so cosmopolitan for England. By the way you'll never guess who I bumped into in Stratford a couple of weeks ago — Mr Plunkett."

"Oh, great. Mr Plunkett. I loved him as a teacher."

"He hasn't changed. Still full of chat and anecdotes and with strong opinions about the world. He's living in Stratford. It's ideal for him as he loves his Shakespeare. He was a teacher at Stratford King Edward VI Grammar School but now he's taken early retirement and he and his wife are enjoying the good life."

"I'm pleased for him," said Hector. "He was a great guy."

Just then a striking, well-built, blonde-haired woman walked past them as she made her way towards the bar. Penelope caught her by the arm.

"This is my sister, Susan. You might remember her from school. Susan, this is Hector Ratcliffe. He was in my class at Grammar School."

Susan gave him a thin smile, nodded and went on her way.

Hector was flummoxed. He was getting on so well with Penelope and yet again a member of her family had given him the cold shoulder. What was their problem with him? He thought of asking Penelope that question but he was keen that there should be no awkwardness between them.

He spent the next half hour chatting to his love until she told him that she had better circulate among other members of the family.

The wake was in full swing. As is normal at such events, even in the most tragic of circumstances like this one, the mourners had become more relaxed now. People who had not met each other for years were rekindling their friendships and the whole atmosphere was becoming almost jolly.

There were even some signs of forgiveness for Tricia, who had been roundly blamed for Derek's demise. She was a selfish and thoughtless person, but had a breezy, outgoing personality and was invariably pleasant to people she met. Women, as might be guessed, had less time for her than men, who quickly became captivated by her in spite of themselves.

She spent most of the wake sitting at a table in the corner of the room, surrounded by men of various ages, while their womenfolk looked on in a resigned sort of way. They understood her charisma, even if they did not approve of it.

When all the food had been consumed it was time for people to say their goodbyes. Hector was determined not to miss the opportunity to bid farewell to Penelope. As he saw her taking her leave of Tricia, he made a beeline and tapped her on the shoulder.

"Goodbye, Hector," she said. "It's been very nice seeing you again."

She offered her soft, pretty face to him to kiss – and he obliged.

"I hope it won't be as long before we meet again," he said.

And, oh, how he meant that. He wished that meeting could be tomorrow, and every day after that for the rest of his life, and through eternity. But as he left the pub the sad reality hit home that it had been 30 years since they had last met and it could many more years before their paths crossed again. More realistically, this might be the last time ever they would meet.

His chagrin became even deeper when he detected that Pamela Douglas gave him what he interpreted as a dirty look when they saw each other in the car park. Had his feelings for Penelope been too transparent, and did her mother see him as a threat to her daughter's marriage? This all seemed far-fetched, but there was clearly something amiss.

Although Hector was convinced there was no realistic prospect of any future relationship with Penelope, he was still intent on solving the riddle of why members of her family were so, at best stand-offish, and, at worst, hostile to him. He had asked her for a date once, more than 30 years ago, and politely accepted her refusal. He had neither seen her, spoken to her, or contacted her in any way since they left school. There was no particular social gulf between them. His family was led by a well-respected and popular former teacher and a mother originally from landowning and farming stock and now a successful businesswoman. He had become a respectable member of the community and, even as a youth, had done nothing so off-colour as to attract lifelong disapproval from another local family.

Hector had always prided himself as being a self-contained person, confident in making his own decisions and not one to complain to others about his lot. But now, perhaps for the first time in his life, he felt an overwhelming need to ask someone's opinion and advice on a personal matter.

Despite his close relationship with his loving parents, he had an Englishman's reticence in sharing his feelings with them. Equally, he would never dream of burdening his children with his concerns. Over the years Aunt Christine had been the person he had talked to most about himself, but that was because she was always determined to involve herself in everyone's else's affairs. He enjoyed his conversations with his aunt, even sparring with her from time to time, but he knew that she was constitutionally incapable of keeping a confidence.

His oldest close friend was Matthew, a decent, humane fellow but of a cynical nature and not greatly interested in affairs of the heart. That only left his other very good friend – Humphrey.

Humphrey Gibb's public persona was the super-confident, extravagantly dressed, ex-public schoolboy, who spent his time playing rugby, yachting and womanising. But not far beneath this image he deliberately projected was a loyal, kind and sensitive man; the sort of man you would feel comfortable sharing a wartime trench with.

Hector decided he needed a heart to heart with Humphrey. He phoned his friend on the pretext of telling him the news Penelope had given him about their old English teacher, Mr Plunkett.

Introducing Penelope into the conversation gave him the opportunity of mentioning the conundrum as to why her family seemed to have taken against him.

Humphrey had no immediate answers to give. He did, though, reveal something of the conversation he had had with Aunt Christine all those years ago when she had cajoled him into fixing a date between her nephew and Esme's friend Miriam.

"She told me that your mother was worried about you being alone since Phoebe left you. She also mentioned something about Penelope. She seemed to think you had an unhealthy craving for her. But that was it. She didn't elaborate at all."

"How would she know what thoughts I had about Penelope? She was the last person I would have discussed that with. In fact, I think you're the first person I've confided in."

(It had slipped his mind that he had also confided in Derek at some length.)

Humphrey regretted that he could offer no further information or insights. But he did promise to give the matter some thought and make a few discreet enquiries.

Chapter seven - Shocking revelations

Penelope's home was a large detached Georgian house in a quiet cul-de-sac on the outskirts of Stratford-upon-Avon. The front of the property was covered in wisteria and well-developed leylandiis made up its boundaries. It all spoke of its owners being a prosperous and successful family.

It was 8.30pm when Penelope reached home from Derek's funeral. Her daughter, Jane, who had driven her and Sarah to and from Sanderholme, dropped her off outside the front door.

On entering her spacious lounge she found husband Stuart laid out on a four-seater settee watching television. He was still a good looking man for his age, tall and muscular with a bronzed complexion and a good head of blond hair.

"Hello, babe," he said. "Have you had a good day, darling?"

Penelope was immediately aware that he had been drinking. His slurred speech and the empty bottle of whisky on the table in front of him were the giveaways. He had been at home all day, and not at all "busy" as she had told Hector earlier. In fact he avoided his in-laws whenever he could as he did not appreciate their studied shows of disapproval towards him.

"Yes, the funeral went as well as it could have done in the circumstances."

"He was a miserable bastard anyway," said Stuart.

"Who?"

"Derek. Billy No Mates. He was an excuse for a man.

Pathetic."

"That's not a very nice thing to say. He never did us any harm. He was always friendly enough to me when he came to mum and dad's."

"He was pathetic. What sort of man would live in a shed when his wife had her boyfriends in his house? Pathetic bugger."

"Have a little compassion, Stuart."

"Bugger compassion. I'm going to bed. Are you coming?"

"Not yet. I just want to wind down a little, if you don't mind."

"Suit yourself, dear. Suit yourself."

When Stuart was out of the way Penelope opened the door which separated the lounge from the kitchen. Immediately a chocolate labrador came bounding in, showing tremendous enthusiasm and affection.

Stuart would not allow the animal in the lounge but Penelope took every available opportunity to spoil the dog when she was on her own in the room.

Benson, the dog, had originally been purchased by Stuart as a gundog when a group of his friends took up shooting as a hobby. A chocolate lab was just the designer dog he needed. But Benson soon proved to be totally uninterested in retrieving game and so, just as quickly, Stuart lost interest in him. So looking after the creature and giving it walks and cuddles soon fell exclusively to Penelope.

When she settled down in front of the television, Benson swiftly leapt up on to the settee beside her and sat contentedly nuzzling her.

Penelope wasn't watching the programme. She just stared at the screen lost in her thoughts. They were not pleasant thoughts.

She was taking stock of her life. Looked at from a distance she would appear to have everything a woman could wish for. She had a good well paid job, as a partner in a firm of solicitors where she concentrated on non-litigious work. She had a beautiful house in a lovely area, two beautiful and intelligent daughters and a handsome husband who had had a good army career.

For a number of years, though, the character of her husband had caused her a great deal of unhappiness. He was a serial adulterer, a heavy drinker, quick tempered, lacking in sensitivity, sarcastic and controlling. And the older he got the worse he became. Penelope often felt she was treading on eggshells when she was around him, particularly when he had been drinking.

He had been a loving parent to his daughters when they were young, but as they became more aware and worldly they came to resent the callous way he behaved towards their mother. As their father's behaviour deteriorated they tended to avoid visiting their parents' home when he was around. They did, however, have plenty of opportunities for seeing their mother as Stuart's job meant he was away for most of the year. When back at home he spent much of his time at the pub, on the golf course or at the 19th hole. And who knew where else?

Penelope had never been a demanding wife; Stuart was the one who always wanted to cut a dash – to have the best house, the fastest car and the exotic foreign holidays. Penelope was happiest having family days out, looking after the garden and reading a good book.

They had been together for 25 years and, although she realised from very early on that she had made a mistake, she was not the type to give up on a marriage. Her traditional upbringing militated against any thoughts of separation or divorce. She was a good Anglican and for her the wedding vows "for better, for worse... till death us do part" were non-negotiable.

A woman of lesser character would have buckled under the strain of such an unsatisfactory marriage. As time went on, through a rehearsed mental toughness, she made herself immune to Stuart's unfaithfulness. She reluctantly accepted that he was a physically strong man with a zest for life in all its aspects.

She found it more difficult to accept his drinking. She realised there was a culture of heavy drinking within the army. But she hated the way this spread into his home life, making him irritable, unkind to his family, frequently incoherent and, very occasionally, physically violent towards her.

As she sat on the settee that night following the funeral she felt particularly low. A horrific thought hit her. She had spent the day at the funeral of a family member who had shot himself. Now she was sitting in her lovely comfortable home in a beautiful part of the country. The awful truth was that she had enjoyed the funeral and she hated being back at home.

She had relished the company of her two daughters on the journey to and from Sanderholme. She had loved meeting up with the rest of her family, even though the event was such a desperately sad one. And her spirits had been lifted by meeting up with a much-liked old school friend – Hector Ratcliffe.

She had always known that he fancied her. She still had no idea how much he had loved her. How much he still loved her. How she was the centre of his universe. She had noticed, though, that he had become a much more rounded personality than the long-haired, slightly geeky boy she knew at school. At last he had made some sort of impression.

****

It's early morning on April 3rd and Hector is in his kitchen opening his birthday cards when the doorbell rings.

It's his father, Charles.

"Hello, son. Happy birthday. Just dropping off your presents and card before I get off to work."

"Come in, dad. Have you got time for a quick cup of tea – as it's my birthday? There's a cup in the pot."

"Oh, go on then. I've got a few minutes."

Hector shows him inside the kitchen and pours out his tea.

"Here's mum's present, beautifully wrapped, as you would expect," said Charles. "And here's mine – not wrapped at all, as you'd expect. It's a new edition of Robert Graves' book, The Greek Myths. You haven't got it, have you?"

"No, dad. That'll be great. I've heard about this book but I've never got round to buying it. Thanks a lot."

Hector opens more of his presents and cards as he

chats away to his beloved father. The two men have always had a meeting of minds. In particular they enjoy talking about literature. Since Charles has been a bookshop owner, he spends most of his time between customers reading books – ancient and modern, fact and fiction, hardbacks and paperbacks, new and second hand. Each time he sees Hector he has a book to tell him about, or to give him. And Hector never tires of this.

They discuss the Classics, philosophy, politics and religion – all those subjects which are supposed to be banned from the four-ale bar. For Hector, their conversations take him to a parallel universe, so divergent from his everyday work of selling and siting caravans, delivering Calor Gas, and mowing acres of grass.

His father is the only person he meets regularly with whom he can converse at this level of knowledge and intellect. Adding to Charles' considerable charm is the fact that he is no intellectual snob. He has his own esoteric interests and strong opinions on a wide range of topics, but he does not look down on anyone who does not share his passions and views. He talks to everyone in a polite and kindly way and treats all as his equal. He also has a great sense of fun and a love of children of all ages, who, in their turn, are happy in his company.

These characteristics have gained him a good deal of popularity in the community. His pupils at Sanderholme Grammar School liked and respected him and, in a very difficult marketplace, he succeeds in attracting a loyal clientele for his shop and an excellent footfall. Hector has sometimes been surprised to overhear his mother and

Aunt Christine mildly complaining that Charles does not bring much money to "the family pot".

During this birthday visit Charles mentions that an old colleague of his, Mr Martin, the former Head of Geography, has popped into the shop.

"Ah, Trumper Martin!" declares Hector.

"How did he ever get that name?" laughs Charles.

"I couldn't possibly tell you," chuckled Hector. "Is he okay?"

"He looks fighting fit but he's had a very bad time recently. His wife, Josie, committed suicide last summer. She had mental health problems for years. I remember that from school days. Such a shame. Nice chap."

The sad story of Mrs Martin's suicide brings Derek's death into Hector's mind and this in turn leads him to recall some of his conversation with Penelope at the funeral.

"That reminds me, dad," he says. "When I was at Derek Stanmore's funeral last year I had some news of Mr Plunkett."

"Mr Plunkett. There was a force of nature if there ever was one. Lovely man. I know he used to inspire you, didn't he?"

"Yes, he did. I think he inspired a lot of people. Well, I was told he lives at Stratford-upon-Avon now. He retired, but he was teaching at the Boys' Grammar School there, Shakespeare's old school."

"Actually, I did know that," said Charles. "I imagine he must have loved teaching there. I can't think of a better niche for him than William Shakespeare's old school, his alma mater."

"I didn't realise he was a pupil there."

"Oh, yes. I think that was why he was so immersed in the Bard."

"So he's gone back home then."

"Yes, indeed. I'm so pleased to hear about him. Who told you all this?"

"It was Penelope Douglas – Penelope Broadlake now. You remember her. She lives at Stratford too. You probably remember her sister, Susan, better. She was a few years older and you would have taught her."

"Yes, I did," replied Charles. "Fancy that."

"Penelope was in my class, you know."

"Oh, yes. Anyway, son, I must be going. I have a shop to open. I hope we'll see you this evening. Come and have a birthday drink with us, unless you have anything else planned."

"Thanks, I will. Bye dad."

Charles shook his son's hand and left.

Hector was left perplexed. His father was well known to be a loquacious person whose timekeeping sometimes suffered as a result. But he felt this time he had left quite abruptly. And his hasty exit had followed directly after the mention of Penelope. Hector tried to tell himself he was being paranoid, although what had just occurred appeared to confirm a pattern of behaviour in which people were trying to put a distance between him and Penelope.

Why should his dad be involved in what he was beginning to identify as a conspiracy? In Hector's opinion, Charles was the least judgemental, most tolerant person in the world, with never a bad word to say about anyone. He recalled the time when he revealed to the family that Phoebe was pregnant and that they had no intention of marrying. His mother was profoundly disappointed and his Aunt Christine had been appalled. His father had said absolutely nothing, had always been kind to Phoebe and had become every inch the doting grandparent to Troy and Janis.

Why had he been so non-committal when Penelope's name had been mentioned? Hector even thought of asking his parents when he met them that evening what the problem was. However, he thought better of it. He didn't wish his family to suspect that he might still have some designs on Penelope, a married woman.

****

Fast forward 10 years…

Hector, Margaret, Aunt Christine, Troy and Janis are sitting in a waiting room at Whapmore General Hospital, 30 miles down the coast from Sanderholme. They are the only people in the room and there is total silence.

The door opens and a doctor in a white gown enters.

"I'm afraid I have some bad news for you. Mr Ratcliffe has regrettably passed away on the operating table. I am so sorry."

Hector puts his arm around his mother, who is shaking and quietly sobbing. Tears are running down his face. Aunt Christine, Troy and Janis stand up together and take it turns to hug each other.

Charles had been undergoing surgery following a heart rupture.

Hector had lost his hero, a person whom he knew was

much cleverer than him, much wiser, much better looking and more loved. He was as close to his father as to anyone and on the same wavelength in so many ways.

He looked back on his childhood with great fondness. There had been interesting annual family holidays, especially to Greece. One year he and his father had travelled together without Margaret to enjoy an extended trip when Charles had shown Hector many of the places he had read about in his Greek mythology books: Mount Olympus, The Temples of Apollo and Poseidon, Delos Island, Ithaca and the Acheron River.

Throughout Hector's childhood there had been plenty of fun and games too: trips to funfairs and zoos, crazy golf and putting; donkey rides and candy floss.

Charles had died at the age of 81, after an illness which had been devastatingly swift. Everyone had agreed that he looked nothing like his age. He had a shock of distinguished white hair to complement his still well-chiselled face and willowy, lithe figure. Intellectually he was as sharp as he had ever been, if inclined to be a little absent-minded.

He had closed the bookshop only three years earlier as custom had declined and the rent and rates on the premises had become unaffordable. But until the sudden illness which killed him he had remained active and a familiar figure in town as he did his brisk daily walk.

Many tears were shed at his passing.

As for the rest of the family, Margaret had suffered from an unsuccessful hip replacement and used a mobility scooter. Aunt Christine was as well-dressed as ever, her expertly and heavily applied make-up successfully hiding her wrinkles. Her figure had become decidedly "matronly".

The two old women no longer worked at the caravan site, although they still took a keen interest in the business.

Troy and Janis, now in their late thirties and both married with children, were well-balanced individuals and pictures of sensible healthy living.

Troy was his father's right hand man at the caravan site. He was well respected in the community, being a Lions Club member and a keen golfer. Janis was now deputy head at her primary school and, following in something of a family tradition, keen on am-dram.

Hector, who had always loved his family, had recently plunged himself headlong into trying to be a perfect father and grandfather. He wished to emulate his role model, Charles.

The Douglas family had also suffered a loss in recent times, Richard Douglas having died of bowel cancer.

****

The day of Charles Ratcliffe's funeral arrived and Sanderholme Crematorium was full of mourners. As well as family members there were many of his former customers, a handful of retired school colleagues, members of the Sanderholme History Society and many other friends.

The Rector of Sanderholme conducted the service, Hector and Troy gave moving eulogies and several of Charles' favourite pieces of classical music were played.

At the close of the service the closest family members

lined up under a colonnade so that they could look at the floral tributes and thank the mourners as they filed out of the chapel.

Hector noticed a blonde middle-aged woman, who looked rather distressed, excusing herself as she weaved past the other mourners and made for the exit to the car park. She had not stopped to acknowledge the family members, which struck Hector as a little odd. As she disappeared from view he noticed Aunt Christine nudging his mother in a knowing kind of way.

Later, at the wake held at a local hotel, Hector asked Christine if she knew who the woman was, but his aunt replied: "No, I haven't a clue, dear. Your mother and I were wondering that too."

And she moved away quickly to talk to another relative.

Among the mourners were Hector's best friends Matthew Copson and Humphrey Gibb with their wives, Sally and Esme. Hector made sure he showed his gratitude for their support by spending a good deal of time speaking to them.

Ten years had passed since Humphrey had promised to make "a few discreet enquiries" to see why there should be a strained relationship between Hector and Penelope's family. He had given periodic updates but this had only been to confirm that he had made no progress.

During their chat at the wake, Humphrey drew Hector to one side and whispered: "I've found something out about the Douglas business. Now is not the time and place to discuss it. Tonight at yours perhaps?"

"Yes, of course. Eight o'clock?" replied Hector.

"See you then, mate," said Humphrey.

****

Humphrey was sitting in Hector's lounge that evening with a gin and tonic in front of him. Hector had poured himself a whisky.

His friend usually projected a devil-may-care persona but on this particular evening he looked serious, even worried.

"So what have you got to tell me?" asked Hector.

"This is probably not the day I should be telling you this."

Hector gave him a sideways look.

"Go on."

"I had to go into Warwickshire for business last week which gave me an idea. Old Mr Plunkett lives at Stratford-upon-Avon, as you know, so I thought I would see if I could look him up and possibly meet him.

"He was always my favourite teacher, as you'll remember, and I think he quite liked me.

"I had a look in the phone book and found a G. Plunkett so I thought I would give it a go. I rang the number and Plunkett himself answered. We agreed to meet up at the Mucky Duck for a drink."

"Oh, the Mucky Duck," Hector interrupted. "I loved it there when we went on the school trips. I think it was the first pub I ever went in."

"It hasn't altered very much. It's still packed with people and we spotted a couple of well-known actors in there. Anyway, we met up one lunchtime and had a few drinks. He had walked there and I was staying the night at the Arden Hotel – for old time's sake – so there were no worries about drinking and driving.

"Mr Plunkett was on great form. He's bright as a button for his age and full of good stories like he always was. He had been through a bad time a couple of years ago when he lost his wife. Apparently she died suddenly of a heart attack, quite out of the blue. He's living on his own now and he's got no family to speak of, but he's still pretty active and seems to be coping well. I think he was pleased to have some company, though.

"Anyway, to cut a long story short, by the end of the afternoon we were both, shall we say, a little tiddly. And very talkative."

Humphrey paused and took a drink. For the first time that Hector could remember his friend looked extremely apprehensive.

"I really don't know if I should go on with this," he said.

"Why not?"

"It's the day of your dad's funeral. It doesn't seem quite right."

"Come on. We've all done the right thing by him today."

"Okay. If you say so. I told Mr Plunkett that your dad had passed away and he said how sorry he was to hear of it and what a nice man and good teacher he had been.

"Then he said something really odd."

Humphrey paused and took another swig of his drink.

"He said it was such a pity that your dad had to leave the school the way he did."

"Had to leave?"

"Yes. He stopped talking after he had said that, but I prompted him to tell me more."

"He said, 'you do know why he left, don't you?' and I said I didn't know.

"Then he said, 'perhaps we should leave it at that' but I joshed him a bit to persuade him to carry on.

"He said: 'I shouldn't tell you this but the fact is he got one of his pupils in the family way. They tried to hush it all up, but inevitably some people got to know about it.'"

Humphrey related that Mr Plunkett had gone on to say that Hector's father had agreed to take early retirement. The girl had left school already when it all came to light so there was no great drama made about it all.

Mr Plunkett said Mr Ratcliffe had been a fool but he had felt sorry for him.

He had added: "Perhaps it could have happened to any of us. There were some very attractive girls, especially in the sixth form."

Hector was hanging on to Humphrey's every word in a state of stupefaction.

His friend continued: "I asked him who the girl was. And he told me it was Susan Douglas."

"Oh my god, Susan Douglas," said a shocked Hector.

Humphrey could see how upset he had made his friend.

"I'm so sorry, old boy. I shouldn't have told you about this today. Today of all days."

Hector smiled at him ruefully: "Don't worry about that Humphrey. I'm grateful to you for telling me. I'm just finding it difficult to take in. It's so…it's so not my dad. He was a good guy."

"But he was a human being," interjected Humphrey. "We're all fallible. Even the best people like your dad. Plunkett told me that Susan Douglas was a real looker and quite forward. Sex on legs, he called her."

"It explains so much," said Hector. "Penelope's family must hate my dad for what he did. Who else knows about this? Mum must know. Why didn't anyone tell me? It's been 40-odd years and I've had no idea."

"It's a lot to take in," said Humphrey. "But listen. I know how you worshipped your dad. He was a great guy. Everyone thought so. He made a mistake. He needs your forgiveness."

"He has my forgiveness. I could forgive him anything because he was such a good dad to me. I just wonder why it had to be covered up so much and for so long. I have so many questions I need to ask. Do you know any more? Did Mr Plunkett tell you anything else?"

"No, I asked him. He knew your dad had left the school and that Susan had a baby. He said he hadn't heard anything more after that."

Hector said he needed to see his mother to get more information. Humphrey prevailed upon him not to pursue it that night, as his mother would have had a traumatic enough day already. So Hector agreed to speak to her the following day.

Humphrey took his leave, but not without giving Hector an assurance that he would be on the end of a phone at any time he wished to talk or needed any assistance.

Hector hugged him and said, "thank you".

****

He was full of anxiety when he went to see his mother at her home the following morning. He was determined to obtain as much information as he could, while causing her the least possible distress.

Margaret was pleased to see him and wanted to talk about everything which had happened the previous day. She had been overwhelmed by the number of people who had been at the funeral and the warm sentiments about Charles which had been expressed.

Hector listened patiently to all that she said and made supportive comments at the relevant times.

Eventually his turn came to take the initiative in the conversation.

"There's something I need to talk to you about," he said.

"Yes, love, what is it?"

"I have been told that dad left the Grammar School because he fathered a child with one of the pupils – Susan Douglas."

Margaret responded to this surprise statement with her typical stoicism. She pondered a moment and replied: "So you found out at last. It must have been quite a shock to you. May I ask who told you?"

Hector replied carefully since he wished no blame to attach itself either to Humphrey or to Mr Plunkett.

"It was sort of accidentally. Humphrey happened to meet an ex-teacher at the school and he told him. There were no ill intentions. The teacher must have assumed that people already knew.

"I would like to know why this was kept a secret from

me for all these years."

"You have to understand, darling, that times have changed. Even now it would be a great scandal if a teacher got a student pregnant. Just think what it was like then. And you have to remember that the Douglas family are very religious.

"Your dad felt so ashamed, but that was nothing to the reaction from Mr Douglas. He was absolutely livid and made all sorts of threats about what would happen to your father.

"But his main demand was that the whole affair should be kept secret. His daughter was to have the baby while she was away at university and was never to reveal to anyone, including the child, who the father was. Your dad was never to try to meet his daughter but agreed to make regular payments to Susan for the upkeep of the child until she became self-sufficient.

"There was a meeting between your dad, Mr and Mrs Douglas and Mr Grout, your head teacher. It was agreed it would be best for everyone if your dad left the school quietly, saying he was taking early retirement. That's it."

"Did you never think that I ought to know about all this?" asked Hector.

"That was the agreement – that no one should be told. And that's how it has stayed all these years. Until this latest tittle-tattle. Who has spilt the beans?"

"I'm not going to tell you that. Am I not to be allowed to have my own secret?"

"That's fair enough, I suppose," said Margaret, shrugging her shoulders.

"Couldn't you at least have let me into the secret?"

"We would have liked to. But we promised the Douglases that we wouldn't tell anyone who didn't already know. And your poor dad was so ashamed. He didn't want you to feel ashamed of him too."

"Who did know, mum? Tell me exactly."

"Well obviously me and your dad, and Aunt Christine; Mr and Mrs Douglas; Mr Grout, probably his Deputy, Miss Knowles, and the Chairman of Governors, Cllr Thomas. That's all, I think. I thought so, anyway. You obviously know of someone else now."

"I think there must have been some gossip around the school."

"I see. I wasn't aware of that."

"It explains why the Douglases have been offish with me all these years. I suppose Penelope must have known."

"The Douglases always said they would never tell her and they made Susan promise that too. So, as far as I know, she wasn't told."

"That's almost incredible. I suppose I will never find out if she knew. I love my dad, but he could have ruined my life."

"Ruined your life? How?" asked Margaret.

"Oh, it doesn't matter," he replied in an offhand tone. Margaret correctly guessed at the reason for this.

"Another thing I have to ask," continued Hector. "How did you take all of this?"

"I was devastated at the time, as you can imagine. But I forgave your dad, because in everything but this, he was such a wonderful husband and a wonderful man. I am sure he was led astray by, well, just lust for a tarty young girl. It's happened before and it will happen again.

"Your dad managed to present a cheerful front all these years, but I'm sure that underneath that he was a broken man spiritually."

Margaret momentarily lost her accustomed composure now and shed a tear. Hector took her into his arms and kissed the side of her head.

"Do you forgive me?" she asked.

"Of course I do," said Hector.

****

This conversation with his mother threw Hector into a period of introspection, in which he struggled to reset his views of the father he had respected and trusted so deeply. After much soul-searching he came to the conclusion that he must consider Charles' character in the round. Everyone said what a lovely man he had been and to Hector he had been as close to perfection as a father could be. But, as Humphrey had said, all human beings are flawed and how could Charles be any exception to this universal truth?

Hector's considered view was that his father was a good, decent man who had made a single big mistake, which, undoubtedly, he profoundly regretted. His mother, to her eternal credit, had clearly reached the same conclusion.

Further questions came into Hector's head, mainly concerning the period when Charles' misdemeanour had first been discovered. How had his family managed so successfully to keep the truth from him? Surely someone in the school community would have blabbed? After all, there had been some notorious gossips at Sanderholme Grammar, among both pupils and staff.

When he next saw his mother he put that point to her. She explained that Susan's pregnancy had come to light during the school summer holidays and that had helped to keep things under wraps.

Hector recalled that he had been surprised that his father's "retirement" from teaching after so many years' service had never been announced in school assembly. At the end of a school year there had invariably been a roll call of those members of staff who would not be returning in the autumn. A teacher who had served for as long as his father would usually receive a farewell gift from the head or chairman of governors in front of the whole school.

Hector had mentioned this at the time but had been told that this must have been an oversight by the headmaster, Mr Grout, and that Charles was too modest a man to make any issue of it.

"And then, of course, your father took you away on an extended holiday to Greece to keep you out of the way of any gossip which might circulate," said Margaret.

The penny dropped for Hector. So that was the reason for the Greek trip – the only time that Hector and his father had been on holiday without Margaret.

It had been explained at the time that his mother was too busy running the caravan site at that time of year to go on holiday. Hector had wondered why they were going away in August when the family's holidays were usually taken abroad during the late autumn or winter when the site was shut down. But he was so excited to be going on an adventure with his father that he never thought to make an issue about the unusual arrangements.

"Why did you think I was such a fragile flower that I couldn't have handled being told the truth?" he asked his mother.

"Your father was so ambitious for you, you know. He didn't want anything to put you off your studies and your exams. And it was the shame of it all too. He couldn't bear the thought of you knowing how unwisely he had behaved. He loved you a lot. You should know that."

Hector, who was sitting in the caravan site office, slumped forward on to his desk, his head buried in his hands.

"If only you knew the repercussions that this had for my life," he railed.

Margaret guessed what he was referring to, but was her usual diplomatic self and waited to see if he would say anything on the subject of Penelope.

He didn't say another word. He had revealed too much of himself already.

Chapter eight – Hector dives in

A week or so after Hector received his surprise news he is taking a walk along Sanderholme's wide sandy beach. He is beachcombing, so his eyes are focused on the strandline where all kinds of treasures might be found: unusual seashells, eggcases, bodies of dead fish, a wide variety of types of seaweed and a selection of hopping insects are among the interesting items to be examined.

Hector's attention to this exploration is disturbed by a loudly barking dog. When he looks up he sees a labrador chasing a ball down to the water's edge, where the sea on this particular day is becalmed and friendly.

Its owner, who is calling to it to bring the ball back to her, is a middle-aged woman wearing a headscarf, a smart padded jacket, a tartan skirt and black boots. She smiles at Hector as she passes by, and then quickly does a double-take as she recognises him.

"Hector! So nice to see you," says Penelope.

"Hello, Penelope."

She presents her cheek to him and he kisses it.

"What brings you to Sanderholme?"

"I'm staying with my mother at Hayfleet. I just fancied a walk along the beach to blow the cobwebs away."

"Hey, it's so good to see you," says Hector, brimming over with pleasure. "Mind if I walk along with you?"

"Please do," says Penelope, flashing one of her most winsome smiles.

"I was so sorry to hear that your father had died," she continues.

"Thank you very much. We will miss him."

"I'm sure you will."

There is an uncomfortable silence, which is broken when the chocolate lab jumps in front of them, wagging his tail and demanding attention.

They stroll along the beach for half a mile, keeping Benson happy by continually throwing the ball for him. Each time he catches it he dashes away and puts it into the sea. Penelope suggests he does that to wash the sand off and make it more acceptable for carrying around in his mouth. The tide is going out but Benson seems quite content to swim and retrieve the ball from the water. Then he lets it go a little too far out and his courage fails him. He swims back to the shore and barks for help.

Hector thinks it is time for him to be the hero. He rolls up his trouser legs and paddles out to rescue the ball, returning with a decidedly soggy pair of trousers.

Penelope laughs at him.

"You really needn't have done that," she giggles. "You're soaking wet. But thank you anyway. Benson is very grateful."

Hector preens himself a little on his successful mission on behalf of his love. It hardly ranks with Perseus saving Andromeda from the sea monster Cetus, he reflects later. But it must have counted for something.

They are approaching a beachside café with tables and chairs set out along the sea wall. Hector seizes the opportunity.

"Do you fancy a coffee or something?" he asks.

"Why not," she says. "That would be nice."

They chat about old times and a number of pleasant inconsequential matters but both feel there is some unfinished business between them – the matter of Hector's father. Neither feels comfortable about broaching the subject.

Hector eventually dives in.

"I hope you don't mind if I ask you a serious question."

"No, of course not."

"Do you know anything about a connection between my father and your family?"

Penelope knows straightaway where this conversation is heading.

"Yes," she says. "He was the father of my niece Jodie."

"Would you believe that I only found that out last week – the day of his funeral? It came as quite a shock, I can tell you. How long have you known about it?"

"Not until we heard that your father had died."

"Amazing. Can I ask who knew before then?"

"My mother and father and Susan obviously."

"And Jodie?"

"No, she was told at the same time as I was."

"Why was it kept from her all these years?"

"I believe there was some sort of agreement between the parents when it happened. I have to say I think it was all a bit unnecessary. Well-intentioned, but quite cruel really, especially on Jodie."

Hector says: "If only times had been different, I am sure my dad could have been a good dad to your niece. He was a kind, compassionate man."

Penelope nods in agreement: "That's how I remember

him from school and it's what my sister has told me. She was very upset when she heard he had passed away. I have to say that my own father – I loved him dearly – could be a stubborn man sometimes. Apparently he, especially, was adamant that Jodie shouldn't be told anything. But I also believe he was very strongly influenced by his own father. Grandad had very strong opinions on things and he could be even more stubborn and unyielding than my father."

A picture came into Hector's mind of a cruel old farmer beating a sheepdog to death. This was Richard Douglas' father.

"Did you realise that Jodie went to your father's funeral?" says Penelope.

Hector shows surprise at this but then he thinks of the distressed woman who had made a hurried exit.

"No, I had no idea. What does she look like?"

"Late thirties, medium build, blonde hair – like a younger, shorter version of her mother. I understand that she didn't stay long. She may not have made herself known."

"I did see a lady there. She was wiping away tears and she left quite quickly. I wondered who she could be. But at that time I had no idea about my dad's history."

"Jodie's a good, kind person, but a little mixed up and quite serious. I think she should have been told who her father was from the beginning. She might have had a happier life."

"She's not been too happy then?"

"She had a traumatic divorce – not really her fault – and suffered from depression for a while. But she's better now, I think. She has a son, Jason, from her marriage. He's 16 now. And she has a new partner – a really nice man. He's got a great sense of humour and I think he's really good for her."

"So my dad had another grandchild. Did he ever know that?"

"No, I'm afraid not."

"This whole business is a nightmare."

"I agree with you. It never should have gone on all these years."

"I have to ask you something – something that's been bothering me for years," says Hector.

"Go on."

"Do you remember that I once asked you to go to the pictures with me? When we were at school."

"Yes, I do remember."

"Did your mother and father put you off coming with me?"

"No, not at the time. But I do remember my mother making some remarks afterwards about you not being my type of person."

"So it wasn't your mother who put you off from coming with me?"

"No, I think I wasn't really interested in going out with anyone at that time. I was very much into my school work. A bit of a swot, I suppose."

Hector is not entirely convinced by this answer and guesses she is just trying to be kind to him. After all, she did go out with Thomas Strawson around then. He believes the truth of the matter is that at that time of his life he was just not attractive to women. He was too intense and shy. A nerd. Penelope, on the other hand, could have had the pick of most of the good-looking boys in the area.

As he thinks about this, he sips at his coffee, which has gone cold, and ponders where the conversation will go next. He has "dipped his toe" into an area which he realises could be embarrassing for Penelope. His choice now is to pull away from the water altogether or wade in up to his neck. He chooses the latter, arguing that this might be his last chance.

"I hope you don't mind me telling you this, but I was head over heels in love with you. You can't imagine how much I fancied you."

Penelope blushes and emits a nervous laugh. She says nothing.

Hector is stumped as to where to go from here. His instinct is to say "I still love you" but he fears that would drive her away for good. He respects her marital status, even though he considers she is married to an insufferable oaf.

Penelope comes to his rescue by making a deadly serious proposition, a game changer in their relationship.

"As we've been talking, I've been thinking," she says. "Now everything's out in the open I think it's time we all broke the ice. I will talk to my mother and see if she would consider inviting you over to her house for a meal, where we could all get together and you could meet Susan and Jodie. Jodie is, after all, your half-sister."

Hector cannot hide the elation he feels on hearing this suggestion.

"What a great idea. Do you think it will be all right

with everyone?"

"I think it will. We're not ogres, you know, even if it appears that we have behaved as if we were. I will have to ask my mother, of course. But I am pretty sure she will agree. If we were to do it, then it would have to be in the next few days. Susan and Jodie and Jodie's partner, Phil, are coming over to Hayfleet for a couple of days this weekend, so that's what would make it an ideal opportunity."

"It would be wonderful," says Hector.

When they have finished their coffees they walk along the beach back to the sea front car park where they had left their cars. They swap telephone numbers and Penelope promises to get in touch as soon as she has spoken to her mother.

"I have really enjoyed this afternoon," says Hector as they say their goodbyes.

"So have I," says Penelope, giving him a peck on the cheek.

As Hector drives home the thought strikes him that he has spoken to Penelope more that afternoon than ever before in his life. She has been easy to talk to, kind and thoroughly decent. He is in love with her more strongly than ever.

****

The invitation to have Sunday lunch at the Douglas house came the very next day and Hector anticipated the event with enormous pleasure, laced with just a hint of nervousness.

He told his mother what was planned and she gave

her blessing, saying it was time for old ills to be healed. She did have some second thoughts after discussing the matter with Aunt Christine.

Margaret was an honest, down to earth person but could sometimes be a little naïve. Christine, on the other hand, had a much more suspicious trait, born of being badly used in a number of relationships during the early years of her womanhood.

"Are you sure that there is no hidden agenda in all this?" she asked her sister.

"Hidden agenda. What on earth do you mean?"

"Hector always set his cap at Penelope, you know. Are you sure he's not trying to get his feet under the table – with some other end in mind than just being the good half-brother?"

"Surely not," said Margaret. "He hasn't had anything to do with her since they were at school. Even then nothing ever came of it. It's 40 years ago at least."

"Doesn't make any difference in my book. You mark my word. No good can come of this."

"Oh, don't make such a drama out of everything, Christine. The woman's married for god's sake."

"So was your Charles."

"That's below the belt," Margaret replied angrily. "Can't you ever just trust someone?"

"No, I have always found that trust is seldom repaid in kind. But you know I love Hector and I only ever have his best interests at heart."

"I know you do, but sometimes… sometimes I just wish you wouldn't meddle."

"I was born to meddle, sis. Meddling is my middle

name," laughed Christine.

****

On Sunday morning Hector put on his best sports jacket and trousers, a matching shirt and tie and his shiniest pair of black shoes and set off for his Hayfleet rendezvous.

The Douglas family home was a large five-bedroomed house built in the 1930s. Situated on a busy lane and surrounded by farm buildings and open fields it had replaced a basic old farmhouse which had been home to several previous generations. It had a neat front garden, with a manicured lawn and colourful flower borders carefully tended by Mrs Douglas, who was fit and sprightly even though she was in her eighties.

Penelope answered the door and showed Hector into a large lounge, furnished with an impressive old dark red leather suite. Benson, the chocolate labrador, came charging up to him to give him a full tail-wagging and hand-licking welcome. Then Penelope's mother, who had been sitting in one of the armchairs, got up to greet him. The rather stern lady he remembered from former times had disappeared and been replaced by a smiling and homely white-haired matriarch, who presented her hand and smiled broadly at him.

Next came the introduction to Susan, who looked in rude health, with a friendly open face and lovely complexion, but a good deal more buxom than she had been at school. She gave Hector a firm handshake.

Susan spoke to Hector in a confident manner, seemingly unabashed by meeting him for the first time since the secret of her affair with his father had been revealed to him. She said she was pleased that at last he was to meet Jodie, but sorry that he could not also meet her son, Timothy, who was away at a farmers' conference.

"Where is Jodie?" she asked.

At that moment the woman Hector had seen at Derek's funeral entered the room via a patio door which led into the back garden. She was followed by her partner, a gaunt bald-headed man with a deeply wrinkled face but a twinkle in his eye.

Susan said: "Here she is – your half-sister."

Jodie looked reticent but stepped forward and also shook hands.

"I'm so delighted to meet you, after all this time," said Hector, trying to put her at her ease.

He detected a tear in her eye and had to do the manly thing and suppress one of his own.

"It's a pleasure to meet you," she replied. "Please meet Phil too."

Her partner had been hanging back but joined the group and gave Hector a warm pat on the shoulder.

"Pleased to meet you, Hector. You don't know how much Jodie has been looking forward to this."

Jodie gave a shy smile and took hold of Phil's hand.

Mrs Douglas and Susan excused themselves, saying they would go to the kitchen to finish preparing the lunch.

Hector and Jodie felt a little uncomfortable in each other's company. Neither was sure whether they should just indulge in small talk as they waited for the meal or they should have a serious conversation concerning their "lost years".

Fortunately, the dilemma was sidestepped for the time being by Phil, a gregarious person, who quizzed Hector about the attractions of the Sanderholme area, including the local nature reserve, in which Hector had a particular interest. Phil, a member of CAMRA, was also keen to know if there were any good real ale pubs which required to be visited.

Penelope chatted to Jodie, guessing that she might need some womanly reassurance in these unusual circumstances.

These lightweight conversations kept our party occupied until the meal was served – a traditional country lunch of roast hung pheasant, with a rich gravy and redcurrant jelly, boiled potatoes, purple sprouting broccoli, wild mushrooms, parsnips, carrots and peas, accompanied by a bottle of Côtes du Rhône, and followed by Queen's pudding and a well-stocked cheeseboard.

The conversation flowed agreeably. Mrs Douglas was the perfect attentive host, Penelope was her usual sweet and charming self, Susan was loud and giggly, Jodie, quiet and serious but seemingly content, Phil very talkative and Hector politely engaging with all of them, but with eyes constantly on his love.

At the end of the meal they left the dining room and returned to the lounge where coffee was served.

Hector sat next to Jodie on a two-seater settee and he felt it was time to have a serious conversation with his half-sister.

"You came to my dad's funeral," he said.

"Yes, it was something I felt I needed to do. It was rather traumatic for me actually, but I'm pleased I came."

"It's a pity I couldn't have introduced you to my mother and the rest of the family. My two kids would have liked to have met you, I'm sure."

"I thought it would be awkward for everyone. Not the right time and place. Perhaps I will meet them some time in the future."

"Sooner rather than later," said Hector.

"You never met my father – your father, I should say – did you?"

"No, of course I didn't. Wasn't allowed," she replied with some bitterness.

Hector could see tears in her eyes again. He held her hand and said: "I understand how difficult all this must be for you."

"Yes. And for you. Do you know I haven't any idea what my father looked like? I got some clues at the funeral that he must have been a popular, well-loved man."

"He was. He was my hero."

Hector put his hand into his jacket's inside pocket and produced a wallet. He took out a photograph of Charles, taken on his father's wedding day, and passed it to Jodie.

"Oh my god. Wow! What a handsome man," she said.

He fumbled in the wallet and handed over a second photo of his father, explaining it had been taken just a couple of months before his death.

"Oh, my. He was still handsome – right to the end of his life. And he looks so nice and gentle."

"He was."

Jodie burst into tears and sobbed out loud. Susan and Penelope rushed across the room to console her.

"I'm sorry," Jodie said to her mother when she had restored her composure a little. "He looks so lovely."

Susan put her arm around her daughter's shoulder and said: "He was a nice man. I'm so sorry things were as they were. I hope you'll be able to forgive me one day."

Jodie shot a disapproving look towards her, which Hector noticed. It was obvious to him that there was some understandable bad feeling on the daughter's part because of what had happened to her.

Jodie wiped her eyes with her handkerchief and then produced an envelope from her handbag. She took out a photo and said to Hector: "Take a look at this, Hector. It's my son, Jason."

Hector stared at the photo for some time and then declared: "Gracious! He looks like my father. So handsome. I've seen pictures of my dad at about this age and they are almost like two peas in a pod."

"That's what struck me when I saw your photos just now," said Jodie. "And he's a nice boy. Like I'm told our dad was."

A few minutes later Susan drew closer to Hector and spoke to him in a quiet voice, almost a whisper.

"Your dad was good to us over the years. He always looked after Jodie financially. I just thought you would like to know that."

"I'm so pleased to hear it," said Hector. "Thank you."

It then dawned on him why he was always told that his father's bookshop made very little contribution to the family's income. Money had obviously been diverted towards Jodie.

As he was thinking about this he could hear raised voices in the hall just outside the lounge. The door opened and in burst a burly man with a shock of golden blond hair, followed by Penelope, who looked uncharacteristically agitated.

Hector immediately recognised the man as Stuart Broadlake, his nemesis.

"Hello, mother-in-law. Hello Susan and Jodie. Hello, Phil. And? I don't think I've had the pleasure…"

"Hector. Hector Ratcliffe. I used to be at school with you."

"I remember you. Hello, Hector."

As Stuart gave him a knuckle-breaking handshake Hector noticed that his breath smelt strongly of alcohol. As the big man moved away he tripped on the carpet and stumbled forward into Penelope's arms.

"Come on," she said. "You need to sit down."

"No, leave it," he snarled. "I'm okay."

Stuart walked over to a chest of drawers at the side of the room and fell on to it in a desperate attempt to stay upright.

Penelope whispered to Susan: "He's drunk again. He's been to the golf club on his way here. And he's driven straight from there."

Mrs Douglas retreated into the kitchen.

"Have I missed a party?" slurred Stuart.

Phil replied: "Not a party exactly, mate. Just a very nice Sunday lunch."

"To which I wasn't invited," said Stuart truculently.

"You were very welcome," Penelope intervened. "But you didn't even tell us you were coming. I thought you were in Stratford."

"I got bored. So I thought I would come and see what you were up to. I can see that you're all enjoying yourselves. What brings you here, Hector? I thought your family were personas non gratas around here."

Penelope thought she needed to step in again.

"We thought that now everything's out in the open it would be good for Hector to meet his new half-sister."

"I agree," said Stuart. "Welcome to the family, old boy."

He left the safety of the chest of drawers with the intention of shaking Hector's hand for a second time. But he stumbled again, fell forward, knocked Hector's coffee out of his hand and finished up sprawled face down on the lounge carpet.

Penelope and Phil both rushed to help, taking one of Stuart's arms each and trying to lift him from the floor.

But he struggled and shouted: "Bloody get off me. I can get up on my own."

Phil said: "I don't think you can, mate. Let us take you over to the settee."

Stuart shouted again: "I said leave me!"

Phil persisted in trying to help him up but Stuart struggled to his feet and then lunged a punch at Phil's face. He missed and then tried again, this time felling Phil with a single blow to the temple.

Hector sprung on to Stuart from the rear and tried to hold him back by grabbing his arms. Stuart pulled away from him, swung round and aimed a punch at his head.

This shot also missed and Hector retreated a few paces backwards.

By this time Benson, who had been cowering in a corner since Stuart's arrival, joined in the fracas, barking loudly and jumping up frantically on everyone.

"Why are you even bloody here?" Stuart said to Hector. "You have a cheek after what your father did. You're a freak. Always were and always will be."

Penelope and Susan put themselves between the two men. Stuart fell back into a chair. Phil struggled back to his feet and Jodie stepped forward to dab a cut on his head with her handkerchief.

"Are you all right?" Hector asked Phil.

"I'll live."

Everyone was fussing round, feeling excruciatingly embarrassed, and asking after everyone else's health and mental condition. Jodie took Phil to the bathroom to tend to his wound. As for Stuart, he was already fast asleep and snoring loudly.

Mrs Douglas put the kettle on and tea was offered all round.

This was not a typical Sunday afternoon in a respectable household in rural Lincolnshire.

Hector decided that the polite thing to do was to take his leave and give the family space to "wash their dirty linen" in private. He gave his thanks to Mrs Douglas and said his goodbyes to Jodie, Susan and Phil, expressing the hope, with a rueful grin, that they would meet again "in happier circumstances".

Penelope saw him to the front door. She looked pale and afflicted as she took him by the arm. He was strangely reminded of Jacques-Louis David's painting of Andromache mourning for her husband Hector after he has been killed by Achilles. The usual self-assured, calm Penelope had let her mask slip for a few seconds. Hector saw that in this unaccustomed vulnerable condition she was more beautiful and desirable than ever. Oh, how he loves this woman!

He could see she was so mortified by what had happened that she was lost for words to describe her torment. So he put one hand on her shoulder as a silent way of showing his support and then gently stroked her cheek with his other hand.

"I'm so sorry, Hector, that you had to be part of all that. Stuart doesn't know how to behave sometimes. It's the drink, mainly. And how could he have driven his car in that state? You will be thinking 'I don't want anything more to do with that family after today's performance.'"

Hector said: "You're not to worry, love. None of this has been your fault. You and the other members of your family have been lovely to me today. The lunch was incredible. As for Stuart... I'd better not say anything at all."

A despondent Penelope nodded slowly in what appeared to be a resigned and remorseful acceptance that her husband left a lot to be desired.

Hector still had designs on her and fanciful hopes as to how their relationship might develop. But at this moment he was genuinely saddened to see her looking so desolate and so obviously trapped in her unsatisfactory marriage. He cared about her more than he cared about himself.

"Please stay in touch," he said. "And if there is anything I can ever do for you, you know that I will do it. Anything."

Penelope smiled sadly and whispered: "Thank you so much. You are a good and kind man. I will keep in touch. I'll phone you soon."

She gave him another peck on the cheek and he reciprocated.

****

It was late evening before Stuart woke up. Penelope was sitting at the other side of the lounge, reading. The rest of the family had gone to bed early, partly to keep out of Stuart's way and partly because all, except Pamela, were due back at work in London the next day and needed to make an early start.

"How are you going, Pen?" asked Stuart.

"What do you think?" Penelope replied testily.

"Oh, I remember now. It all got a bit messy didn't it?"

"Messy? Your behaviour was downright disgusting. How could you act like that in front of my family and friend?"

"I'm sorry. I realise I was over the top. But that Phil always riles me. He's so damned reasonable – and full of chelp. And where did you drag up that bloody Hector from? I would have thought your lot would have had enough of that family after what his bloody father did. And anyway, when I think of it, he always fancied you. That prat had your name on his satchel at school."

"So fancying me makes him a prat does it?"

"Oh, no. You know what I mean. He was always a prat.

Swanning around quoting his bloody literature. He's just a younger carbon copy of his bloody father. Hypocrites both of them. Pretending to be intellectuals when all they wanted was to get girls' knickers off."

Penelope then did something which went contrary to her usual placid nature. She lost her temper.

"You're disgusting. You haven't got a decent thought in your head, have you? I can't take any more of this. I just can't bear your... your *coarseness*. You're supposed to be an officer and a gentleman and you speak and behave like the lowest trooper. What has happened to you?

"You're violent and, what's even worse, you're a potential killer."

"What the hell are you on about?"

"This afternoon you drove home from the golf club with a skinful of beer inside you. That made you a potential killer."

Stuart sat up straight and wagged his finger at his wife.

"Just shut up, you stupid cow. You po-faced misery. You think you're so superior don't you? Bloody Mother Superior, that's you, Well, I'm sick of you and your pontificating. Why don't you go and find Hector bloody Ratcliffe? He's more your type – boring, simpering little twat."

Penelope stood up ran towards the door and slammed it after her.

Stuart curled up on the settee and went back to sleep.

The next morning Penelope rose at seven o'clock after a sleepless night in which she took stock of her current unsatisfactory life and pondered what options she had to bring about change. She knew that her marriage had gone past the point of no return. She could no longer tolerate the way her husband behaved, both to herself and to other people. She had not loved him for years and she had no reason to think that he loved her, if he ever did.

Another fault line in their marriage had been that they had never seen eye to eye on money. She enjoyed life's comforts that money could bring, but that was not a be-all and end-all for her and she was careful in her spending. Stuart liked money to make a statement, that he was a rich, important and desirable alpha male. He liked fast cars, dining at posh restaurants, belonging to the best golf club in the area and going on holidays to the "in" places, i.e. those with the whitest beaches and bluest seas in the most exotic locations. The result was that he spent a great deal.

Penelope had always earned more as a solicitor than he did as an army officer but she had never made that a point of contention and for many years had accepted his extravagances with good grace. This changed when she realised that a good proportion of his expenditure went on impressing his "other women". This caused a few rows but Penelope had always stopped short of turning these into wars, or even battles. Mentally, though, his behaviour was inflicting deep scars on her and only her resilient character protected her from any sort of breakdown.

His boorish and drunken outbursts were now beyond the pale and Penelope believed the time had come for some decisive action on her part.

The option of mariticide having been quickly ruled out, the obvious answer was to seek a divorce, for which she had plenty of grounds. However, as noted previously, this was against the principles which had been instilled into her throughout her life, by her family, by the Anglican Church of which she was a faithful member, and by her own philosophy.

The logical alternative to this was a legal separation and this route had some appeal for Penelope. In the short to medium term she could accept this solution in good conscience. She would regret breaking up the family unit but was confident that her daughters would support her as they had recently become disillusioned with their father themselves. Eventually there might be a divorce, but this would have to be at Stuart's instigation, not hers. This would be an outcome she could live with.

Did Penelope's nocturnal deliberations feature Hector at all? There may indeed have been a fleeting fancy of some close relationship. However, the fears and fancies of the night can swiftly disappear in the cold light of day. This was the case when Penelope awoke and her thoughts of legal separation and a new start had largely dissipated.

Events very soon led to those night-time notions being resurrected. When she went downstairs she discovered that Stuart was no longer on the settee. Her immediate thought was that he had found a bed or some other place to sleep in one of the other rooms. She searched the house but he was nowhere to be found. She went outside and found that his car had gone.

When Stuart had misbehaved in the past it was his usual tactic to show contrition the next morning, even to the extent of bringing Penelope breakfast in bed or giving her a husbandly cuddle. Just driving away without any apology, or even a goodbye, was a new low for him. Penelope took this as a sign that he no longer cared what she thought about him. It was all over.

Her mother found her sitting in the lounge, staring into space.

"Good morning, Penelope. Are you okay?" asked Pamela.

"No, not really, mum. I'm very upset and annoyed about what happened yesterday."

"I don't blame you, dear. Stuart was awful. You know we stopped liking him a long time ago, but he was like an animal yesterday. Just a drunken animal. Where is he now anyway?"

"He's gone."

"Where's he gone?"

"I don't know. He's supposed to be having a holiday this week. He's probably gone to find some pub somewhere.

"Mum, there's something I've got to tell you."

"Yes, dear?"

"I'm going to leave Stuart."

"I'm not surprised. I could see it coming. I think you're doing the right thing. He's been treating you like dirt for years. I know you well enough to realise that you wouldn't do something like this lightly. We didn't bring you up to give up without a fight. He's a beast. He's always been a beast in my book. But now he's a drunken, violent beast too."

"Thank you, mum. I never thought I would do this. It's giving up, and I don't like giving up."

"Sometimes you have to. You have to think of yourself. Will you divorce him?"

"No, mum. It's against my principles – till death us do part and all that."

"I respect you for that. They're my principles too," said her mother.

****

A few days went by, during which time Hector had thought about little else than the events at Hayfleet. His sadness over Penelope's plight was coupled with a ray of hope that she might turn to him for comfort.

He was taking his turn in the caravan site office when the phone rang. It was her.

Penelope said she had rung to apologise again for Stuart's behaviour and to thank him for his patience and understanding. Then she broke the news that she had decided to separate from her husband.

For two days after Stuart left Hayfleet she had tried to make contact with him, but to no avail. Eventually, on the third day, she had phoned home and he had answered. He was drunk again. When she told him of her decision to leave him his reaction had been to shout "suit yourself" and slam the receiver down. She had heard nothing from him since.

She explained she had taken some leave from work and would stay at her mother's for a few more days "to let the dust settle". Then she would return to Stratford, go to work and set in train the process for a legal separation. She had spoken to her daughters, who had been quite shocked by the news because she had always shielded them from their father's worst excesses. However, having now heard her full story, they had accepted her decision and declared their unconditional love and support for her.

Unsurprisingly, Hector backed her too, in the strongest of terms. He was scathing about Stuart, whose behaviour had confirmed him as the bully he had always thought him to be.

Hector was quick to take advantage of Penelope's new "freedom", inviting her to his home for dinner the following evening. Although admitting that his culinary skills were limited, he promised to cook his "signature dish" of fish lasagne. Penelope graciously accepted his offer and thanked him for the consideration he had shown towards her.

Hector anticipated the dinner date with great excitement laced with a little anxiety. He thought that it could be the "make or break" occasion for Penelope and himself. He was up at dawn cleaning and tidying the house, where he had been living alone since his children had flown the nest to get married. This was followed by a trip to the supermarket to buy provisions for the meal. The finishing touches were a bath, hair wash and a general spruce-up, even involving removal of nose and ear hair.

When Penelope arrived it was clear she had made an extra effort too. Her usual style had always been understated, comfortable as she was in her own skin and signifying a self-confidence that her good looks needed no artificial embellishment.

Today she had a smart new hairdo and was wearing a stunning, short, flowery summer dress. Her bare legs were as shapely as they had been when she was a teenager. And her face was as smooth and her smile as alluring as ever.

Hector, in smart summer shirt and slacks, looked relaxed and cool. Inside, though, he was far from calm, sensing that this evening was one of the most important of his life.

Independently they had both decided to enjoy the occasion and try to put to one side Penelope's troubles and the trauma of the Douglas family gathering. Their conversation flowed easily during the meal and afterwards. There was a good deal of reminiscing about school days but also some positive talk about their families and their aspirations for the rest of their lives.

Hector's principal aspiration remained unspoken as he didn't wish to appear presumptuous that Penelope would wish him to be part of her future plans.

Towards the end of the evening the conversation turned to Stratford-upon-Avon. Penelope said she had fallen in love with the town during the Grammar School excursions they had both enjoyed. Hector agreed that the trips organised by Mr Plunkett had been the highlights of his schooldays.

"He was a great teacher," said Penelope. "He brought English literature to life with his enthusiasm and his tremendous depth of knowledge. He was incorrigibly self-opinionated but a really lovely guy."

"He inspired me to take an interest in poetry. It wasn't my cup of tea before I had him as a teacher, but it's been a part of my life ever since," said Hector.

"I even tried to write a poem – once."

Penelope laughed: "Did you decide it wasn't your forte? Or perhaps it was an epic poem and you're still working on it?"

Hector didn't immediately realise that she was being facetious and replied: "No, I think the subject matter was too painful for me to do a repeat performance. I still have the poem as a matter of fact."

"I'd love to see it," said Penelope.

"All right then. I'll find it. Well, now I think about it, there are actually two poems. Don't worry they're both very short! Just give me a minute."

Hector went over to a bureau, opened a drawer, sifted through a pile of papers and found the poems.

"Let me read them to you. I must warn you, though, that they're not very good. He sat beside her on the settee and recited...

Hopelessness?

Waiting, waiting, for a time,
Which I know will never come,
Weighted down by Sorrow's garb
Foolishly I press on.
Heaven's dreams have turned to nightmares,
Torture me by night and day;
Waiting, waiting, but truly knowing,
Knowing you're for ever gone.

Ever since the Autumn day
When your brightness lit my life
I have snuggled down in bed
With glowing expectation.
Now minutes of gloom and hours of apathy
Stilt my every waking thought,
Hoping, hoping, doubting, willing,
Is this life all God can do?

Willing, there's a potent word,
Although it's powerless without faith;
I conjure you nightly in my bed
And then yawn at my failure.
Give me, please, some chink of hope
Some tender message of regard,
That I may cherish a subject's hope
Of a sweet, moist kiss from the lips of his Queen.

Misery
Futureless, I seize at mole-hills,
Make my pleasure in childhood ways,
Don the comic face of misery
Put my trust in fetish signs.

Pitiless, you left me standing,
Said goodbye in mocking tones.
Now my life's devoid of beauty
An empty shell, a continuous moan.

"They're not bad poems but they're so sad," said Penelope.

"They're about you," said Hector.

Penelope covered her face with her hands and declared: "Oh my lord. It makes me sound so cruel. I wasn't really like that, was I?"

"It seemed like it at the time, but then I was over-sensitive and quite immature, I suppose."

"I certainly didn't intend to behave like that. But then I didn't realise how intense your feelings were. I thought those words on your satchel were just a silly schoolboy thing. Did you never think of telling me how strongly you felt?"

"I was too shy. And I didn't want to risk being rejected. My only serious throw of the dice was when I asked you to go to the pictures. You wouldn't believe how much courage that took."

"You make me seem like an ogre," said Penelope, smiling shyly.

"No, you were never that. Far from it. I thought you were an angel."

"I'm far from being an angel, I can assure you."

Hector looked straight into her round, brown eyes and said: "I still think you're an angel."

Penelope returned his direct gaze and replied: "I always liked you, Hector. But you've matured like an old wine and you've grown on me in the last couple of weeks."

She moved her face close to his and he kissed her on the cheek. Then she turned her head slightly so that their mouths came close. He kissed her twice on the lips. She put her arms around him and their kissing became passionate.

Hector put his hand on her knee, and slipped it gently along her thigh, which was as smooth as fine silk. He was in heaven.

Chapter nine – Matchmaker, matchmaker

Having spoken to Penelope about the secret kept by the two families regarding his father and Susan, Hector was even more forgiving of his mother for having left him in the dark.

However, a subsequent conversation he had with Aunt Christine left him feeling a little prickly on the subject.

He had been careful not to tell his mother that Mr Plunkett had been the one to reveal the secret, or that Humphrey had been the messenger. These were two of the people he most respected in the whole world and he didn't wish there to be any bad feelings towards them.

He was surprised and rather annoyed when Aunt Christine suddenly revealed that she knew of the involvement of the two men and that she and Margaret had discussed it.

"How could you possibly know that?" Hector demanded of his aunt.

"Ah, dear, you should know by now that Aunt Christine knows everything."

He wasn't to be deflected: "Seriously, how do you know?"

"Seriously then, Humphrey's grandmother, Gloria, told me. I think she gave Humphrey the third degree and he crumpled."

"Unbelievable!" said Hector. "The Spanish Inquisition had nothing on you women."

"Did you not know, dear, that I was thrown out of the Spanish Inquisition for cruelty? Anyway, let's change the subject shall we? I was really interested to hear about George Plunkett. I was always very fond of George.

"Do you remember that Sanderholme Players' production we did together – 'Troilus and Cressida'? We played the lead roles."

"Yes, I remember it well," said Hector, slightly put out that she had deftly changed the subject.

"You could have played your namesake Hector in that production, you know," said Christine.

"I remember you trying to bully me into it," he said. "I was at the most 14 at the time, I recall. I would have been the puniest Hector ever seen!"

"You could have had padding to fill you out a bit."

"Oh, yes, sure. I'm not even sure if my voice had broken at the time. Hardly hero material."

"Rubbish. You were just too shy. I could never get you on to the stage."

"I think Sanderholme can think itself lucky for that."

"I hear that George lost his wife, Marjorie, and that he's living alone now. That's sad. They never had children, you know. I would love to see him again."

Hector merely replied: "Yes."

He had some doubt as to whether Mr Plunkett would necessarily wish to see her.

But she persisted.

"Do you know his address in Stratford, or a telephone number?"

"No, I don't actually."

"Humphrey must know them because he went to see him. I will ask Gloria. She can find out from Humphrey. I would love to go and see him."

Hector nodded in acquiescence.

****

For the first time in her life Penelope was feeling frightened. She was afraid of the reception she would get from Stuart when she returned home and as a result she kept putting off that day. She took all the remaining annual leave that she was entitled to and remained at her mother's.

During those weeks Hector and Penelope saw each other every day and through intimate conversations began to understand the experiences which had shaped their personalities both during their time at school and since.

There was the conundrum regarding Penelope which had always puzzled and slightly worried him. What had she seen in Stuart Broadlake that would ever have suggested to her that he would make a suitable husband? It was the mote in her eye as far as he was concerned.

Penelope began her explanation by saying that, of course, Stuart had his obvious appeals. He was tall and muscular with extremely handsome manly features. Although she was primarily a cerebral person, she had not been immune as a girl to the charms of what she described as "a bit of beefcake".

This description, emanating from such a pure and innocent mouth, somewhat shocked Hector. Then he harked back to the time when he had "the hots" for Tricia Stanmore, a veritable "cheesecake". What right had he to go all holier than thou because Penelope had found Stuart attractive?

He still thought, though, that it was inconceivable that she should actually have wished to marry such a man.

"He could be very charming when he chose to be," said Penelope. "And in the early days, when we were first courting, he chose to be charming most of the time.

"And do you remember that we studied Pride and Prejudice for A level? I was too impressed, I think, by a quote I read in that novel – *'it is better to know as little as possible of the defects of the person with whom you are to pass your life'*.

"I did know that Stuart could be moody sometimes but it was only after we announced our engagement that friends started to warn me about his violent temper and his tendency to bully people.

"I was brought up to be patriotic and I was proud to be married to someone who chose to serve his country in the armed forces. You see where I'm going with this. I was to marry a very attractive young man, who had always been courteous to me and who shared my ideas of patriotism.

"My parents had encouraged our relationship too. They were impressed that he was head boy of the school. Also my father and his father, who, as you probably know, was ex-Army and a bank manager, were members of the same Masonic lodge.

"Did I love him? I can't really be sure. I think I was in love with an idea of what he was. If I'm honest I don't think I have ever loved a man. Don't misunderstand me. I *am* confident that I'm capable of loving a man. But back then it didn't seem that important. I was never a rebel, you see. My mother and father always expected me to get a good degree, get a good job, get married, get children. It was what people did and I saw no reason to reject that path.

"If I'm honest I still cleave to that simple view of life. If Stuart had been a half reasonable husband I would have been perfectly happy with my lot.

"After we were married I began to see some of the flaws in Stuart's character — his selfishness, his unpredictable tantrums and his endless flirtations. But he also had this other side. He was dedicated to his job and immensely proud of his regiment. And he was brave. He saw active service in Northern Ireland during the Troubles and in the Falklands War.

"He loved his daughters too. He always used to play with them and encouraged them to get involved in sport at school. He taught them to play golf and took them for riding lessons.

"Gradually, though, he changed. He started drinking more. His flirtations turned into full-blown affairs. And I heard on the grapevine that he was using prostitutes. When he was drunk he often became abusive to me, mostly verbally, but occasionally physically as well. He was just someone who could never be satisfied with what he had. It's all right to have aspirations, but he was just greedy.

"I threatened to leave him several times unless he mended his ways. And recently, until what happened the other Sunday, he did seem to be getting the message. He would come to Hayfleet with me each time I visited my mother, whereas previously he always had an excuse not to come. Of course that may have been because he joined Sanderholme Golf Club and always took the chance of having a round there.

"I almost thought he might have turned over a new leaf – until this latest debacle.

"Anyway I must stop. You don't want to hear all this."

Hector told her she had no need to stop. He would always be interested to hear what she had to say. His ears had already pricked up when she had said that she *was* capable of loving a man. He dared to think that *he* might be that man.

Nothing ventured, as they say, he jumped in: "I just wondered if there was any chance that I might be the man who you might be capable of loving?"

Penelope smiled at him bashfully: "I think you might be. But there's no rush is there? There's a lot in my life I have to sort out."

Hector replied: "I understand that. I won't rush you. I will just love you and be as patient as I need to be."

"Thank you."

****

It was autumn and the new organist at St Martin's Church, Hayfleet, was practising for the following Sunday's harvest festival service. This was to be her first service since her appointment and she was keen to be note perfect.

The organist was none other than Aunt Christine, who had gone full circle from being an Anglican, pagan, Methodist, Scientologist, Zen Buddhist and Spiritualist, to her childhood home as a fervent member of the Church of England. St Martin was a High "bells and smells" Church, with a vicar who liked to be called Father, much to the distress of some Low Church members of his congregation.

Having practised "We Plough the Fields and Scatter" to her satisfaction, Christine was munching on a lunchtime snack of spam sandwiches, a Scotch egg and a Cadbury's Dairy Milk bar.

The flower ladies were busy preparing their arrangements for the following Sunday, which involved a certain amount of squabbling as to whose pride and joy was to take precedence among the displays.

When Christine noticed that Mrs Pamela Douglas was amongst the arrangers she quickly gobbled up the remainder of her lunch and went over to introduce herself.

"It's Mrs Douglas isn't it?" she enthused.

"Yes, dear. It is."

"May I introduce myself? I'm Christine Ashburn. I believe you know my sister, Margaret Ratcliffe, and my nephew, Hector Ratcliffe."

"Oh, yes. Of course. I think we have met once before. Quite a few years ago."

"Yes, I think we may have done."

"So you are going to be the new organist?"

"Yes, I'm giving it a go. We'll have to see whether I'm up to it."

"I'm sure you will be."

"It's very good news that our Hector and your Penelope are getting on so well, isn't it?"

This was a fishing question, designed to ascertain the

lie of the land.

"Yes, Penelope is seeing quite a lot of Hector. He seems to be a nice man," said Pamela.

"Hector is absolutely lovely," declared Christine. "There isn't a better man in the whole of Sanderholme. You know he has been fond of Penelope ever since they were at school?"

"Yes, I understand so. It is very nice that they are getting on."

"Do you think Penelope will be divorcing her husband?"

"I don't think she believes in divorce. I do think there may be a separation, though."

"I'm not a big fan of divorce myself. But in extreme circumstances it may be the only alternative. I would love to see Hector and your daughter getting together permanently. I think they would make a lovely married couple," said Christine.

Pamela smiled.

"Perhaps you're jumping the gun a little."

"Well, there's no point in them hanging about – not at their age. I think they should get on with it as soon as possible."

"No doubt they will come to their own decision in good time," said Pamela.

"Perhaps we might just nudge them along a little," said Christine. "The sooner she gets away from that horrible Broadlake man, the better."

"I agree with you there. He is a horrible man. We have been worried about Penelope for a long time."

Pamela clicked her thumb against her middle finger,

denoting that she had just remembered something.

"You know I said I thought we had met once before. Well, I remember now. You came unexpectedly to our house one day when Penelope was still at school. You came specifically to warn me that your nephew was interested in Penelope and that it should be very much discouraged. You've changed your tune now haven't you? "

"Yes, I have. I know that. The situation has changed, though, hasn't it? Now it's not such a secret any more about Charles and Susan."

"Yes, you're right. I must admit that things have changed," said Pamela.

"So, what do you say?" said Christine. "Shall we all give them a little push in the right direction? I'm sure Penelope will listen to you."

"I don't think I'm really the pushing type," said Pamela.

She added with a grin: "But let's agree that I won't do anything to discourage them."

"That's the spirit," declared Christine.

"I will tell Margaret about our plan of campaign. She will help us, I'm certain. She so wants Hector to be happy. It's been lovely to meet you," she said, offering Pamela her hand.

Mrs Douglas was somewhat flummoxed to be told that she was now part of some conspiracy. However, she decided to take the line of least resistance as she realised she was up against a formidable force of nature in the form of Hector's aunt.

"It's been a pleasure meeting you," she said.

Christine bounded off to the church car park, jumped into her hot pink VW Beetle and zoomed off, leaving gravel spraying in the air behind her. She was on a mission.

When she arrived at the caravan site she rushed in through the reception door, finding Margaret and Hector inside.

"You'll never guess who I've been talking to," she said.

"No, I can't guess," said Margaret.

"Mrs Douglas, Penelope's mother. She was at church this morning."

"Oh, that was nice for you," said Margaret, with some foreboding as to what was coming next.

Looking towards Hector, Christine continued: "She's absolutely over the moon about you and Penelope getting together."

"I'm pleased," said Hector. "It's early days yet, though."

"Mrs Douglas thinks you two have no time to waste. She thinks Penelope should get a divorce and marry you as soon as possible."

Hector was taken aback: "She actually said that, did she?"

"Yes, she agreed with me that it was the way forward."

"She agreed with *you*, did she?"

"Yes, she did."

"Aunt Christine, you've been doing your thing again, haven't you?"

"What thing is that, dear?"

"Interfering."

"Interfering? Being helpful is what I would call it," said Christine.

Hector gave a sigh of resignation. There had been many occasions in the past when Christine had annoyed him immensely with her 'helpful' interventions. But over the years he had stopped fighting against them, knowing that trying to stop them was like King Canute trying to stop the tide coming in.

Sneakily, though, he was rather pleased that his aunt was fighting his corner this time. For the course she was urging was precisely what he wished to see happen. He would never, on principle, admit it to her.

"You really are getting ahead of yourself," he said. "We have only known each other properly for a few weeks. And, by the way, she's against divorce. She's trying to have a legal separation."

"You need to nip that idea in the bud straightaway," said Christine. "That way you never will be able to tie the knot."

Margaret intervened: "Really, Christine. I think you're going too far now. You can't run people's lives for them. I think at their age they're quite capable of making their own decisions."

"Hear, hear," said Hector.

"I'm only trying to help," said Christine.

"I can't listen to any more of this just now," said Hector. "I've got work to do."

When he had left the office, Christine said to Margaret: "Right. What's our next move going to be? Perhaps you should give Mrs Douglas a ring, Margaret."

****

Penelope's car pulled up in the caravan site's car park which was a few yards away from Hector's home. She got out, walked round to the passenger side and opened the door.

Out leapt an excited Benson who had been strapped into the front seat. His attention was immediately drawn to a white Staffordshire bull terrier who was straining at the leash in an attempt to say "hello" to his fellow canine. The dog's handler was trying his best to keep his dog under control by pulling hard on its lead and shouting loudly at him to "Behave".

The dog's owner was none other than Cecil Roberts, now in his late-eighties, unshaven but generally still looking well-turned-out, slim and quite sprightly.

"Don't scold him," said Penelope. "I don't mind him coming over and making friends."

Cecil allowed his dog to go towards Benson and the two animals made a great fuss of each other, rubbing noses and inspecting bottoms.

"He's a lovely dog," said Cecil, pointing to Benson. "What sort is he?"

"A labrador," replied Penelope.

"Oh, a labrador. Are you staying on the site?" asked Cecil in his usual direct style.

"No, I've come to see Mr Ratcliffe, the site owner."

"Hector?"

"Yes, Hector."

"Are you on business then?"

"No, we're friends."

"Friends?" said Cecil. "I don't have friends. They let

you down. But Hector's a very good man. He's the nearest thing I have to a friend. He's looked after me over the years."

"Yes, he is a decent man," agreed Penelope.

"The best," said Cecil. "So you're friends, then. You're a good looking woman. Hector needs a wife to look after him. You should marry him."

Penelope laughed: "You don't beat about the bush, do you?"

"Are you married?"

"Yes."

"You can't marry Hector then. That's a pity. He's a lovely man and you're a lovely lady. You should be married."

Penelope laughed again and decided it was best not to make any more marriage-related observations.

"You've got a lovely dog there," she said.

"Yes, he's a good dog. Margaret, Hector's mother, found him for me. They've been very good to me, the Ratcliffes. They're a lovely family. I won't hear anything bad about them."

"Do you have a van on the site?" Penelope asked.

"Yes, that's my van over there," replied Cecil, pointing to a smart green caravan a few yards away.

"You spend your holidays here then?"

"Oh, no. I live here all the time. I was one of the managers."

"Oh, I see."

"I was responsible for hygiene."

"Oh, I see."

"Cecil Roberts is my name."

Cecil offers his hand to Penelope, who gently shakes it.

"I'm pleased to meet you, Cecil."

"Tell Hector that you met me. And tell him I think you would make a lovely couple."

Penelope said she would indeed tell Hector that she had met him. As frequently was the case with Cecil, it was once met, never forgotten.

****

Immediately after this encounter Penelope enjoyed a pleasant dinner at Hector's house. She did indeed tell Hector that she had just met an unusual "character" but made no mention of his suggestion that they should become man and wife.

Inwardly she found the idea – and the direct manner in which it had been presented to her – highly amusing. But she was far from ready to share the suggestion with Hector. The fact that she was still a married woman weighed too heavily with her.

It was when she returned to Hayfleet later that night that the full impact of her bizarre meeting with Cecil struck home. It was obvious to her that he was, to say the least, a little dotty.

He had referred to Hector as "a lovely man" and the considerate way he had treated her certainly confirmed that description.

There was also no doubt at all that Hector was deeply in love with her. This was no mere schoolboy crush. It was a worship which had been sustained undimmed for more than half a lifetime.

The introverted, mildly eccentric but rather interesting and kindly youth she had known at school had blossomed into a quite well-rounded, quite good looking and still rather interesting older man.

Penelope, despite her good looks, intelligence and confident manner, remained humble and not quite able to understand why she should be the object of such utter devotion, loyalty and undiluted romantic love which Hector offered to her.

She had fallen completely out of love with her husband and questioned whether he had ever truly loved her. She felt she had merely provided him with a respectable domestic arrangement, a comfortable base to go back to between his extra-marital adventures.

She wondered, though, if she could live up to the expectations that Hector had of her. She realised she had been put on a pedestal and worried that she was undeserving of it and that Hector might quickly become disillusioned should they ever come to live with each other.

Yes, she knew she was highly intelligent. Yes, she knew she was good looking for her age. Yes, she was capable of loving someone. And, yes, she could still enjoy sex. But for all that she strongly suspected that she was BORING – that she lacked that spark which could inject a sense of adventure and excitement into a relationship.

If only she could have known that whatever she felt might be her own shortcomings, Hector would never share her opinion. All aspects of her character and her appearance captivated him. Whatever she thought, whatever anyone else in the world thought, to him she was the perfect woman, and would be to the end of days.

As she curled up on the red leather settee in the family home late that night, pretending to read a novel but engrossed in her thoughts about the future, her mother came in from the kitchen on the pretext of wishing her goodnight.

She sat down at the side of her daughter and asked her if she had had a pleasant evening with Hector.

"A very enjoyable evening, thanks, mum," she replied. "Hector cooked a really good meal. He's had to do a lot of cooking for his family over the years, so he's become quite an expert."

"You get on very well with Hector, don't you, dear?"

"Yes, we do get on well. He's a sweetie."

"When this business with Stuart is over and done with, do you think you might possibly have a future with Hector?"

"Possibly," said Penelope cagily, pretending to read another line of her book.

"I do like him, you know," said Pamela. "I believe he's quite a gentleman in a quiet sort of way. I don't think he would ever mistreat you."

"I think you're right. I don't know if I'm ready to plunge into a new relationship. Everything seems to be changing at such a pace."

"I understand, dear. People do speak highly of Hector. I bumped into his aunt at church. She thinks he's marvellous."

"I've heard about Aunt Christine," said Penelope. "Quite a formidable character, I'm told. Hector's told me all about her. She's a notorious matchmaker!"

Pamela laughed.

"She is perhaps a little pushy. But I think she means well."

Penelope laughed too and suddenly found her mood lightening.

"I must tell you this," she said. "I met this strange old man in the car park at Marshview Caravan Site today, outside Hector's house. He told me that Hector was a lovely man and that I should definitely marry him, even after I had told him I was already married.

"He was someone who used to work on the site. To be quite honest he seemed to be a sandwich short of a full picnic."

"Perhaps wiser than you imagine," suggested Pamela, smiling and looking her daughter straight in the eye.

"Perhaps," said Penelope, turning towards her book because she thought it was time to change the subject.

Pamela took the hint, said her goodnight and retired to bed.

Chapter ten – Mr Plunkett

On a warm summer's morning, an open top sports car drew up outside a terraced townhouse in a quiet cul-de-sac in Stratford-upon-Avon.

A noticeable couple alighted: a man in his sixties of medium build with a tousled mane of curly brown hair, wearing a pale blue sports jacket, blue and red checked shirt and orange moleskin trousers; and an ample elderly woman, wearing a headscarf, a floral dress and high-heeled shoes and carrying a large designer handbag.

The man held the car door open and as she emerged gingerly she carefully removed her scarf.

Humphrey Gibb and Christine Ashburn were paying a visit to George Plunkett.

Aunt Christine had tracked down George and then prevailed upon her friend Gloria's grandson to provide transport. She had thoroughly enjoyed the journey from Sanderholme with the wind blowing in her face.

As they walked down the path the front door opened and a dapper, bony man, wearing a light grey suit and a red carnation buttonhole, opened the front door.

Christine and George greeted each other enthusiastically, exchanging kisses, which resulted in George being left with a swathe of bright red lipstick on his freshly laundered white shirt. This was followed by a manly handshake between George and Humphrey.

Mr Plunkett led his guests into his neat dining room where the best china tea set was ready for action.

Talk of the old days soon began, with Christine particularly keen to recall various Sanderholme Players' productions in which she and George had performed.

Her favourite had clearly been Shakespeare's "Troilus and Cressida" in which they had played the leads.

"That part was made for me," she declared. "And, of course, it didn't end well for Cressida – just like my love life."

She stood up, thrust out her chest and declaimed:

"Time, force, and death,
Do to this body what extremes you can;
But the strong base and building of my love
Is as the very centre of the earth,
Drawing all things to it."

Humphrey clapped and George shouted, "Bravo" and then stood up himself to recite some lines of Troilus he had remembered:

"Even such a passion doth embrace my bosom:
My heart beats thicker than a feverous pulse;
And all my powers do their bestowing lose,
Like vassalage at unawares encountering
The eye of majesty."

This provoked more applause from Humphrey. Christine took her turn again:

".... for to be wise and love
Exceeds man's might; that dwells with gods above."

"So true, so true," said George. "Shakespeare knew a thing or two about life!"

"Your turn," said Christine.

"No, I think I have taxed my memory quite enough," said George. "I think it's your turn now, Humphrey. What can you remember from your virtuoso performance as Romeo in the school play?"

Humphrey hesitated and then admitted shamefacedly that he couldn't remember a single line.

"Not even this," said George...

"O, she doth teach the torches to burn bright!
Her beauty hangs upon the cheek of night
Like a rich jewel in an Ethiop's ear;
Beauty too rich for use, for earth too dear!"

Humphrey said: "Oh, I remember that now. You've got a better recall than I have. I can only think of a couple of lines"...

"My lips, two blushing pilgrims, ready stand
To smooth that rough touch with a tender kiss."

"Trust you to remember those lines," George laughed. "No doubt you were savouring the chance of a kiss with Penelope Douglas. Oh, sorry, I mean Juliet."

"I couldn't possibly comment," said Humphrey. "Particularly as now she seems to be taken by my dear pal Hector."

"Indeed," said George. "Who would have thought it? After all these years. Good luck to them both, I say. I am sure they will make a great couple."

Christine said: "He has never given up the hope that he might finish up with Penelope, even when it seemed a daft idea."

"Ah," said George. *"To be wise and love, exceeds man's might."*

Humphrey interjected: "But as the Bard also said, *'All's Well That Ends Well'*."

"Very true in this case, I think," said Christine.

"The King of France is one of the characters in 'All's Well That Ends Well', isn't he?" asked Christine.

"He is indeed," said George.

"It reminds me of something I was told on the caravan site last week," said Christine. "The scruffiest looking old van on the site is owned by the scruffiest looking man on the site, Mr Clarke. When he came in to pay his rent he casually revealed to me that he is the direct descendant of the last King of France, Louis-Philippe, and he claimed that if France had kept the monarchy he would have been the King today.

"I think he could tell that I thought he was a nutty as a fruitcake. I had a job keeping a straight face. But he was absolutely adamant about it. Anyway the next day he comes in with this family tree on one huge piece of paper stuck together with loads of bits of Sellotape. And there was his name at the bottom of the tree, Louis Clarke. It made me think that perhaps he isn't as nutty as I thought he was.

"But he had another surprise for me. He said he had been very ill recently, while he was staying in his caravan. He was waiting for the results of tests to see if he had bladder cancer and he had some sort of urine infection which made him delirious. He said that while he was in bed suffering from this condition Jesus Christ came and sat on the edge of the bed, touched him gently on the hand, and told him not to worry because he and his Father would look after him."

"He related word for word quite a long conversation he had had with Jesus."

"So he was nutty after all," said Humphrey.

"No, he wasn't. Despite his scruffy appearance he is quite an articulate, reasonable type of man. Even though

I'm religious myself, and definitely believe in miracles, I was sceptical about what he was telling me. Just imagine, Jesus Christ coming to a caravan site in Sanderholme.

"Then he showed me something which really got me wondering. He took out his mobile phone and showed me a slightly blurred photograph of a man, dressed in Middle Eastern clothing, sitting on the edge of a bed."

"Oh, come on, so Jesus agreed to pose for a piccy?" said Humphrey. "I think you were having your leg pulled, Christine."

"You would think that. But not if you knew Mr Clarke. He's a very earnest person, not one to pull anyone's leg. I believe him."

Humphrey laughed out loud.

"So he's the King of France and he's had a personal visit from Jesus. Do you feel there's something of a pattern developing here? Could your Mr Clarke perhaps be something of a fantasist?" said Humphrey.

"You may mock, Humphrey. But I believe him. And there's an end to this story that I haven't told you about yet. He didn't have cancer and he made a complete recovery. The Son and The Father obviously looked after him as Jesus promised."

"If you and Mr Clarke believe all this then that's fine. That's what religion's all about – to bring people healing and comfort – isn't it?" said Humphrey.

"There was still a mocking tone in what you said," said Christine. "You think religion brings comfort, but that it's not really about truth, don't you?"

"I'm sorry to disappoint you, but I'm afraid I'm a total

'don't know' when it comes to religion," Humphrey replied.

"How can you have reached your age and not know?" said Christine.

George, who had been uncharacteristically quiet during this conversation, could see that Christine was preparing to mount a very high horse, and judged it was time to come to Humphrey's aid.

"Christine," he said. "I seem to recall that at one time you used to change your opinions on religion quite frequently."

"Indeed I did. Indeed I do. But what I have never doubted is the existence of God, or gods. How else could we be here except by some immaculate design? You have to use your imagination, dear George. I was a pagan once, now I'm an Anglican. Tomorrow – who knows? You have to believe in something, though."

"Okay, okay, perhaps you're right," said Humphrey. "All this must run in the family. I remember when we were at school that Hector was always talking about the gods. Some people thought he was off his trolley, but he always had interesting ideas and he never knocked anyone else's opinions."

"That's how I remember, Hector," said George. "He always had perfect manners. That's what's so lacking in the modern world."

"Yes, he's always been a well-mannered lad. It's what I like about him," said Christine.

"I have a bee in my bonnet about manners," said George. "They are one of the few things which distinguish a civilised society from the barbarous state of nature.

"I remember Desmond Morris in 'The Naked Ape' suggesting that civilisation is just a thin veneer. But I have always thought it is a veneer well worth having and encouraging.

"A quote from an American journalist called Bill Moyers also stuck in my mind: 'Civilization is but a thin veneer stretched across the passions of the human heart. And civilization doesn't just happen; we have to make it happen.'

"That's fundamentally what I believe and what has guided the way I live my life. If we are not to live a life which is, as Hobbes had it, 'nasty brutish and short' then we must have civilisation, and the greatest prop of civilisation is good manners.

"Goethe said: 'A man's manners are a mirror in which he shows his portrait.'

"I'm sorry to go on about this. It's something I'm passionate about. I think the one thing which could make the earth a better place to live in, and die in, is manners.

"I'm sorry. Rant over. I am lacking in manners myself in pressing my views upon you. I will shut up."

"Don't do that," said Christine. "I agree with every word you have said. I blame The Beatles. Respect for authority and one's betters ended with them. And those dreadful satirical programmes like 'That Was The Week That Was'. The rot started in the Sixties."

"I agree," said George. "I look back to the Fifties with nostalgia – and to the Sixties with horror. Sorry to hog the conversation. What do you think, Humphrey?"

"I haven't given this a lot of thought to be honest. I try

to make the best of life as I find it." replied Humphrey.

He took a deep breath and said: "But here goes then. Isn't it obvious that in a healthy society, the cream must be allowed to come to the top? And that's what's wrong with our present set-up. We don't allow that to happen. We are ruled by mediocrities in all our institutions – people with no manners because they are ill-bred and aren't the natural leaders who should emerge from a society which has a proper elite in charge."

Humphrey had breezed through life making lots of friends and making no enemies. Many people might have suspected that he had a superiority complex born of his well-to-do background, but he had never given them any ammunition which would have confirmed those suspicions.

On this occasion he had had no wish to reveal his true opinions, but felt, out of his own sense of good manners, that he should respond seriously to George's question. He was comfortable enough in the company of George and Christine, two old reactionaries, to know that the controversial opinions he had expressed wouldn't cause undue antagonism.

George was surprised to hear Humphrey's candid opinions, as this was the first time he had heard him open up in this way.

"I think there is a great deal of truth in what you have said. I would just put this to you: there are people of all classes and levels of intellect who have perfect manners; and there are some in the elite who are incredibly rude. You have spoken of natural leaders. I am speaking of natural gentlemen and gentlewomen."

Humphrey said: "I think you have a very good point about manners. But perhaps manners aren't everything. Natural leaders have to be rude sometimes in order to get things done."

"You have a good point there yourself," said George. "I think we are largely in agreement. What do you think, Christine?"

Having been uncharacteristically quiet, Christine was keen to have her say.

"I do like good manners," she said. "I hate the way some people behave these days. They just have no respect for others. It all starts in the home, I think. Parents need to teach their children good manners, but that's difficult if the parents don't have any manners themselves. That's where the schools should come in, and, I know it's unfashionable to say so, the churches.

"Manners are surely about kindness and consideration to other people and that's what the Christian religion teaches us. We need a religious revival in this country in my opinion. There are too many ministers in the church who are just glorified social workers. They should spend more of their time preaching the gospels and less time trying to be all things to all men."

"Was Christ showing good manners when he overthrew the tables of the money changers in the temple?" asked Humphrey.

Christine replied: "As you said, manners are good but they aren't everything."

"Okay," said George. "Perhaps I have to concede to both of you that manners aren't everything. But my standpoint is that they are damned near everything if we wish to live in a relatively civilised and peaceful world. Anyway, shall we get some lunch somewhere?"

That option pleased everyone and so they soon retired for a pleasant bar meal at the Mucky Duck.

They spent a very enjoyable afternoon, exchanging anecdotes and appreciating that they had much more in common than they would ever have imagined.

Humphrey, often seen as hail-fellow-well met but lacking in gravitas, had revealed inner depths and some surprisingly controversial opinions and Christine showed there was much more to her than a domineering, if good-hearted, gossip. In fact this was all down to George Plunkett, who in everyday life as well as in his teaching career had the quality of being able to draw out people's true characters.

At the end of the convivial afternoon the unlikely trio pledged to do it all again in the near future.

****

The time came for Penelope to return to Stratford-upon-Avon.

She had been nervous about going home as she had no clue as what to expect. She had not seen or heard anything from her husband since he had put the phone down on her shortly after the Hayfleet incident.

Hector agreed to go to Stratford with her and they travelled in convoy in their cars. Penelope had phoned the landline at her home and Stuart's mobile but there had been no response. She had also contacted her daughters, but they too knew nothing of their father's whereabouts.

It was therefore with a great deal of apprehension that Penelope and Hector arrived at the house on a wet October afternoon.

Penelope gingerly unlocked the front door and opened it. In the lounge they found a trail of empty bottles of beer and spirits both on furniture and across the floor.

Penelope shouted Stuart's name while Hector searched around the house. He wasn't at home.

At first this gave them a sense of relief. But this was short-lived as they began to weigh up what might happen next. If Stuart had been there at least they would have known what his state of mind was and faced up to any dangers he might have presented. Now they were in a quandary about what to do next. If Hector left Penelope there alone then Stuart could turn up at any time, with unknown consequences. However, if Hector stayed with her this might provoke her husband into one of his worst tempers.

They tried again to phone and message him but there was still no reply. It was decision time.

Hector felt it he needed to live up to his name and be the hero.

"I can't just leave you here. I'll stay until you can find out what's going on."

"You don't have to do this, you know," said Penelope. "I feel so stupid. I like to think I'm always in control. But I have to confess that I'm scared. I would like you to stay, if you're sure you don't mind."

"Of course I don't mind."

****

Night falls and they entertain themselves by playing Scrabble. Their minds are not on the game, though, and their scores are low.

It's 10 o'clock and there's a call on Penelope's mobile phone. It's Stuart.

"Hi, Penelope. I got your message. I'm on my way home."

He sounds drunk.

"You've not been drinking have you?" says Penelope.

"I've had a couple. But I'm not drunk."

"You're not driving are you?"

"Yes, darling. I am. But I'm not drunk."

"You sound it. Please don't drive. You're not driving now are you?"

"Stop bloody whinging, will you? I'm fine. I'll be home in a minute."

Penelope covers her phone and says to Hector: "He's nearly home. He's drunk and he's driving."

"Oh god," says Hector.

"You must go, quickly. He'll go berserk if he finds you here."

"I won't leave you. Who knows what he might do?"

"I'll try to humour him."

She picks up her phone again.

"Stuart, come home then, but please drive carefully."

"I heard you talking to somebody just then. Who was it?"

"Oh, it's just Hector Ratcliffe. He was kind enough to see me back home. He's leaving any minute now."

"Bloody Hector Ratcliffe. Is he sniffing round again?"

"Don't be ridiculous. Of course he isn't sniffing round. He's just been a helpful friend and now he's on his way back to Sanderholme."

"I don't bloody believe you," he shouts angrily. "I'll sort him out in a minute."

"Oh, Stuart, no."

He ends the call.

"Lock the front door and leave your key in the lock so his key won't work," says Hector. "Can we get out by the back door?"

"Yes, but then what?" asks Penelope.

Just then there is a tremendous crash and the sound of glass shattering. Wood and bricks come flying towards Hector and Penelope. Lumps of the ceiling crash down in front of them. Everything seems to be in slow motion.

To their horror they see a car has smashed through the lounge wall and window and is lodged half way into the room and half way out of it.

A cloud of dust envelopes them and they both start coughing. Hector grabs Penelope by the arm and drags her into the kitchen. She is shocked and crying.

Hector sits her down on a kitchen chair and then dashes back into the lounge. He looks in through the car's front window and sees Stuart slumped motionless over the steering wheel of the yellow Porsche. Blood is running down his face. Benson is jumping up at the side of the car and whining loudly, concerned about the master who cares so little for him.

Hector takes his mobile phone out of his pocket and taps out 999, asking for an ambulance and police. Having given the necessary details he returns to the kitchen and explains to Penelope that Stuart is in the car and looks in a bad way.

She rushes through into the lounge to see for herself.

"Stuart, Stuart. Are you all right?"

There's no response.

An ambulance arrives within ten minutes. The crew members see that Stuart is trapped and call for the fire brigade. The fire crew cut him out of the car and he is stretchered into the ambulance. He is unconscious but Penelope is given reassurance that he doesn't seem to be badly injured.

While this is going on the police arrive and collect statements from Penelope and Hector. They also give them contact details for a breakdown service for removal of the car and a joiner who can secure the house until proper repairs can be carried out.

The ambulance takes Stuart to the accident and emergency department at Warwick Hospital. Hector and Penelope follow on in Hector's car.

When they arrive at the hospital, they are greeted by police officers who tell them they have taken a blood sample from Stuart to determine whether he has been drink driving. Then a nurse tells Penelope that he has regained consciousness. She goes to the ward to see him, leaving Hector alone in a waiting room.

****

When Penelope returned after half an hour, she looked tense and upset and Hector's immediate reaction was to hug her.

She explained that Stuart had only superficial cuts to his head, with the possibility that he might suffer from whiplash later. It was expected that he would be discharged from hospital the next day.

"Did he say much about what happened?" asked Hector.

"Yes, he claimed that he accidentally put his foot on the accelerator rather than the brake. That's his story. I don't believe him for a moment.

"He's blaming me for it all. He admits he was driving too fast in a temper because I had invited you into our house. He's just incapable of accepting how badly he has behaved."

"He's an absolute bastard," said Hector.

"What am I going to do?" asked Penelope. "I'm scared of going back home to be alone with him."

"I'll stay with you," said Hector.

"No, Hector. You can't possibly do that. It will make him even more aggressive. Heaven knows what he might do. He might kill you."

"Then why not come back home to Sanderholme with me? I could protect you there."

"He would just come and look for us. Although he neglects me and is horrible to me he's still possessive. He would hate the thought of me being with anyone else. You can see from tonight how violent his temper can be. There's nothing he would stop at doing."

"I do understand what you are saying," said Hector. "But what other alternatives are there? Could you stay with one of your daughters for the time being?"

"Stuart would probably just follow me there and insist

I went back home."

"What about getting police protection from him?"

"I'm not convinced that would work either. When he's drunk and in a temper nothing would stop him. The thing with Stuart is that he's fearless. He's won bravery medals for it in the army. I used to admire that about him, but this is the downside."

"I can be fearless too," said Hector, a statement which not only surprised Penelope a little but also surprised Hector to hear himself saying it. "Please let me take you back to Sanderholme and I promise to do everything I can to look after you.

"Marry me."

Penelope looked startled by this new bombshell.

Pausing to help restore her usual equilibrium, she replied calmly: "I can't marry you. I'm already married, as you know."

"Then get a divorce."

"You know my views on divorce. I've taken a vow and in all conscience I can't break it."

"Then just come and live with me. I will always love you. Whether we were married or not it would be 'till death us do part' as far as I am concerned."

Penelope looked at him with her most serious expression and whispered: "I love you too. Very much. And I really appreciate what you have offered to do for me. Right now, though, I think we need to get back to Stratford to my broken house."

Hector kissed her on the cheek and nodded in agreement.

****

When they arrived back at Penelope's house in the early hours of the morning, they found that the Porsche had been extricated from the lounge and the walls and window boarded up. The lounge remained in a calamitous state, covered in dust and debris, with broken furniture, ruined carpets and curtains and smashed ornaments.

Penelope viewed the scene in desolation.

"I can't bear to look at this," she said. "Let's get some sleep and decide what to do when we wake up."

In their separate bedrooms Penelope and Hector had sleepless nights for very different reasons. Penelope was wracked with worry about what would happen next. She was certain that an extremely unpleasant confrontation with Stuart awaited her later that day. Hector, on the other hand, was in a state of ecstasy. For the very first time Penelope had told him she loved him. At the worst he might be murdered within the next few hours, but even if that should happen he would die happy in the knowledge that his life's ambition had been achieved. The woman he loves loves him.

After a few hours of this sleep deprivation they swiftly breakfasted together. Hector made tea and Penelope produced bowls of cereals. As they sat opposite each other at the kitchen table, Penelope put her hand on his and said gently: "I will."

"Will what?"

"Come back to Sanderholme with you – and live with you."

Hector beams: "For ever?"

"Always. At least that's what I had in mind."

Hector's initial reaction to this news was to smile the biggest smile he had ever smiled. Then the more pragmatic side of his nature kicked in, as he started to consider the practical problems of the life-changing decisions they had just taken. What would happen regarding Penelope's very good position as partner in a successful firm of solicitors? What would happen to the house which she and Stuart owned jointly? What would her daughters think about her upping sticks and moving away from the area where they all lived? Who would have custody of Benson?

When he put these questions to Penelope it was clear that she had already thought of the answers herself. She said she would leave the law firm where she had already stayed on past normal retirement age and would be content to have a change of direction. Ownership of the house and its contents would be sorted out through the legal separation process. Her daughters would be supportive and anyway would be only three hours away. And, of course, Benson would come with her.

Hector was happy to agree to all of this. He was impressed that in all the chaos of the last few hours she had come to such common-sense solutions.

"We can have a lovely time together. I promise we'll enjoy ourselves and we'll embrace each other's families," he gushes.

Even though little had been eaten, it had been a very productive breakfast. Now they must hurry away before Stuart's return.

He leant over and kissed her on the lips.

****

There was no time to lose now. Penelope scurried around the house collecting those clothes and other important personal belongings which she needed to take away with her. Hector meanwhile was charged with boxing up Benson's accessories, including food, bowls, leads, beds, balls and cuddly toys.

They filled up both of their cars and were away by ten o'clock. Any fears they might have had about Stuart's next moves, were, for the present at least, secondary to feelings of excitement they both had about the prospect of a new life together.

Three hours later they arrived at Hector's house, unpacked the car and sat down to eat a lunch of fish and chips they had picked up from a sea front shop on their way.

On the journey home Penelope had phoned daughters Jane and Sarah to tell them everything which had happened. Although both had expressed concern about their father's condition, they had given their mother the full backing which she had hoped for and expected.

Over the next few days Penelope and Hector were on tenterhooks expecting some violent reaction from Stuart. But there was none.

Penelope contacted a colleague at her firm to set up the legal separation process, which she expected to take at least four months. She pointed out to Hector that it would normally be a bad idea for her to start a new relationship until the separation was sorted out. But it didn't take much persuasion for her to agree that

Hector's protection outweighed this consideration.

Three weeks went by and still there was no contact from Stuart. Jane and Sarah had both phoned, texted and emailed him but with no success.

Hector found himself strangely conflicted at this time. On the one hand he felt nervous about what Stuart's next move might be. He knew that if it came to any kind of violent confrontation he would be on the back foot against the physically strong, bad-tempered war hero. Despite his heroic first name he had never been a fighting man and had absolutely no skills in the martial arts. On the other hand, he was no coward and instinctively knew that if he, Penelope or any family member or friend came under threat, he would face up to whatever challenge presented itself.

However, he also felt rather ashamed that he had scuttled back to Sanderholme with Penelope as quickly as possible in order to avoid Stuart. He tried to convince himself that he only behaved in that way because Penelope was fearful of meeting her husband. But he knew that wasn't true. He was a coward, a disgrace to the name his parents had given him. They should have called him Paris instead, after Hector's feckless and rather cowardly younger brother.

Then he is reminded that in "The Iliad" even Hector, the super hero, had some less than valorous moments, fleeing twice from Ajax and once from Achilles. Once from Achilles! Having remembered this he snapped out of his mood of self-flagellation. After all, whatever might have happened between Hector and Achilles, Hector was clearly the better man.

Having temporarily settled his mind in this way, his thoughts strayed in a different direction. It suddenly struck him that his obsession with the Trojan war, which may have never even happened, was childish and immature. As an Englishman born in the 20th century what on earth had a war fought more than 3000 years ago, and even maybe just a myth, got to do with him? Prosaically, he was only interested in that conflict because his father had been even more fixated by it, so much so that he insisted on his only son being named after its premier hero.

Hector told himself he finally had to grow up and live in the present with its real tribulations and challenges. In truth he was deluding himself. He would never completely break away from his childhood obsession with the Classical world or from his father's strong and largely beneficent influence. It went to the very core of his personality.

One day Hector and Penelope received a welcome telephone call from her mother inviting them to another Sunday lunch at Hayfleet. This time, though, the only people present would be the three of them together with Pamela's grandson Timothy Grenville. He lived at the Douglas Home farmhouse and had been a great prop to his grandmother since Richard died.

Timothy was a handsome 40-year-old, wiry, above average height, deeply tanned and with neat black hair. He could easily have passed as actor Ty Hardin, of the Bronco Layne TV Western series, with an added black moustache. He was charming, honest and friendly and had proved to be a very good farmer.

He was now running two farms, the Douglas Home Farm and Bank Farm, which he had inherited from Derek Stanmore. He also managed the small caravan site at the old Havenside Farm.

He had been away at a National Farmers' Union conference when the previous eventful Sunday lunch had been held, so this would be the first time Hector had met him since Derek's funeral.

Timothy and Pamela gave their guests a warm welcome and another splendid lunch was enjoyed.

In the postprandial conversations, Timothy and Hector got on famously, finding that their respective interests in farming, nature conservation and the caravan trade had many areas of overlap. It helped that Penelope and her mother were interested in these subjects too.

Inevitably the discussion at one point got round to Stuart and his latest bad behaviour. Timothy clearly shared the general Douglas family view that the army captain had badly let down both himself and his wife and put himself completely beyond redemption.

Hector showed Timothy a mobile phone picture he had taken of the destruction which Stuart's car had wreaked in the Stratford house.

Timothy looked carefully at the photo and after a few moments of deep thought asked to look at it again. Having had his second look he passed the phone back to Hector and said nothing for a few moments.

Then he remarked: "It's certainly a distinctive car. How long has he had it?"

"Only about a couple of months. He bought it new from a garage in Solihull. It was his pride and joy. He nearly broke the bank with it – and now look at the state of it. The idiot," replied Penelope.

"Just let me have another look," said Timothy. "I can't believe what he did."

Timothy, who had previously been bright and loquacious, now became curiously detached from the conversations. Hector was looking closely at him as he had sensed the sudden change in the farmer's mood.

The talk moved on to Penelope's intention to separate from Stuart and what would happen to the Stratford house.

Then Timothy changed the subject back to the car.

"Was Stuart around this area about a month ago?" he asked.

"The last time he was here was when he came on that Sunday when we had lunch here," said Penelope.

"I was away then. Is that the only time he's been over?"

"As far as I'm aware," said Penelope. "Why do you ask?"

"Oh, it doesn't matter," replied Timothy.

"It does matter, Timothy," she said. "Anything about Stuart matters at the moment. It's important for me to know where he has been and what he has done."

"I just thought I recognised the car. It's the sort of car you would remember. There aren't many yellow Porsches around here. And the number plate seemed familiar – WG. I'm probably wrong though. Forget about it."

"It's a personalised number plate. WG stands for Welsh Guards – Stuart's regiment," said Penelope, becoming very interested in what Timothy might know. "Where do you think you might have seen it?"

"I thought I saw it along Havenside Lane a couple of times," he said.

"About a month ago?"

"About then. It might have been a little longer ago than that."

"That's strange. But perhaps it's not so strange. I never did know what he was up to most of the time," said Penelope.

The matter was dropped as Penelope said she would have to go to the kitchen to help Pamela clear up after the meal.

When mother and daughter were alone, Pamela's thoughts turned to the "pep talk" she had received from Aunt Christine when they met at the church. Although not entirely impressed by Christine's interference in her daughter's love life, she had taken on board the basic message and actually agreed with it.

"Are you and Hector still getting on well?" she asked Penelope.

"Yes we are, mum. Very well. He's so kind and considerate. Such a contrast to my husband."

"I like him too, dear," said Pamela. "Have you thought that perhaps you might have a future together?"

"Yes, I have mum. Yes, I think we will."

"Then you should marry him."

"I am married."

"I know, dear, that both of us have always said that divorce is out of the question for us because we believe in the sanctity of marriage and that it's for life," said

Pamela. "But there are times when sticking to a principle willy-nilly is cutting off the nose to spite the face. And I think this is one of those times. Stuart has disqualified himself from being your husband by the way he has treated you for years. Have you and Hector discussed marriage at all?"

"Yes, we have. And I know he would love to marry me."

"Well, there we are then. A separation is all very well but it can go on for years. Better to make a clean break."

"I will give it some thought, mum. I'm grateful for your opinion."

When Hector and Penelope arrived home that evening they discussed what Timothy had said about seeing Stuart's car on Havenside Lane. It was a lane to nowhere and they could not fathom why he would have bothered to drive along there.

"Perhaps he was taking a look at Bank Farm, now there's more of a family interest in it," suggested Hector.

Penelope shook her head, saying that he had never shown any interest in the farm or farming in general.

Just then the doorbell rang and Hector shepherded in his son, Troy.

He had come to ask his father for a day off work the following week so he could take part in a golf tournament.

Penelope asked him if he played at Sanderholme Golf Club and he said he was currently the club captain.

"Are you? That's great. You must be a very good player," said Penelope.

Troy didn't reply, smiling modestly.

"You must know my husband, Stuart Broadlake. He's a member at your club."

"Dad's told me about him but I don't believe I know him," said Troy. "Is he a new member?"

"Fairly new, I suppose. I think he joined about a year ago."

"I don't recall him at all. I do know most of the members."

Penelope took her phone from her handbag and showed Troy a photo of Stuart.

"No, sorry. He's quite a distinctive looking man. But I don't recall him, or the name Broadlake from the membership for that matter. But perhaps my memory's going."

"Perhaps so," said Penelope, looking perplexed.

After Troy had left, Penelope and Hector had even more to discuss. They were increasingly puzzled by Stuart's behaviour.

****

Two weeks later, on an unseasonably warm autumn day, Timothy is hosing down the crew yard at Bank Farm when a woman's voice calls: "That looks thirsty work. Fancy a nice refreshing lager?"

Timothy turns off the hose and walks over to the farmhouse where the voice has come from.

A tall, slim, attractive woman emerges from the back door of the house, carrying a half pint beer glass. She is wearing tight white trousers revealing shapely long legs and a white, almost transparent, tie-front blouse.

The woman is Tricia Stanmore, now in her sixties, but

looking not a day above 40.

They sit opposite each other at an outdoor table and Timothy thanks her for the drink. He is sweating from his hard work and sinks the beer very quickly.

She smiles at him in a fetching manner, touches his hand and says: "Are you coming inside today?"

He returns her smile and she leads him inside the house and straight up the stairs into a bedroom.

They both hurriedly strip naked revealing their well-honed bodies. Timothy is bronzed and muscular and Tricia lily white with smooth, flawless skin. They clamber on to a double bed and are quickly into passionate love-making, both purring with pleasure, when suddenly the bedroom door is flung open.

The large frame of Stuart Broadlake looms over them.

"What the hell's going on?" he shouts.

Timothy leaps off the bed and tries to guide Stuart out of the room.

"I think you need to leave us," he says.

Stuart leans backwards and lands a heavy punch on Timothy, his large knuckles pounding into the younger man's right eye.

"Stuart, leave him alone," screams Tricia.

But the larger man then knees Timothy in the stomach and leaves him winded on the bedroom floor.

Broadlake goes down the stairs, followed by Tricia, still naked.

"You must go," she says.

"Don't worry. I am going. Bitch."

He slaps her hard across the cheek and then charges out of the back door.

****

That same evening Hector and Penelope were sharing a bottle of wine in the conservatory overlooking the patio at Hector's house when a Range Rover arrived in the driveway. Timothy got out and walked over to the conservatory door. He had a swollen black eye and a plaster over his eyebrow.

"Blimey," said Hector. "What have you been up to?"

Timothy, who usually had a ready smile and cheery demeanour, looked strangely serious.

"May I sit down? I've got something to tell you," he said.

"Of course," said Hector. "Sit down here. Would you like a glass of wine?"

"No thanks," said Timothy.

"I'll tell you why I'm sporting this black eye. It's all very embarrassing, but I feel I need to be honest with you."

Hector and Penelope looked bemused.

"To start with, a confession. I've been having – what shall I call it? – a bit of an affair with Tricia Stanmore."

"Tricia!" said Hector. "A great looking woman."

"Yes. I was with her this morning and, well, something happened. To come straight to the point, your husband, Penelope, came bursting in and did this to me."

"Stuart?" said Penelope incredulously.

"Yes, I'm afraid so," said Timothy. "To cut a long story short he's been having an affair with Tricia himself and he was in a jealous rage."

"Oh god!" said Penelope. "What next? I wonder how long that's been going on?"

"Tricia said for about a year."

Penelope, deep in thought, went quiet for a few seconds and then said: "It's all beginning to fit into place now. That's why you saw his car going down to Havenside."

"Yes, to be honest I had actually seen the car parked at Bank Farm a couple of times. So when I saw your photo of it crashed into your house I put two and two together. But I didn't want to make any accusations because, although I might have had some suspicions, I really had no proof then that anything was going on between your husband and Tricia.

"I'm sorry to have to tell you this. I feel I owe it to you as a relative and a friend to put you fully in the picture. And I can assure you I'll be keeping to the farmyard and out of the farmhouse in future. It's too dangerous."

Penelope said she was grateful for his honesty. Hector asked Timothy if he had reported the assault to the police.

"No, I was playing with fire and I just want to forget about the whole episode. I'm sure there's no permanent damage done."

"Are you sure?" asked Penelope. "Your eye looks dreadful."

"I think it'll be okay. But if it isn't I'll go and see a doctor. Let's not involve the police, though. As I said, I'm quite embarrassed about it all."

"Very well," said Hector. "Now will you have a glass of wine?"

"Yes, I will now. Thank you."

Learning about what had happened at Bank Farm was

the spur which goaded Penelope to decide that divorce was her way forward. She was no longer trapped by her fine principles. Pragmatism had won the day. She contacted her legal colleagues the next day to start the proceedings.

During the following months Penelope and Hector were in a constant state of apprehension. On his past form they expected either further violent reactions from Stuart or perhaps even a late renaissance of the charming side of his character in an effort to win Penelope back. Surprisingly they got neither. They never saw or heard from him in person, merely receiving letters from his solicitors accepting the reality of the divorce.

It was all something of a mystery until Penelope received a phone call from her daughter Jane. Stuart had visited her the previous day and introduced a new woman friend. The extrovert 50-year-old was the landlady at his old local pub at Guilford, not far from the army barracks at Pirbright where he used to be based. From Jane's account it seemed that he was in a happy mood, content with his new lot and unlikely to cause Penelope any more trouble.

Chapter eleven – Synchronicity

Fast forward twelve months…

It is a beautiful July afternoon and the sound of a string quartet wafts across the garden of Douglas Home Farm. It is coming from a large marquee in the grass field next to the house.

Inside, more than one hundred guests are celebrating the marriage of Hector and Penelope.

Penelope looks every inch the mature English rose in her ivory lace A-line bridal gown, while Hector has an immaculate grey three-piece suit with top hat and tails.

In stunning matching dresses are Penelope's bridesmaids, her 10-year-old granddaughter Petra, daughter of Jane, and Hector's granddaughters Tilly, 14, and Robina, 12. The page boys are Troy's son, Peter, and Sarah's son, Ralph.

Looking resplendent in their own suits and top hats are Hector's two best men, Humphrey Gibb and Matthew Copson.

The mothers look their best too. Pamela is escorted by Timothy, and Margaret, now in a wheelchair, is being pushed by Aunt Christine who has the most spectacular hat on display that day, comprising bright red leaves and feathers to match her red dress. She has baked a special cake of makeup for the big occasion.

Everyone has been keen to meet Jodie's son, Jason. He brings a tear to Margaret's eye, looking, as he does, like a handsome carbon copy of Charles as a young man.

Bringing up the rear of these important guests is none other than George Plunkett, looking his usual debonair self in a grey three-piece suit topped off with a pink carnation. He and Aunt Christine had developed a close friendship in the preceding months and he had been invited to the wedding at her instigation.

It is a typical English country wedding breakfast with traditional English food and a friendly warm-hearted atmosphere. Penelope is a practising Anglican but as a divorcee has been unable to remarry in her local church. Although the ceremony has been held in Sanderholme Register Office, the vicar of Hayfleet, Father Henry, is among the guests and, after some cajoling by Aunt Christine, has agreed to bless the union at a later date.

Hector's wedding speech is a tour de force. He has always been exceptionally well read but far too well-mannered in his later years to let everyone know about it. But now he cannot let his moment of triumph pass without producing a scintillating performance, full of wit and teeming with literary, historical and mythological allusions.

He has a surprise in store for the guests when he declares he has a very special announcement to make.

"I have some breaking news for you all. I have just been told – and on good authority (my mother) – the wonderful news that my dear Aunt Christine has become engaged to my favourite school master, Mr George Plunkett."

A loud cheer goes up.

"Now much as we welcome this great news, we should not get too excited yet, as I have to warn you all, and particularly you, George, that this is at least the sixth time that my aunt has been engaged to be married, and that she has yet to walk down the aisle of a church as a married woman.

"I also have to tell you there is a great irony in this as over the years she has had considerable success in arranging marriages for other people.

"Those of us who were lucky enough to have attended Sanderholme Grammar School know what an inspirational teacher and great man Mr Plunkett is and so I am sure that we will all be filled with trepidation that he will fall under the influence of my esteemed aunt and will never have another minute's peace."

"You horrible boy!" Christine interjected in mock outrage.

"No, no," says George. *"Hanging and wiving goes by destiny"* – 'The Merchant of Venice'."

Christine whacks him on the head with her large handbag.

Hector continues in a literary vein, finishing his speech with a heartfelt plea to Penelope, straight from the mouth of his beloved Wordsworth: "Come grow old with me. The best is yet to be."

****

A great deal had been organised in the past year. Coincidentally, Hector and Penelope both had unfulfilled dreams of living in the countryside. They were also up for a new challenge. And, in what could perhaps be described as a perfect example of synchronicity, both had looked longingly for a number of years at the Havenside Farmhouse with its small caravan site next to the Marsh Eau river. The house was a substantial one but had been uninhabited and neglected badly since Penelope's grandfather had died many years earlier. What had been the living room was now used as a reception for the caravan site, but the rest of the building was empty and unloved.

The house had an extensive garden, with a fine orchard and plenty of space for growing vegetables, something which appealed to Penelope in particular.

Pamela agreed that following their marriage the couple could live in the house and run the caravan site, allowing Timothy to concentrate on the two farms. So they had spent the past few months supervising the renovation and furnishing of the farmhouse.

After the wedding Troy and his family were to move into Hector's house and Troy was to take full control of the Marshview Caravan Site.

****

A week before the wedding Hector had enjoyed a low key "stag do", meeting up with friends and relations at Sanderholme's Buckthorn Arms, still a flourishing venue when so many other pubs which he had frequented in his youth had long since closed down.

After a three-course meal and a few rounds of drinks to toast the bridegroom-to-be, only three guests remained, Hector and his bosom pals Matthew and Humphrey. They continued drinking and were in a mellow, reflective mood as the early hours of the morning approached.

Matthew had passed an interesting but drama-free life, having married young to Sally, Bernice's friend they had met in the Stag's Head all those years ago. He had retired comfortably from his most recent post as Editor of the Sanderholme Times, where his son was following in his footsteps and was now working as chief reporter. Matthew and Sally lived quietly in his late parents' old home in Sanderholme, where he had passed his childhood. He was basically contented with his lot, but still possessed a deep-grained cynicism which prevented him from presenting a totally sunny disposition.

Humphrey had sailed through a life with lots of ups and downs with his carefree personality intact. The main "downs" had related to the fact that he had nailed his colours to his father's mast too many times. Mr Gibb Snr, the professional financial adviser, had run numerous businesses over the years, making and losing millions of pounds in the process and eventually dying as a bankrupt. His son had worked for him in most of these enterprises and as a result his own fortunes had ebbed and flowed in step with his father's. He had always managed to keep up appearances, though, dressing as a toff, pursuing a variety of country sports and taking expensive holidays with his family in the years when funds allowed.

The one constant in his life was his wife, Esme, who stayed stoically loyal in the difficult times and enjoyed life to the full in the better periods. They had been blessed with a son and a daughter, and now had two little grandchildren on whom Humphrey doted.

When the three chums managed to get together, once or twice a year, they had a lot to talk about. There was a great deal of discussion on "the old times" and much "putting the world to rights". They had many lively arguments but these were always conducted in good humour and never became personal. However, they did enjoy shocking each other with controversial remarks to help set these debates alight.

On this particular night, the discussion turned to the relative merits of the fifties and sixties: the decades when they enjoyed their childhoods and their youth.

Hector championed the fifties, liking the calm and certainty of the decade, where there was still respect for authority and for elders. Like his Aunt Christine, he believed the United Kingdom had been in decline "ever since The Beatles".

Matthew, on the other hand, was a supporter of the sixties, saying that was a time of opportunity for young working-class people, liberated from the stuffy hierarchical structures of the past.

Humphrey had no preference for either of these decades, or for any other decade before or since. His view was that positive, active and fun-loving people, such as himself, would enjoy themselves whatever decade, or century, they happened to live in.

Eventually their conversation, as it always did, turned to Cecil Roberts.

On this occasion, though, the discussion was a sad one, as their hero and honorary president had passed away peacefully a few months earlier.

If Hector was the real hero of "The Iliad", then perhaps Cecil Roberts is the real hero of this story. He was a man to whom Fortune had dealt a very bad hand in his early years. Consigned to a mental institution for half of his life, Cecil had emerged into the real world as a virginal greenhorn, a novice in the affairs of men.

His distrust of other people and his almost brutal view of sex and human relationships smacked of someone who had suffered some form of abuse in the institution to which he had been so unfairly confined.

Despite all of this he survived with his head held high, being creditably self-sufficient and facing his life's towering obstacles with searing honesty, astonishing courage and a self-confidence born of naivety. His unusual character, and especially his eccentric ideas and abrupt manner of speech, made him a figure of much amusement within the Sanderholme community. But people loved him and respected him as a fundamentally decent human being, striving valiantly in the world where the odds were stacked so heavily against him.

Not Hector, not Achilles, but a true 20th century hero, born in the underclass but struggling to become a valued working man.

"Who would have thought, all those years ago, that Cecil would still be in our lives until so recently?" said Matthew.

"We owe you a great deal for looking after him so well for all these years," said Humphrey to Hector.

"He was a nice old boy, right up until the end," replied Hector. "I had my doubts about him when his first wife died so suddenly, but he proved to be a good loyal friend to our family, and to everyone on the caravan site."

This had been borne out when his simple funeral service at Sanderholme Crematorium had been attended by hundreds of people, including many caravan owners from the Marshview site, a large contingent from the Pentecostal Church, and, of course, the entire membership of the Mad Hatters' Cecil Roberts Appreciation Society, Sanderholme branch.

A star guest at the service was Ajax, Cecil's beloved Staffy, who lay quietly at Hector's side throughout. Cecil maintained to the very end that he had no friends, but very many begged to differ.

The three friends sat in silence for a few minutes as they contemplated the phenomenon that was Cecil Roberts. Then Hector said: "Do you know, I believe I might not have been getting married next week had it not been for Cecil?"

"How come?" asked Matthew.

"One day Penelope met Cecil outside my house and he told her that she should marry me. That was even though she was married to Stuart at the time! But, you know Cecil – straight John Bull as they used to say.

"Penelope actually told me that his advice had done more than anything else to open her eyes and decide where her future lay."

"Incredible," said Humphrey. "But entirely believable."

He proposed a toast: "To Cecil, a true gent, wherever you are."

The three friends shook hands and vowed that after the wedding they would meet again very soon – at the annual general meeting of the Mad Hatters' Cecil Roberts Appreciation Society, Sanderholme branch.

Chapter twelve – Hector's reckoning

Fast forward nine years…

It was a gloomy evening in June 2019, and in Lincolnshire two months of rain had fallen in just two days.

Hector looked out of his bedroom window and saw that the normally benign Marsh Eau river was menacingly swollen and fast flowing. The water was muddy brown and was carrying along pieces of green vegetation, straw and wood which it had scoured from the banks.

The Environment Agency had put out a severe flood warning and so he had been busy throughout the day handing out sandbags to caravan owners on the Havenside site and placing others up against the outside doors of his house. All he could do now was wait and hope that there would be no overtopping of the river.

Penelope joined Hector at a bedroom window as he continued his vigil throughout the evening. Heavy rain was forecast for around midnight. And rain it did – in torrents. The couple looked on in horror as the water breached the bank with such force that it upended several caravans which were closest to the river. But it didn't stop there: within just a few seconds it swamped the lawn in front of the farmhouse, caused havoc to Penelope's beloved kitchen garden and then swept aside sandbags to enter the kitchen and dining room on the ground floor.

Hector and Penelope were powerless and had little choice but to shelter upstairs as the flooding did thousands of pounds worth of damage to their home.

Next morning by wading through a foot of water they managed to leave the house by the back door. The sight which greeted them was shocking. The caravan site was completely under water to a level halfway up the side of the vans. Owners had managed to evacuate the night before. Some had managed to book in at local hotels while others had spent the night in their vehicles along the nearby lane. Now they had returned to survey the doleful scene.

Some caravans were write-offs and all of them suffered considerable damage.

There was a lengthy clear-up operation to undertake, with both Troy and Timothy providing sterling assistance.

For Hector and Penelope and for van owners, it was to be several months before insurance claims had been settled and there was to be any semblance of a return to normality.

Hector and Penelope were resilient people and were looking forward to a successful new season in 2020. Their Havenside site was looking inviting again and the Marshview site at Sanderholme, from which they derived the lion's share of their income, had been unaffected by the floods.

In the September following the flood Hector had taken an evening walk on his familiar route along the riverbank, from his home towards the coast.

He was immediately struck by the eerie silence. There was no birdsong, no ducks quacking and splashing and none of the usual plops caused by fish jumping. The river was lifeless and brown. The surface of the water was undisturbed either by darting small fry or busy insects, and there were no bubbles caused by bottom feeding fish.

When he was a young boy his father would sometimes take him fishing on the Marsh Eau. Their favourite spot was next to the bridge which took a private farm road across the river. The bank was less steep there than in most stretches and there were some excellent nooks in which to place a fishing basket. Hector was saddened to see that these spots had disappeared. In their place was forbidding looking rock armour strengthened by mesh to protect the bank against future flooding.

Towards the end of his outward journey Hector walked past the shed where his friend Derek had lived for so many years. It was a forlorn sight, almost flattened and in pieces, presumably a victim of the flood. A stark reminder of the transience of man's life.

As North American author Marty Rubin wrote: *"Time is a river that carries us along. We have to leave everything behind."*

Hector began to feel that Nature had abandoned the Marsh Eau river. The floods must have frightened away the resident River God. Death was in the air. But even recognising this, his spirits could not be dampened. He had been literally "living the dream" with Penelope for more than nine years and nothing, not even the prospect of death itself, could overcome his deep feeling of joy.

He thought of a line by John Donne: *"Only our love hath no decay."*

As he continued his walk two things happened which

filled him with hope. Soundlessly, two muntjac deer airily tiptoed across the ploughed field opposite the riverbank and disappeared into a copse. Then in the water next to the far bank there was a single heavy splash indicating a large fish jumping, probably a tench. Nature was, after all, still engaged in its eternal struggle against Death. Perhaps in time she would be victorious and the River God would come out of hiding.

Then, in February 2020, came Storm Dennis, described as "one of the most intense extratropical cyclones ever recorded". The usual flood warnings were issued and the Marsh Eau again looked threatening. There was no overtopping this time, but furious gusts of winds of up to 90 miles per hour again disrupted the caravan site. Vans, although well anchored, were blown on to their sides. Slates were blown off the roof of the house, leaving a gaping hole above the main bedroom.

Hector and Penelope were faced with more bills and headaches and a second major clear-up. This was all completed in time for the opening of the site at the beginning of March. The couple were gratified by the patience and loyalty shown by the van owners, who recognised that in "normal" times the well-equipped site was an idyllic location.

All was set again for the season. From the first weekend of the month the site began to buzz as owners arrived to open up their vans. Spring cleaning was done inside, and outside decking was being scrubbed down and painted. Hector was busy delivering Calor Gas, repairing fencing damaged by the storm and generally making himself useful to the customers. Penelope manned the reception and assisted the capable local woman who ran the bar and tearoom situated in a converted barn next to the house.

The birds were singing and the river sparkled and looked happy in the bright sunlight.

Then there was coronavirus.

The "season" came to an abrupt halt on 24th March as the site had to be closed, holidaymakers went home and Hector and Penelope went into lockdown in the house. For the first few days they were miserable and frustrated. They loved their business and way of life they had created at Havenside and resented the trials and tribulations which had recently afflicted them.

However, after the first week of isolation their mood lifted and, now they had the time and opportunity for contemplation, they began to count their blessings.

For Hector there was an overwhelming feeling of smugness that here he was, after all these years, in lockdown with the woman he had loved since he was a teenager. If perfection was possible in this world, then this was it.

He looked back with some wry amusement at his youthful obsessions with Greek concepts of love: *eros, ludus, agape* – none of those were for him. He had for years nurtured a modern, Western-style, romantic affair with an English beauty.

Penelope, after years of heartache and turbulence, felt at peace with a man she had come to love dearly and whom she trusted with her life. If a tinge of sadness remained, it was only because she wished she had appreciated Hector all those years ago at Sanderholme

Grammar School. Her earlier life could have been so much better.

During the coronavirus lockdown the couple spent their days in a leisurely fashion such as neither of them had found time to experience previously. They rose at whatever time suited them and breakfasted at their ease while watching daytime television. They pottered in the garden, pottered on the caravan site, pottered in the kitchen preparing nice meals. They did a lot of pottering.

They went for their daily walk along the riverbank; read books in their conservatory or out on the patio in the sunshine, usually with a glass of wine for refreshment; listened to CDs which had been collecting dust on shelves for years; and watched TV programmes which they had recorded but never had time to see.

Most of all they just enjoyed talking to each other, reminiscing about old times, but, more importantly, laying plans for the future. Lockdown was unsettling for everyone but also left plenty of time for taking decisions and assessing relationships.

Hector felt confident that their marriage really would last until one of them passed away. Just occasionally he felt he should reassure Penelope that this was the case, even though no such reassurance was necessary.

Lockdown also lent itself to serious reading. While he was enjoying "Love In The Time Of Cholera" by Gabriel Garcia Marquez he came across a short passage that he could not resist reading out aloud to his wife: *"I have waited for this opportunity for more than half a century to repeat to you once again my vow of eternal fidelity and everlasting love."*

Penelope blushed and just said "thank you".

Although Hector and Penelope were fit for their ages, they were both just over 70 and so were required to leave home as little as possible owing to the pandemic. Although they kept in daily contact with family and friends via Facebook and emails, the only people they saw regularly were the post lady and Hector's son and daughter, Troy and Janis, who took it in turns to do their shopping and drop it off on the doorstep.

Coronavirus brought suffering and tragedy to so many families and Hector and Penelope were empathetic enough to be sorely troubled by that. Their lockdown, though, had many features which gave them a sense of perspective – a sense that they were among the luckiest people alive.

On the first day of their isolation they used up their ration of one walk per day to take a stroll hand in hand along the riverbank. What a change Hector found since his journey along there the previous autumn.

Songbirds were in full voice, little birds were twittering and swooping across the river, thousands of tiny fish were causing ripples in the shimmering water, larger fish were jumping for joy, ducks were squabbling, and mating swans gliding by in formation. Nature had beaten Death! Hector, who had become more worldly than the teenager obsessed by gods and goddesses, was sure that Mankind, with its incredible ingenuity, would defeat and soon rid the world of the coronavirus pandemic.

****

During the early stages of the epidemic, Sanderholme and its hinterland was faring better than most parts of the country, with a tiny number of deaths and relatively few admissions to hospitals. This was perhaps surprising as it continued to attract a large number of day visitors from areas of the country with a much higher infection rate.

Nevertheless a strangely unnatural atmosphere prevailed throughout the area. People walking in the residential parts of the town found themselves swerving to avoid getting too close to other pedestrians. Mostly this was received with an understanding smile and a thank you or an appreciative nod. There were some grumblings from elderly people about youngsters who failed to make room on the pavement. But then young people always did possess a naïve sense of their own immortality and so perhaps cannot be expected to appreciate that this is not shared by those approaching the end of their time in this world.

Except for those most used by tourists, the area's extensive beaches were deserted and desolate, with only the odd dog walker providing a reassurance that some alien force had not landed on earth and committed a terrible act of genocide.

Normally busy roads were deadly quiet. As Hector drove along them he was reminded of those idyllic times of his youth when it was safe enough to play football and French cricket on the streets with Matthew and his other friends, taking care not to step on the scary sheepdog Mossy.

As these daydreams led him back to those days of

childhood freedom he thought of today's young people, confined to their homes, logged on to Fortnite, Snapchat and Instagram, not daring to play on the traffic-filled roads and scared into thinking there is a paedophile around every street corner.

He thought of university students, locked into their colleges owing to coronavirus, instructed not to go to the pub or even have sexual relationships, their student loans hanging over them and little prospect of being able to afford their own home until middle-age.

He berated himself for being so smug as to be actually enjoying lockdown, cosy in his cocoon of love with the woman of his dreams – healthy, wealthy and happy while others were so less fortunate.

However, he was soon to be jolted out of this complacency. Death, the great leveller, was to play his hand.

A few months after Hector and Penelope had tied the knot, Aunt Christine and her latest beau, George Plunkett, went ahead with their own marriage.

George loved his home at Stratford-upon-Avon and Christine, with her theatrical pretensions, had come to love it too. But she had been faced with an awful dilemma. Several years previously her sister Margaret had become wheelchair-bound following a failed hip replacement operation.

Christine would have been happy to take Margaret with her to Stratford, but her sister was adamant that she would not leave Sanderholme and the rest of her family. This put Christine into a turmoil of indecision and split loyalties.

Margaret, typically, came to the rescue by insisting that she check herself into one of the local care homes. She assured Christine by telling her that she was certain she would not be lonely in her new home. She already knew several of the other residents there and she also expected to have regular visits from Hector, her grandchildren and great-grandchildren.

And that was indeed what happened after Christine was finally convinced to leave Sanderholme.

For a number of years Margaret lived happily in the comfortable and well-run care home, although more recently it had become apparent to the staff and her family that she was suffering from the onset of dementia.

When coronavirus struck, visits by relatives were restricted to occasional socially distanced meetings in the home's gardens. And only when weather permitted.

It was on one warm, sunny afternoon that Hector paid one of these visits to his mother. The care home manager, Mrs Jessop, met him at the front door and guided him to a strategically placed chair on a patio. A male carer then pushed Margaret out in her wheelchair, leaving her at a suitably safe distance from her son's seat.

Margaret was on good form, delighted to see her son and pleased to be let out into the fresh air. She appeared to be more lucid than the last time he had met her. They exchanged news about the family, eventually getting round to discussing Christine and George.

"I need to tell you something about Christine – something you should know before I die," said Margaret.

"Oh, come on," said Hector. "What's all this talk about dying?"

"You have to face facts. At my age it's not going to be far away."

"You could be around for another ten or 15 years."

"Oh, rubbish," said Margaret. "But now listen what I've got to tell you.

"Aunt Christine and George Plunkett - they had history."

"History?"

"Yes, years ago when they were in the Sanderholme Players together they had an affair."

"An affair? Mr Plunkett was married at the time, wasn't he?"

"Yes, he was. And his wife, Marjorie, found out about it. She insisted that George left the town to get away from Christine. That was why he left the Grammar School – the year after your dad left – and went with Marjorie to live in Stratford."

"Wow. I knew Aunt Christine had a chequered past, but I'd never heard about this. But can I ask you why you're telling me now, after all this time?"

"It's because I feel so guilty about leaving you in the dark for all those years about your father and Susan Douglas. I couldn't bear to keep another family secret from you. You deserve to know everything that went on."

"You certainly come up with some surprises. Are there any other skeletons in the family cupboard?"

Margaret laughed: "I don't think so, son. Oh, apart from the murder I did."

Hector looked at her askance.

"You nearly believed me then, didn't you?" she joked.

Hector giggled. His mother had never been noted for a sharp sense of humour and so she had taken him completely by surprise.

"You're awful," he said. "What am I going to do with you?

"So, anyway. What did you really feel about Aunt Christine and Mr Plunkett getting hitched?"

"I thought jolly good luck to them," said his mother. "They'll entertain each other for the few years they have left.

"You know, I never really blamed either of them for the affair. Christine was badly done to by several men. She shouldn't really have had an affair, but I excused her because she had gone through such a rough time.

"As for George, I didn't really blame him either. Marjorie was a horrible woman. She was bossy and always belittling him, even though he had a much greater intellect than her. She had married above her station, as they used to say."

Hector thanked his mother for telling him this latest family secret. The previous revelation about his father's affair had rocked him to the core and caused him a great deal of sadness. This story about Christine was very small beer by comparison. Nothing would have surprised him about his crazy aunt!

Early the next morning Hector had just got out of bed when he received a telephone call from the care home to say that his mother had suffered some sort of attack during the night and was struggling for breath. An ambulance was on the way to the home and they advised that Hector should get there himself as soon as possible.

He quickly dressed, found Penelope who was showering, and told her he was on his way to the home. When he arrived he was greeted at the front door by a grim-faced Mrs Jessop, wearing the obligatory mask.

"I'm so sorry, Hector, but your mother has just passed away," she said, fighting back a tear. "A paramedic is here and he believes she had a heart attack."

A numb Hector gave her a thin smile and thanked her for telling him the news. He realised that his mother was one of the most popular residents owing to her stoical and uncomplaining nature and he appreciated that Mrs Jessop's emotion was genuine.

In spite of her advanced years and onset of dementia there had been no clue that Margaret had underlying medical conditions, so her death came as a shock to Hector and the family.

She had been the mainstay of that family throughout Hector's life – undemonstrative and sensible but offering unquestioning love to all.

Hector recognised that her eve of death "confessional" about keeping Christine's affair a secret was typical of her. It may not have been an earth-shattering piece of news to give to her son, but something she needed to get off her chest before, as she must have believed, meeting her Maker.

****

Margaret's death was an unwelcome break with the lockdown routine, but this was to be interrupted again and in a dramatic and, for Penelope in particular, traumatic way.

Three weeks into their isolation, Penelope received a phone call from her elder daughter, Sarah. Stuart had died suddenly at home, alone, his liver having given up. The news was not entirely a shock as his lifestyle made it somehow inevitable.

Penelope felt profoundly sad, not so much from a sense of loss, as from a feeling that her ex-husband's life, once so filled with action and promise, had ended in such a disappointing way.

She felt that at heart he was not a bad man, but one who had been set on the wrong course by being too much worshipped by his parents in his early years. Hector thought there was more to it than just a spoilt childhood and that there might be genetic reasons for his bad behaviour. Back in his schooldays, for instance, he had heard rumours that Stuart's father had been a wife beater.

The funeral service was held three weeks later at a crematorium at Leamington Spa, a few miles from Stratford-upon-Avon. Owing to coronavirus the number of mourners was restricted to six. In the event only five people expressed an interest in attending, Penelope and Hector, Stuart and Penelope's two daughters, and Stuart's sister, Fleur.

It was a brief but dignified affair, conducted by a humanist celebrant, with very little emotion displayed.

When it was over and the others were thanking the woman celebrant, Hector stood quietly in the background.

As he looked at Penelope, still beautiful in her early seventies, and thought about Stuart, lying in his coffin, he allowed himself a guilty inward smile.

Hector had defeated Achilles this time.

THE END

.

www.blossomspringpublishing.com

Printed in Great Britain
by Amazon